The Enlightenment:
A Tori Cooper Novel

By Vicki Stewart

Other books written by Vicki Stewart

First Sight: A Tori Cooper Novel, 2013

This book is dedicated to my family and all of my friends who have been so supportive this past year.

Thank you all for encouraging me to continue writing my story.

~~~~~

Chapter 1

Hidden behind his Oakley sunglasses, Agent Hunter's dark blue eyes critically surveyed his surroundings. *'It is a beautiful day,'* he thought to himself. A day some would call picturesque and unforgettable. Others would refer to it as the most horrific day they would want to quickly forget.

He knew from experience that as soon as the press found out about this latest murder, this small, elite and peaceful community would never be the same again.

As the breeze gently fingered through his raven black hair, he took in the idyllic beauty of the surrounding estates and panoramic ocean views. There were only a small handful of houses on the street, and each had been positioned to provide the most scenic view of the Atlantic Ocean's Crystal Coast.

"Paradise lost," he murmured quietly to himself as he reached into the jacket pocket of his suit to retrieve his notebook and double-check the house number against the address he had written. Confirming this was the place, he walked up the driveway to the front door, where a non-uniformed officer stood guard.

Pausing long enough to flash his badge at the officer, he said, "My name is Agent Gabriel Hunter. Would you please tell me where I can find Detective Sloan?"

The officer nodded his head towards the hallway behind him and replied, "Back there, in the master bedroom."

Acknowledging the officer's response, Agent Hunter walked through an elaborately furnished living area, then down a long hallway carpeted in a thick plush caramel that absorbed the sounds of his approaching footsteps. He stopped at the threshold of the master bedroom, taking in the details of the scene.

The first thing his eyes were drawn too were the back and far right 'walls' of the room, which were constructed of floor to ceiling panels of glass that seemed to be floating in between richly-stained wooden frames. Long brass rods, positioned at the top of the frames, ran along the entire length of both walls, and supported heavy caramel-colored silk curtains which were currently pushed off to the sides, allowing the light from outside to fill the room.

The view directly outside overlooked the shoreline of the coastal waters and today's clear blue sky contrasted against the dark blue water, made quite a spectacular picture within the wooden frames.

His gaze transitioned over towards the far left wall of the room, which was lined with floor to ceiling bookcases, in the same richly-stained wood-tone as the window frames.

The shelves were filled with an eclectic assortment of knick-knacks and pictures as well as various paperback novels.

Agent Hunter's gaze stopped at the bed where a once beautifully displayed jacquard caramel and gold patterned comforter was now carelessly strewn on top of the mattress, massively stained with dried blood.

"May I help you?" demanded a voice from the other side of the room.

Agent Hunter turned to the sound of the voice and was met with a defiant glare from a very shapely brunette with almond shaped eyes the color of toasted coconut. "My name is Agent Gabriel Hunter with Behavioral Analysts Unit of the FBI. Are you Detective Sloan?" he asked, showing her his badge.

"FBI? What's the FBI doing nosing around in my case?" she exclaimed.

Agent Hunter smiled amicably and in a patient tone, replied, "I spoke with your Captain earlier this morning who gave me your name and the location of the crime scene. He said he was going to inform you of my arrival."

"Oh, did he?" she asked, narrowing her eyes at him suspiciously. Pulling her cell phone from her pocket, she dialed a number and stared at Agent Hunter while the call connected. "This is Sloan," she barked into the phone. "Did you authorize an Agent Hunter from the FBI to have access to my crime scene?" Detective Sloan turned to stare out the window, while Agent Hunter continued to patiently wait.

Less angrily, she added, "Yes, sir. A call in advance would have been helpful. I understand you're under a lot of pressure, sir." Pausing to turn back to Agent Hunter, she said, "Yes of course. I understand. I'll keep you informed of any new information. Goodbye, sir."

With forced humility, she ended the call and stuffed her phone back in her pocket. "I'm sorry for the attitude, Agent Hunter. The courtesy call seems to have slipped my Captain's mind. The press has already caught wind of a murder in this area. It's only a matter of time before they find out who it was and where it happened."

Agent Hunter gave her an understanding smile and replied, "No apologies necessary, Detective Sloan. This isn't the first time this has happened."

"Why are you at my crime scene?" she asked, curiously.

"We have reason to believe your victim fits the profile of a series of other women who have been killed by a man the FBI is currently looking for," he replied, looking back at the bed and surrounding area.

"What makes you think my VIC fits your profile?" she asked.

Agent Hunter paused and looked back through the doorway he had entered, trying to gauge the distance between them and the officer at the front door.

Understanding his caution, Detective Sloan walked over and quietly closed the bedroom door.

"Better?" she asked.

Agent Hunter nodded and in a low voice, replied, "Yes thank you. As I was saying, there are certain details about your victim's murder that fit other murders we've seen. Your victim's name was Marsha Foster, is that correct?"

Detective Sloan nodded her head and replied, "Yes, that is correct."

"The preliminary details of your police report indicate Mrs. Foster was twenty-eight years old, blonde, athletic, married but no children," he added.

"Still correct and not yet seeing anything calling out serial killer," she continued.

"How about the fact that her throat was cut from left to right with a very sharp thin blade that the medical examiner has determined to be a scalpel, and the killer posed Mrs. Foster in a sleeping position on her back and placed a single red rose in her right hand," he said.

Detective Sloan stared at Agent Hunter and quietly replied, "My report doesn't say anything about how Mrs. Foster was positioned or about the rose."

"Yes, I'm aware of that," he replied. "Based upon your reaction, am I correct?"

Deliberating her choice of words, Detective Sloan admitted, "Yes, those details will eventually be added to my final report. How did you find out about Mrs. Foster's murder so quickly? It just happened the day before yesterday and I hadn't submitted my initial report until yesterday afternoon."

"We have a fairly sophisticated database management system designed to continually query certain law enforcement databases for certain criteria in ongoing investigations," said Agent Hunter. "For example; certain details of a crime scene, or even a particular physical characteristic of a victim, that could be related to another case."

Agent Sloan turned back to look at the bed, and said, "Well, her killer didn't leave us any evidence. We didn't find any fingerprints other than Mrs. Foster's and her husband's. There were no signs of forced entry, no shoe-prints and nothing out of place except in this room."

"Where is the husband now?" he inquired.

"He's out of the country on a business trip. I spoke with him yesterday afternoon and he's understandably distraught. He's on his way back to the United States now," she replied.

"So you think he's clean? What about any marital discourse?" he asked.

Detective Sloan shook her head emphatically and said, "Uh uh. They've only been married for a couple of years and according to family and close friends, they were still in the honeymoon phase of their marriage. I don't think the husband is our guy. What about this killer you're tracking? What do you know about him?"

"Our profile indicates that the killer is a white male, he's between twenty-five and forty-five years old, has a menial job where he doesn't feel respected or in control. His method of killing indicates that he may have had a dysfunctional relationship with his mother, who was more than likely younger in age, blonde and attractive."

"What about the significance of the single red rose?" Detective Sloan asked, curiously.

"Perhaps it's a calling card. Or it could just be a guy who likes red roses. We're looking into all possible scenarios," Agent Hunter replied.

"So what is it you want from me?" asked Detective Sloan.

Agent Hunter reached into his pocket and removed one of his business cards. Handing it to her, he replied, "Just your cooperation and inclusion in any new developments you and your team uncover, Detective. I'm not here to take over or remove you from your case. Please take my card and call me when you have something you feel is of significance."

"Let's say I do that. What's in it for me?" she challenged.

Agent Hunter chuckled and replied, "I will return the favor by contacting you with any new leads we come up with as well, Detective. We're on the same side here and my main goal is to catch a killer, as I hope is yours as well."

Detective Sloan deliberated for a moment and then nodded her head agreeably. She took one of her business cards from her own pocket and handed it to Agent Hunter. "Deal," she replied.

"Thank you," he said, taking the card. "I'll be in touch."

Chapter 2

'I am a mystery even to myself,' Tori thought inwardly as she regarded the object she was holding. Even now, after four months of feeling its familiar weight in her hands, she found herself conflicted. *'Is this really what God has planned for me? What if I've ventured down the wrong path? Would I know the difference?'*

"Cooper!" she heard bellowing from a voice behind her.

"Yes, sir!" she immediately replied, pointed the Glock at the target in front of her and squeezed out six carefully aimed shots.

As the instructor engaged the mechanism to retrieve Tori's target, she heard several murmured comments from the cadets beside her.

"Seriously?"

"Unbelievable."

"She did it again."

Tori winced as the target stopped in front of her, revealing a perfectly unmarked human silhouette. Turning to look at the instructor, she met his eyes, guiltily.

He narrowed his eyes back at her slightly, moved onto the next cadet in line and shouted, "Reynolds!"

"Yes, sir!" the cadet replied and fired her weapon at the silhouette in front of her.

Tori looked back at her target and sighed in defeat. "Yeah, I'm seriously not the traditional gun-wielding, dark navy suit with fashionable yet comfortable shoes, FBI type."

"Don't be so hard on yourself, Tor!" Piper exclaimed while admiring the perfectly executed shots on her own target. "You've only been at this for a few months."

Also admiring her friend's target, Tori replied, "Says the star pupil with the flawless aim. Look at that perfect pattern! Let me guess, your first toy was a sniper rifle, wasn't it?"

Piper snorted a laugh, shook her head and replied, "Uh, uh. It was a Colt Forty-five. I had to wait for the sniper rifle until I was eight when my arms were long enough to handle the barrel and pull the trigger."

"Why do I think that you're not making that up?" Tori said, rolling her eyes. "I mean seriously! Why can't I complete a round like that just once? I think Agent Easton is losing his patience with me. Could he have me fired from the academy because I'm a lousy shot?"

"Aw, don't worry about him. It's his job as the firearms instructor to teach us how to handle our weapons. Besides, if he really wants you to improve, he needs to do something other than give you the stink eye every time he walks by," Piper noted, scowling at the instructor behind his back. "Tell you what. Why don't we book some range time one afternoon this week and we'll work on it together?"

Tori smiled at Piper and said, "I would appreciate any help I could get at this point. Thanks, roomie!"

"No problem, roomie!" Piper replied.

While they waited for the rest of their group to finish range practice, Tori reflected upon how fortunate she was that she and Piper had been assigned as dorm-mates. She chuckled to herself, thinking back to the first time they met. Piper was standing on top of the desk in their room, hanging a prism from the ceiling in front of the window to catch the sunlight because she believed that there should always be color around her.

Not that Piper lacked color to begin with. Her short spiked hair was dyed flame red which Tori had to admit, although it would never have been a color she would have chosen for herself, the vibrant red matched Piper's bubbly, fearless personality perfectly. The resulting effect also played well with Piper's pale, freckled complexion and chocolate brown eyes. The funniest thing about Piper was the paradox between her enormous personality and her stature. She claimed she was five feet tall, however Tori was fairly sure she was at least an inch below that. 'She's Tinkerbell with a gun,' Tori laughed to herself.

"What's so funny?" Piper asked, noticing the smile on Tori's face.

"I was just thinking to myself that you're like Tinkerbell with a gun," Tori replied, humorously.

"Well I'm fresh out of pixie dust so I guess I'll work with what I've got!" Piper replied with a grin, motioning to her Glock.

Craning her head to look at the range next to them, she added, "I wonder how the guys are doing with their practice today. Do you think Ben will remain the leader?"

Turning to look in the same direction, Tori watched the other cadets 'high-fiving' each other and replied, "It looks like someone's doing well today. You never know. Logan has been giving Ben a run for his money lately so it could go either way."

Tori smiled warmly as Ben looked over and their eyes met. He smiled back, gave a small wave in greeting and then resumed the conversation with his friends.

She was still getting used to the idea of thinking of Ben as her 'boyfriend.' Both of their parents had been next-door neighbors long before either family had any children, so Ben had always been more like a brother to her and her older sister, Aubrey, than anything else.

Then, one tragic night when Tori was fifteen years old, her sister snuck out of the house to meet who she thought was a boy she met in an internet chat room, but instead, he turned out to be a psychopath who murdered Tori's sister.

A murderer who not only would Tori meet ten years later and assist in his arrest, but who also still had in his possession, the body of her dead sister.

Tori idly slid the heart charm on her necklace back and forth against the chain and thought back to the past few months of how quickly her life had changed.

Starting out as a private investigator with Ben at their agency in Cheyenne, then moving halfway across the country to enroll at the FBI academy was something she would never have expected.

The irony of the situation was what had started out as merely accepting a missing person's case for one of her father's colleagues, had turned into a life-changing moment. Not only had Tori found the woman she and Ben were hired to find, they stumbled upon a crime scene in an abandoned warehouse, uncovering three other victims the killer had murdered, eventually leading them to a fifth victim and then finally to her sister's remains.

That life-changing moment was when Tori learned she was able to both see and communicate with the spirits of victims of violent deaths. Not to mention the fact that the spirits of the murdered women had helped Tori identify their killer.

Tori laughed thinking back again to that day, remembering her initial disbelief that she could talk to the dead, trying to convince herself that she was having a mental breakdown instead. Thankfully, Ben had trusted her enough to believe her.

Then, when she met Agent Hunter, Tori learned that there used to be another agent on his team, Karla Neviah, who had a similar ability to Tori's, except Agent Neviah was only able to talk to spirits of violent deaths, she was not able to see them. Her ability was short lived as she too became one of the killer's victims.

Tori looked down at the heart-shaped charm in her hand and tenderly traced the inscription 'Always Sisters,' thinking of how blessed she was having her new-found 'ability,' as it was giving her an opportunity to get to know her sister again, even though she was only in spirit form.

She smiled and reminded herself that it was giving her mother that same opportunity to get to know Aubrey too. As it turned out, the 'ability' to communicate with the dead was something that ran in Tori's maternal side of the family, which her mother had kept from Tori and her sister.

She wasn't angry at her mother because of the secret. Tori's grandmother had used the 'ability' to help others and it had become something her mother grew to resent, rather than embrace. Watching Tori accept her own 'ability,' was helping her mother learn too as well.

'God gives us all special abilities, we just need to find out what they are and what we can do with them,' Tori thought to herself.

Breaking from her trance, she looked back over to where the guys were practicing and said, "I still think you should consider the sniper training, Piper. You would easily demolish both Ben's and Logan's stats. You have a gift and you should use it."

Piper shook her head firmly and replied, "I'm not really interested in being a sniper. I love to shoot, don't get me wrong. I just don't want to get pigeon-holed and that be the only thing I do. I want to start out as a field agent, work crime scenes and learn as much as I can before committing to one team. Speaking of committing to a team, have you heard from Agent Hunter yet?"

"No, not yet," Tori replied. "But graduation is still four weeks away so I'm not really worried about it too much."

"What about your mom?" Piper asked quietly, making sure no one around them could hear her. "Aren't she and your sister in Arizona with Agent Neviah and her parents?"

"Yes, they arrived a couple days ago," Tori replied, quietly. "My mom sent me a couple of text messages but they don't have a lot of detail for obvious reasons. We talked on the phone before they left. She said she and Aubrey were going to help Mrs. Neviah come up with some ideas to make her husband and daughter's skeletons more easily transportable.

"They're also going to work on researching both the Neviah and Ramiel family histories to see if there's a long-lost ancestral connection we're not aware of."

Piper shook her head in disbelief and said, "I'm still trying to get my head around the fact that your mom actually carries your sister's skeleton around in a suitcase. Can you imagine how the average person would react if they knew what was in that bag?"

Tori laughed in response, having seen Agent Hunter's reaction when he first learned of her sister's improvised traveling arrangements, the last time they met in Denver. "I'll be the first to admit that it takes some getting used to. If anything, it will be good for Mrs. Neviah so she and her husband can travel together from now on."

"It's so sad that both her husband and her daughter were murdered," Piper said, sadly. "Do you think she's lonely being the only remaining survivor in her family?"

Tori paused for a moment and said, "I'm not sure. I guess I hadn't thought about that before. I mean she has both her husband and her daughter's spirits with her but I guess it would be difficult not being able to see or touch them or feel their touch in return."

"So tell me again why Agent Neviah has her mother's maiden name and not her father's name?" questioned Piper.

"It's a tradition in Mrs. Neviah's family that the women keep the maternal family name and not the paternal family name. Had Agent Neviah lived and married, she would have kept her name and any female children she had would have kept her maiden name," replied Tori.

"What about your mother's family? Did they do the same thing?" Piper asked.

"Yes, they did," Tori replied. "At least they did until my mom married my dad."

"Well, I hope they find something. I think it would be cool to find out there's a whole other side of your family you knew nothing about," said Piper.

"Well, both sides literally have skeletons in their closets so it's already starting off like an old Vincent Price macabre movie," Tori replied with a grin.

"Carson, Cooper, Pepper and Roper, you all remain where you are. The rest of you, turn in your targets and check in your weapons. You're free to go," Agent Easton directed to the group.

"Great," Tori sighed. "I'm in detention."

Laughing sympathetically, Piper patted Tori's shoulder and replied, "At least you're not the only one! Good luck. I'll see you later."

~~~~~

Later that afternoon, in her psychology and cultism class, Tori's mood quickly improved as she listened intently to her instructor, as he explained a homework assignment on the psychological impacts of cultism in modern-day society.

Psychology and cultism was one of the classes Tori had selected from a list of available electives and she picked it mainly out of curiosity.

Agent Hunter had advised her that only a few select instructors at the academy had been made aware of her special 'ability' and as it turned out, this instructor, Agent Sullivan, was one of them.

"Does anyone have any questions on the requirements of the assignment?" Agent Sullivan asked, looking around the room.

A male cadet a few chairs down from Tori raised his hand so the agent prompted, "Yes?"

The cadet cleared his throat quietly, and said, "I guess I'm curious how we're supposed to research cultism while were here on base. I mean it's not like we're going to come across a bunch of robed Satanists wearing masks and sacrificing small animals on an altar of fire or anything like that."

A series of muted chuckles filtered through the room as Agent Sullivan gave a patient smile and replied, "I would agree that the likelihood of that scenario would be very difficult to come by, Mr. Dixon. Fortunately, that is not one of the requirements of this assignment.

"I am giving you all three weeks to complete this assignment and it will be the last assignment before your final exam. I do not want or expect you to turn in a final paper on the expected views of cultism today. Instead, I want you to do your homework and research the unexpected areas where perception today may not look like cultism where it actually is. You can use the internet, our base library or any other means of information you have available to you."

Secretly pleased by the confused and anxious looks on his students' faces, Agent Sullivan asked, "Are there any other questions?" When no other brave soul raised their hand, he added, "Very well then. Class is dismissed."

While everyone quietly picked up their materials and shuffled from the room, Tori waited in her chair as she did at the end of each class.

When all but she and Agent Sullivan remained, she waited as he finished packing his course work into his satchel and walked over to sit in the seat next to her. His grand-fatherly eyes met hers, humorously and he asked, "So, do you think I made this assignment challenging enough?"

Tori laughed, recalling the faces of some of the cadets around her and replied, "I think there may be one or two students breathing into a paper bag right about now."

Chuckling at the visual, Agent Sullivan asked, "What about you? Do you have any questions?"

Tori paused for a moment and replied, "Not about the assignment, no."

Agent Sullivan looked at Tori with concern and asked, "Has something happened since we last talked? Are you still having troubling dreams?"

Tori glanced around the room to make sure they were alone and replied, "I've started having this one dream over and over, however lately I've begun recalling more of the details than I was able to at first."

Reaching into her backpack, Tori pulled out her notebook, found the pages in question and handed the book over to Agent Sullivan. "This is what I remembered from a couple nights ago," she added.

Agent Sullivan was quiet as he read the few pages Tori had written. When he was done, she heard him sigh deeply and met her eyes, which were filled with concern. "You realize what this sounds like to me, right?"

Tori nodded her head soberly and replied, "I don't know what to do. I'll be honest, I'm a bit confused as to the meaning....not to mention a little scared."

"It's okay to be scared, Miss Cooper," Agent Sullivan added. "Fear is a natural reaction to the unknown." He deliberated a thought for a moment adding, "Hmm."

"What?" Tori asked.

"I think this would be the perfect opportunity for you to research this for your class assignment," Agent Sullivan replied.

Tori looked at the agent in confusion and said, "My assignment?"

Agent Sullivan gave her a small smile and replied, "Fight fire with fire, Ms. Cooper. To be forewarned is to be forearmed. Do your research, plan ahead and prepare yourself for what appears to be a very possible encounter with a very old soul. I'm serious about doing your research. If this turns out to be what it sounds like, you'll need to be prepared."

Tori nodded her head and replied, "I understand. Thank you, Agent Sullivan."

As Tori rose from her chair, she paused and looked down at Agent Sullivan's face. "Sir, you don't seem very surprised about my dream. Did Agent Hunter warn you that this may happen?"

"Yes, he did," Agent Sullivan admitted. "Agent Neviah shared a similar dream she had with Agent Hunter, so he advised me to be prepared in the event you mentioned anything along those same lines. I hope that doesn't bother you that he asked me to do that."

Tori shrugged and replied, "No, that doesn't bother me. It would have been nice to know that as well but I guess I can understand why he didn't say anything to me. Planting the seed and stuff like that. Thank you, sir."

"You're welcome, Miss Cooper. See you tomorrow," he replied.

"See you tomorrow," she said, giving a small salute as she headed for the door.

Agent Sullivan watched Tori leave the room and then pulled his phone from his pocket to make the call he was secretly hoping he would never have to make.

Once the call connected, he said, "Hello, Agent Hunter? It's Agent Sullivan. Yes, sir. They've begun...."

Chapter 3

Later that night, Tori was doing research on the internet, jotting down notes in her notebook and bookmarking sites she thought she would want to research again later. She was deep in thought, when suddenly, Piper bounced into the room.

"Hi!" She greeted Tori, happily. "A bunch of us are going over to Hogan's Alley for a nighttime surveillance simulation. Do you want to come with us?"

"Thanks for the offer but I think I'll take a rain-check. I've got a lot of research I want to get through tonight," Tori replied.

"What's the research for?" Piper asked curiously, looking at the website Tori had pulled up. "Fallen angels? Why are you researching fallen angels?"

"It's for my psychology and cultism class," Tori replied. "Agent Sullivan gave us an assignment where we're supposed to find examples of cultism in today's society where others would not consider it to be cultism."

"Hmmm....," Piper said. "So like certain religions and stuff like that?"

"That would be one area, yes. However, he said religious cults are too obvious so he suggested we explore other areas," Tori replied.

Piper looked at Tori quizzically and asked, "How do fallen angels fit into other areas of cultism?"

Tori realized that she hadn't told Piper about her most recent dreams and wasn't sure she was ready to discuss them at the moment. Instead she replied, "That's what I'm trying to figure out. Anyway, thanks again for the invitation, have fun!"

Noticing Tori's sudden change in subject, Piper went along with her, and replied, "Okay, see you later then!"

~~~~~~

Later that evening, Tori felt her eyes getting tired from hours of staring at the laptop screen and decided to call it a night.

Piper was still out, so she sent her a quick text to make sure Piper had her room key with her. While she was at it, Tori sent a text to Ben to say goodnight. After receiving a confirmation text back from Piper and a 'Goodnight, I love you,' text back from Ben, Tori locked the door and went into the bathroom to get ready for bed.

Flipping on the light switch and waiting the usual few moments for the fluorescent bulbs to flicker to a steady pulse, Tori gazed upon her reflection in the mirror, noticing the small dark circles under her sea-green eyes. "This is becoming a bad habit, Tori," she said to herself.

When her 'other self' refused to respond, she sighed, ran her fingers through her long auburn hair, pulled it into a ponytail away from her face and began her facial cleansing and tooth brushing ritual. She then changed into her academy sweats and a t-shirt, crawled into bed and turned out the light.

While she was lying there waiting for sleep to overtake her, she stared up at the ceiling fan slowly rotating above her head and thought more about God's fallen angels.

'What could have made them become so unhappy with God that they would turn against him?' Tori wondered. *'And since no human was there, how do we know what really happened?'*

Deciding that she had more questions than what the internet could answer, she concluded that a visit to the base library the next day was in order. A few minutes later, she drifted off to sleep.

~~~~~

Tori looked around her and realized that she was in the garden again. As in her dreams before, she was surrounded by the most beautiful and fragrant flowers she had ever seen. Mixed in with the flowers, were a multitude of berry bushes and fruit trees – some of which were so exotic looking, she couldn't identify their origin.

31

The gentle hum of honey bees and the flutter of butterfly wings set an underlying wave of musical energy in the air around her.

Off to her left, she saw a path leading deeper into the garden that she didn't recall seeing in previous dreams. Curiously, she began to follow it.

While she walked, the slight breeze, moving through the branches of the trees above her, alternately dappled patterns of shade and light on the path before her. She stopped to inspect a tree offering the most intoxicatingly inviting fruit which looked somewhat reminiscent to dragon fruit. As she was about to turn away, she noticed that there weren't any pieces of the fruit lying on the ground rotting beneath the tree as she would have expected. Looking around her, she realized none of the other trees or bushes had old, fallen fruit either. *'That's interesting...'* Tori thought.

Tossing the question around in her head for a few moments, she continued walking along the path.

A short time later, she reached the end of the path and found herself standing in front of a large, beautiful tree. The massive trunk and supporting branches were gnarled and twisted and reached up high above her into the clear blue sky.

On the ground at the base of the tree, there was an ornate wooden bench that looked as if it had been lovingly carved and polished by an expert hand.

Mentally debating whether the bench was intended for her to sit upon or not, Tori was momentarily distracted by movement from the breeze as large, succulent looking fruit peeked out from among the leaves.

"Tempting, aren't they?" She heard in a soothing tone behind her.

Tori whipped around quickly but there was no one there. "Who said that?" she called out.

Feeling something brush up against her leg, she looked down and gasped as a large serpent circled around her feet. Jumping backwards, she tripped and nearly fell down, but a strong hand caught her around her elbow.

Regaining her balance, she turned and found herself looking into the face of the most handsome man she had ever seen. No, handsome wasn't right either – this man was, dare she say it, beautiful?

"Did I startle you? Please forgive me," the man said in a tone so smooth it was almost musical.

Tori instinctively pulled her arm from his grasp and retreated several steps away, regarding him critically. Her earlier summation had been correct in thinking no man she had ever seen looked so polished and perfect – not even the most carefully campaigned politician could look this good. 'That's funny that a politician was my first thought,' Tori thought inwardly as she noted the man's carefully groomed dark hair, custom made Italian suit and expensive shoes.

Instantly, the realization sank in that this same man was another form of the serpent that had been circling her feet a few moments earlier. His name, although unspoken, could clearly be heard in her mind. Looking back and forth between him and the tree, she knew where she was.

"Hello, Eve," he crooned, humorously.

"What? My name isn't..." Tori began to reply.

"I know who you are, Tori," he chuckled, cutting her off. "I was just teasing you."

"Is that so?" Tori challenged. "Are you the one responsible for bringing me here over and over?"

"Have you been here before?" he asked, mockingly. "Had I known that, I would have introduced myself sooner."

"What do you want?" Tori demanded.

"It isn't what I want that seems to be the question here, is it, Tori?" he taunted.

"What are you talking about?" Tori asked.

He laughed gently and began slowly walking in a circle around her, tapping the tips of his fingers together in time with each step. "You're the one with all the questions without any answers. Perhaps I should be asking you what it is that you want. Like that tree for example. The fruit looks delicious doesn't it? Would you like to try it? It will give you all the answers you're looking for."

"No thanks," Tori replied, sarcastically. "I'm very familiar with the book of Genesis by the way. Been there, done that. The last girl you talked into eating fruit from that tree didn't fare so well. Nice try, Satan."

"Aw...you do know who I am, don't you?" he chided, menacingly. "I'm the big bad wolf! Aren't you afraid of me, Tori?"

"Not particularly," she replied, defiantly. "I'm strong enough in my faith to know that you can't hurt me."

Satan stopped in his tracks and turned towards her slowly. "Is that so?" he snarled. As his face slowly morphed from the chiseled, modeled features into a twisted expression of evil, he asked, "Would you like to put that faith of yours to the test, dearest Tori?"

Tori gasped in surprise as he lunged towards her and she immediately felt herself being pulled away.

Moments later, Tori opened her eyes and choked out a cry as she became aware of her surroundings back in her dorm room. Gasping for breath, she glanced over to Piper's side of the room and saw her roommate sitting crossed-legged on her bed, staring at Tori with a terrified expression on her face.

"What just happened?" Piper asked, bewildered.

"What do you mean?" Tori asked in confusion.

"I mean your aura, which is usually the most amazing shade of vibrant green, just went completely black and now it's back to green again!" Piper exclaimed. "I've never seen that happen before! What on earth were you dreaming about and don't blow me off like you did earlier today. What's going on, Tori!"

"My aura?" Tori asked in surprise. "You can see people's auras? Why is this just coming out now, Piper?"

"Hey! Stop changing the subject!" Piper accused. "See? You're doing it again!"

Tori sighed and ran her hands over her face in frustration as she felt her heart start to return to its normal rhythm. "I'm not doing anything on purpose, Piper. Just give me a minute to catch my breath."

"Fine, you have one minute," Piper declared, crossing her arms across her chest, defiantly.

Tori sat up in her bed, pulled her knees up to her chest and wrapped her arms around her legs tightly. Looking at Piper with a slightly guilty expression, she said, "I just wasn't ready to tell anyone about these dreams I've been having. They've kind of been freaking me out."

"Well after what I just saw, I would venture a guess to say that was once heck of a dream! You looked absolutely terrified when you woke up!" Piper exclaimed.

"Looking into the face of the devil would do that to anyone," Tori replied as she shuddered at the memory of his face.

Piper quickly got up and crossed the room to sit on Tori's bed beside her. "Are you talking literally the devil - as in the guy with the horns and a pitchfork?"

"The one and only," Tori confirmed meeting Piper's eyes.

"Well that explains the darkness around your aura," Piper replied. "So what made the darkness go away? Did you do something in your dream to pull away?"

Tori thought for a moment and replied, "I don't think I did anything. Satan asked me if I was scared of him and I perhaps a bit too arrogantly, said no and then he lunged at me. The next thing I knew, it felt as if someone had put their arms around me and pulled me away. Then I woke up."

Piper stared at Tori wide-eyed in amazement, noting that Tori hadn't done the mental math yet. "You think you felt someone's arms around you pulling you away."

Seeing the look of expectation on Piper's face, Tori asked, "Yeah – so?"

"So!" Piper cried. "So someone like, I don't know, maybe a guardian angel?"

Tori scowled at Piper and said, "A guardian angel? Yeah, right! Next thing you're going to tell me it's my long lost great-great-great-whatever Grand-father Ramiel! It was probably due to all the research I was doing earlier."

"What if it wasn't? Would it be so outrageous to consider, considering you just had a face-off with Satan?" Piper challenged.

"I don't know what to think right now," Tori admitted, rubbing her hands over her face. "I'll think about it later, in the daylight so I can get the visual of Satan's face out of my head. Seriously, though. Let's go back to your little secret. You know about my secret, why didn't you tell me about yours? Don't you trust me?" She asked in a wounded tone.

"It's not that I didn't want to tell you, Tori," replied Piper in defense. "I haven't told anyone at the academy about it. Honestly, think about it for a minute. Most people are so close-minded that they believe the study of the meta-physical energy signals around people goes hand in hand with crystals, Tarot cards and Ouija boards."

"Well how long have you been able to see people's auras?" Tori asked.

"As far back as I can remember," Piper replied, shrugging her shoulders. "My mom said that when I was old enough to talk, I used to tell her that I saw rainbows around people. She tried to down-play it like I was just making it up, but one day when my aunt Sky was at our house, I mentioned it and she freaked out. She was the one who put two-and-two together and figured out what I was seeing.

"My mom would be what you would consider as the logical child in her family. She's a geologist and has always been grounded in the tangibles of science.

"Her sister, however, my aunt Skyler, would be what one would consider as my mother's polar opposite. Sky is into spiritual healing and alternative medicine. She owns a store that sells herbs, aroma-therapy candles, crystals and stuff like that. My mom wasn't really comfortable with the whole thing but she was understanding and let me figure it out as I got older. I used to work for my aunt for several summers when I was a teenager which was pretty cool. I learned a lot about what I could do and found that I can tell a lot about a person just by the color of their aura.

"Anyway that's the abridged version of my story. Now, be honest. Do you seriously think the FBI would ever have taken me seriously if they knew all that?"

Tori regarded Piper for a few moments and replied, "I think it's possible you're the one who's being close-minded about this and you need to put some trust in the people around you. I've told you about my experience with Agent Hunter and his team, so you know he for one would believe you."

"I'm just not ready yet," Piper replied. "Please promise me you won't say anything to anyone."

"I promise I won't tell anyone, it will be your story to tell. But I seriously think you should consider talking about this with Agent Hunter the next time he's on base. At least promise me that you'll think about it," Tori said, hopefully.

"Okay, I promise I'll think about it," Piper agreed.

Chapter 4

The next morning, Tori had a few hours before her first class so she took advantage of the opportunity to continue her research at the academy base library. She was pleasantly surprised to find an entire shelf dedicated specifically to the theological research about the archangels and several Jewish writings not included in the modern day Old Testament.

Surrounded by a mountain of books, Tori quickly became entrenched in the translated ancient writings, one of which was a verse that mentioned two archangels – Ramiel and Remiel.

'That's strange,' she thought. *'Ramiel was called the 'Thunder of God' and Remiel was called the 'Mercy of God'. They're not the same angel!'* Sitting back in her chair with a puzzled look on her face, she added out loud, "Then why is my mother's maiden name not 'Remiel' with an 'e'?"

"Ah! I was wondering how long it would take until you asked that question!" sounded Agent Sullivan's voice as he approached her table. "I had a feeling we would find you here."

Tori turned around, surprised to see both Agent Sullivan and Agent Hunter approaching her table. "Agent Hunter, what are you doing here?" she asked in a surprised tone. "Has something happened? Is everyone all right?"

Agent Hunter gave her a small smile and replied, "Everything is fine, Miss Cooper. May we join you?"

Looking around at the disarray and towers of books around her, she looked back at him sheepishly, began moving a few of the stacks to one side of the table and replied, "Yes, of course! I'm sorry about all the books. Let me get some of them out of the way."

"Allow me to help you," replied Agent Sullivan, quickly stepping forward.

Picking up the book nearest to him, Agent Hunter read the title and replied, "Hmmm. Your collection of Old Testament writings has grown considerably, Agent Sullivan. Where did the academy obtain this latest group of writings?"

While Agent Sullivan helped Tori move the books, he replied, "I acquired that particular book you're holding on my last visit to Jerusalem about three years ago. After the September eleventh tragedy, I realized that we had a rather diminutive selection of historical Hebrew resources around religious beliefs and prophetic writings outside of the Old Testament, so I began adding new materials to our library. I also receive donated materials from various seminaries, private collections and academic institutions from time to time."

Once an appropriate area of space was cleared and everyone was seated at the table, Tori asked again, "Not that I'm not happy to see you Agent Hunter, but you didn't answer my question. What are you doing here? We weren't scheduled to meet for another couple of weeks."

Agent Sullivan cleared his throat and said, "Actually that was my doing, Miss Cooper. I called Agent Hunter and asked him to come."

Tori turned to Agent Sullivan in confusion and asked, "Why? What's going on?"

"Agent Sullivan called me yesterday afternoon in response to a request I made of him when I found out you had been assigned as one of his students," replied Agent Hunter.

"After you and he spoke yesterday afternoon about your most recent dream, Agent Sullivan felt it was time to alert me to the fact that you've been having a similar dream to one Agent Neviah shared with me while she was still alive.

"The dream was about a particular garden with a large tree in its center. She was never able to fully determine its significance; however, she was certain there was one."

Tori shook her head and laughed as she flipped back a few pages in the notebook beside her. Pushing the book towards Agent Hunter, she replied, "I think it's safe to say that I've figured out the meaning of the dream, Agent Hunter. I had another, very detailed one again last night."

Agent Sullivan looked over Agent Hunter's shoulder and they both silently read the details of the dream that Tori had carefully recorded. Tori watched the men's faces intently, looking for any reaction and was secretly satisfied when both men reacted with raised eyebrows and an exchanged look of concern.

"Agent Hunter?" said a familiar voice.

Tori and the agents looked up to find Ben standing at the table. "Hello, Mr. Vincent," replied Agent Hunter, rising from his chair and extending his hand.

Ben returned the handshake and replied, "This is a pleasant surprise! What's going on?"

Agent Hunter looked down at Tori's face and could tell by her expression that Ben was not aware of their topic of conversation. Deciding that she must have her reasons why, he smiled at Ben amicably, and said, "I had some business to discuss with Agent Sullivan and we were fortunate enough to happen upon Miss Cooper. Would you care to join us?"

"Actually, I stopped by to get Tori for our next class," Ben replied, looking at Tori for confirmation. "Are you going?"

Tori looked down at the time on her cell phone and replied, "I totally lost track of time. I'm sorry, Ben! I have to put all these books back before I leave. You go ahead – I'll meet you there."

Ben looked back and forth between Tori and the agents and made a quick decision not to question her. He flashed a crooked grin and replied, "No problem! I'll see you there. Agent Hunter, will we see you again before you leave?"

"I would like that very much, Mr. Vincent," replied Agent Hunter. "I'll give you a call this afternoon."

"That sounds great!" Ben replied. "See you later then. Bye, Tor!"

"Thanks, Ben!" Tori replied, grateful that the awkward moment had passed.

Watching him walk away, Tori turned to find Agent Hunter watching her closely. She narrowed her eyes suspiciously at him and asked, "What?"

"You haven't been telling Mr. Vincent about your dreams," he stated matter-of-factly.

"I haven't wanted to worry him un-necessarily," Tori replied. "Besides, it's not like there's anything he can do about it. Not to mention that both you and Director Gibbs were very clear that I needed to assert myself more individually and not lean on Ben as much as I have in the past. This is me taking charge of my life."

"Taking charge of your life is commendable, Miss Cooper. Just remember that we didn't intend for you to take on all of your challenges alone. Being part of a team also means that you learn to rely upon each other when needed," advised Agent Hunter.

"I understand that, Agent Hunter," Tori replied. "I had planned to tell him, we've just been so busy, we haven't had a lot of time to see each other. It's taken some time getting adjusted to living in the dorms."

"Speaking of which, how are you and Miss Stirling getting along?" Agent Hunter asked curiously, locking his eyes with hers. "I imagine by now you've both had an opportunity to get to know each other?"

'He knows about Piper!' Tori thought inwardly, careful not to register a reaction to his question. *'Of course he knows,'* Tori reasoned, in her mind. *'He knew everything about you before the day he sat down with you in the Greeley police station. He would have researched any cadet assigned to your dorm room, regardless as to who it was. Do I tell Piper that he knows? Do I let on to Agent Hunter that I know?'* "Oh, she's great!" Tori replied, casually. "She's got quite a gift!"

Agent Hunter raised his eyebrows in surprise and replied, "Oh really? She told you?"

Laughing to herself at his reaction, Tori waved her hand dramatically in the air above her head and replied, "Told me? She didn't need to, she showed me!"

"She showed you?" asked Agent Hunter, puzzled. "How did she do that?"

"At the firing range during firearms instruction," Tori replied, innocently. "I keep telling her she should consider sniper training but she said she's not interested in specializing in just one thing. She wants to experience other areas in order to determine where she would be best suited."

Seeing Agent Hunter's puzzled expression deepen, Tori decided not to tease him any further so she gave him a quick wink and added, "Yeah, she's quite the colorful character!" Agent Hunter smiled as he realized what she meant.

Meanwhile, oblivious to what Tori and Agent Hunter were talking about, Agent Sullivan interjected, "Colorful would be exactly the word I would use for Miss Stirling! You can see that flame red hair all the way across campus!"

"I look forward to meeting her," Agent Hunter laughed, returning Tori's wink.

"Well I better return these materials to the shelf and get to class," Tori said, rising from her chair and grabbing the set of books closest to her.

"Why don't you go on to class, Miss Cooper," replied Agent Sullivan. "I'll put these back for you."

Tori looked at Agent Sullivan in surprise and replied, "Are you sure? There's a lot of material here!"

"I don't mind a bit – you go on. We'll talk more about your most recent dream later this afternoon after class," he replied.

Tori hesitated for a moment, but then decided to take him up on his offer. Stuffing her notebook and pen into her backpack, she replied, "Okay then. Thank you very much, Agent Sullivan. I'll see you this afternoon. We'll talk later, Agent Hunter?"

"Yes, we will, Miss Cooper," Agent Hunter replied.

"Okay. I'll see you later," Tori replied.

As Tori walked away, Agent Hunter sat at the table and stared at the wood-grained surface, deep in thought.

Agent Sullivan methodically returned all the books and materials to the shelf, watching Agent Hunter out of the corner of his eye. When all the materials were in their proper place, he sat down across from Agent Hunter and quietly said, "You're worried about her, aren't you?"

Agent Hunter met his eyes and replied, "Aren't you? You've had enough time to get to know Miss Cooper and formulate your own impressions. If what we know about her turns out to be true, do you think she'll be strong enough to handle it?"

Agent Sullivan sighed deeply and replied, "I sure hope so. She really doesn't have much of a choice."

"You never answered her question," Agent Hunter said curiously.

"You caught that, huh?" laughed Agent Sullivan. "She seems to have forgotten she asked it."

"She'll remember," replied Agent Hunter with a knowing smile. "You just better be prepared to answer it when she does."

Nodding his head in agreement, Agent Sullivan asked, "So, what do we do next?"

"I think it's time to call the others and bring everyone up to speed. Miss Cooper is going to need all the support we can give her," replied Agent Hunter, somberly.

Chapter 5

Sarah took a sip of her coffee and sighed contentedly as she watched the sun rise over the mountains. There was just a hint of coolness still left in the air around her feet where the sunlight hadn't yet reached, which would quickly warm as the sun rose higher in the sky. Taking advantage of those last few minutes, she closed her eyes and enjoyed the moment.

Having seen her mother perform this same ritual the past few days, Aubrey waited patiently in silence beside her.

"Ah, another beautiful day," Meda said happily as she emerged from the house, carrying a large tray. Placing the tray on the table, she added, "Perfect for breakfast on the patio!"

Sarah looked at the abundant assortment of fresh fruit, breads and other foods on the tray and replied, "My goodness, Meda! There are only two of us actually eating any of this food which looks amazing by the way! What is that heavenly smell?"

"It's a quiche that Aubrey thought you might enjoy. It's made with caramelized onions, cremini mushrooms and Gruyère cheese. She and I made breakfast together today," Meda replied proudly as she cut two pieces from the dish, handing one to Sarah. "Besides, I rarely get a chance to cook for more than one person so I'm enjoying the opportunity to cook for someone else."

Sarah placed the plate on the table in front of her, smiled appreciatively at Meda and Aubrey and said, "That was very thoughtful of you both, thank you!" She took a bite of the quiche and again, closed her eyes in contentment. "Oh, this is wonderful! The combination of the smoky, caramelized onions and the creamy Gruyère is perfect! You'll have to give me this recipe!"

Sighing happily and looking at the mountains around them, Sarah turned back to Meda and said, "Meda, you've gone out of your way to make me and Aubrey feel so welcome the past few days. Thank you! I sincerely hope you'll allow us to return the favor and come visit us in Cheyenne."

"Well, now that you've helped me make Karla and Tobias more mobile, I think that would be a good first family vacation for us," Meda promised.

"Speaking of which, where are Karla and Tobias?" Sarah asked.

Meda chuckled, "They're testing out the range of distance they can move beyond the recent modifications we've made to their travel bags. Tobias is excited about the new arrangements and has asked if we can take a drive together today so he can see how much things in town have changed since he last saw them. We were thinking that we would do that after breakfast. Would you and Aubrey like to join us?"

Sarah and Aubrey exchanged a look of understanding and Sarah replied, "Thank you for the offer but I think Aubrey would agree that the three of you should share that moment together the first time. We'll join you on the next trip."

"It's a deal," Meda agreed.

"So what are we going to research today?" Aubrey inquired, eagerly. "Do we have any other sources to look into regarding our family history or details on the statue and the amulet?"

"Your father sent me a few websites we can look into after breakfast," Sarah replied. "He's friends with a genealogist who offered to help us trace lineage of the Ramiel and Neviah families. According to your father, this friend majored in patrilineage in college and was able to trace a chain of descendant links from his family through known male ancestors all the way back to Jonah. Of course your father wasn't able to share some of the more sensitive details of our two families with his friend; however, it will be interesting to see what he finds."

"Anything is better than nothing," Meda interjected. "I'm still troubled by the fact that Karla and I found an entire period of the Neviah family history that is missing from our archives. Our family has always been very careful to record as many of each generation's history for the benefit of our children and grandchildren who follow us. Neither my mother nor my grandmother ever mentioned the missing information."

"Perhaps they didn't know," suggested Sarah. "Let's go back through that period of time where it sounds like there's something missing and we'll see if we can come up with anything new."

"Everything is in the storage boxes in the living room if you want to start some of that while I take Karla and Tobias into town. Maybe a fresh set of eyes will see something we missed," Meda replied, hopefully.

"I think that sounds like a wonderful plan," Sarah agreed.

~~~~~~~~~~

Later, while Meda, Karla and Tobias were out, Aubrey and Sarah began working through the first box of the Neviah family history.

They were halfway through the box when Sarah paused with a confused look on her face.

"What's wrong?" Aubrey asked with concern.

"I'm not sure," Sarah replied, continuing to read the paper in her hand. "This document is titled 'The Letter of Baruch to the Nine and a Half Tribes,' and there's a handwritten note in the margin that says it was written in either the late first century AD or early second century AD after the destruction of the Temple in AD seventy. Apparently, this letter is associated with the Old Testament, but not regarded as scripture by Jews or most Christian groups."

"What does it say?" inquired Aubrey.

"It mentions an archangel by the name of Remial, with an 'e,' not an 'a,' who was said to be the angel of hope and was responsible for divine visions and guiding the souls of the faithful into heaven," replied Sarah quietly.

"Wait a second," argued Aubrey. "Tori said that was what the archangel Ramiel with an 'a' did. Who's this Remial character with the 'e'! Were they two separate angels?"

"I don't know, honey," Sarah admitted. "Let's search them on the internet and see what we find." Sarah turned to her laptop and opened two browser windows, entering a search for both names. "Hmmm...it does appear that they were two distinctly different angels although not all the sites I'm seeing agree one-hundred percent on the details between the two. Remial with an 'e' was said to be the 'Angel of Hope' and Ramiel with an 'a' was the 'Thunder of God.'"

'Well, that doesn't sound good," admitted Aubrey, reading over her mother's shoulder.

"Um, I would have to agree considering here it says that more than two hundred of God's angels became fallen angels after taking wives, mating with human women and teaching forbidden knowledge," added Sarah.

Aubrey gasped in surprise and exclaimed, "Is that how our family gift originated - from the offspring of a fallen angel and human mother?"

Sarah sat back against her chair and replied, "I guess that's entirely possible, honey. I mean it makes sense when you think about it. I wonder if either Meda or any of her ancestors came to that same conclusion."

"Wonder if Meda came to what conclusion?" Meda asked as she entered the room, followed by Karla and Tobias.

"Oh! You're back! How was the drive?" Sarah asked.

"It was wonderful!'" Tobias declared, excitedly. "I can't believe how much the town has changed! There are so many more people than I remembered! And our school looks so nice! It was recess time so we stopped to watch the children playing on the playground!"

Karla laughed at her father's excitement and said, "We even stopped at the cemetery so Mom could put flowers on mine and Dad's graves, in case anyone was watching."

"Ah, keeping up the ruse – good thinking!" Aubrey applauded.

"So what were you wondering if I had already concluded when we walked in?" Meda inquired.

"Mom was reading a site on the internet that claims several of God's angels became fallen angels after taking wives, mating with human women and teaching forbidden knowledge," replied Aubrey. "I was asking her if that's where our family gift originated - from the offspring of those women."

Meda nodded her head in confirmation and replied, "Yes, that is what my ancestors have believed as no other explanation could be found."

"Do you know anything about the differences between the angels 'Ramiel' with an 'a' and 'Remial' with an 'e'?" Sarah asked.

Meda gave Sarah a surprised look and replied, "I've never heard that there were two angels so similarly named. What were you able to find out about them?"

Sarah handed Meda the document she and Aubrey read earlier and said, "We found this letter in the first box here, but didn't know what to make of it."

While Meda read the document, Karla and Tobias flanked her on either side of her and read along.

"Hmm....I recall reading this letter before but I have to admit that I never went so far as to research the origin of the names of the archangels," Meda confessed.

"Well, I guess we'll set it aside for now and see what other things we find that we need to dig into further," added Sarah. "It does seem odd though that my family has always used the spelling of our name with the 'a' and not the 'e' as it appears we should have."

"Perhaps someone made a typographical error at one point and nobody ever caught it?" suggested Tobias.

"That has been known to happen, especially families who migrate from one country to another."

Sarah shrugged her shoulders and agreed, "I guess that's possible too. Either way, I'm not going to worry too much about it right now. I want to see how much progress we can make going through these boxes before dinner. It's my turn to cook tonight!"

~~~~~~~~~~

Later that night, several hours past dinner, the group was surrounded by stacks of carefully placed historical documents, originating from the storage boxes which now lay empty and discarded nearby. Karla looked up to ask her mother a question and noticed that both Meda and Sarah had fallen asleep on the couch, each with a piece of paper still in their hands. Karla and Aubrey exchanged a smile as Karla whispered, "They look like a set of books ends posed like that, don't they?" Aubrey chuckled and nodded in agreement.

Tobias looked up from the documents he had been reading and grinned. Gazing lovingly at his wife, he turned to Karla and quietly said, "They're well suited for one another, don't you think - for what they're destined to find out about each other?"

Karla gave her father a puzzled look and replied, "What do you mean, Dad?"

Tobias came closer to Karla and Aubrey so the sound of his voice wouldn't wake either woman and asked curiously,

"Come on, my Karla. You don't think we're all here by coincidence do you? There's obviously a connection between your mother and Sarah that fate has determined now is the time to discover! Don't you see it?" Turning to Aubrey, he asked, "What about you, Aubrey, do you see it?"

"I don't know what to think yet," Aubrey admitted, honestly. "I agree that it seems as if events are unfolding that all tie into one another but how do we know that it's a good thing or a bad thing?"

"We don't and that scares me a little," added Karla. Turning back to her father she said, "Which is why I'm not admitting to anything yet until I have more information to base my conclusions."

Tobias chuckled and replied, "Always the investigator. That's my Karla."

Out of the corner of Aubrey's eye, she saw movement from the corner of the room along the wall by the sofa. Turning to look fully at the corner she asked, "What was that? Did you see that?"

Both Tobias and Karla looked in the direction Aubrey was looking and asked in unison, "Did we see what?"

"Something moved in the corner, like a shadow — but how could that be? The light is coming from that end of the couch and there's nothing there," replied Aubrey.

"Are you sure you saw something move?" asked Karla as she walked over to the corner for a closer look.

"Positive," replied Aubrey. "Something was definitely there."

Karla turned to Aubrey and replied, "Well there's nothing here now so I don't know what you could have seen."

"Hmm...that's strange," Aubrey replied.

The conversation was interrupted by the sound of Sarah's voice. "What was that all about?" Sarah asked, staring at Meda, who was also now awake.

"I have no idea," Meda replied cautiously, looking at Sarah.

"What was what all about?" asked Karla.

"Sarah and I just shared the same dream," Meda replied.

"Shared the same dream?" Aubrey asked. "How do you know you shared the same dream?"

Sarah turned to Aubrey and replied, "Because we were both in it and talked to one another."

Karla eyed the women carefully and asked, "Mom – what was the dream about?"

Puzzled by her daughter's question, she calmly replied, "We were both sitting on a wooden bench at the base of a large tree in the center of a beautiful garden. Why?"

"Were you the only two people in the garden?" Karla probed.

"I think so," Meda replied looking at Sarah for confirmation. "Did you see anyone else, Sarah?"

Sarah shook her head slowly at Meda and replied, "No, just you."

Sarah looked at Karla and asked, "Why are you so concerned about our dream, Karla? Have you had that same dream?"

"Something similar, yes," Karla admitted. "Before I died, I was having dreams where I was walking through a beautiful garden. At the end of the path, I would always end up standing in front of a massive tree. At the base of the tree was a carved wooden bench."

"That certainly sounds like the same dream," said Tobias.

"So what's the big deal? You all had a dream about a garden and a big tree." Aubrey asked, curiously.

"I don't think it's just 'a garden' we've all seen. I think it's 'the garden,'" Karla replied, emphasizing the difference.

Aubrey's eyes widened in surprise and she asked, "Wait a second. Are you saying 'the garden' as in the garden of Eden?"

Karla nodded her head and replied, "I'm not one-hundred percent sure but I think so." Looking back and forth between Meda and Sarah, she added, "Based upon what just happened between your mother and mine, it sounds like we'll find out soon enough."

Chapter 6

Tori watched Ben's expression carefully as she chewed and swallowed a bite from her sandwich, nervously sliding the charm on her necklace back and forth while she waited.

She had surprised him with an impromptu picnic lunch between two of their classes, to tell him about her recent dreams, and to take advantage of some much needed one-on-one time together.

Both she and Ben quickly found out how difficult it was finding time for dating while they were at the academy. In a nutshell, it was nearly impossible. Even after four months, they were still getting used to the regimented schedule, intense course work and living in the dorms apart from one another.

That's not to say that dorm life didn't have its perks. Tori had totally lucked out getting Piper as a roommate and Ben and Logan seemed to be getting along pretty well. It reminded Tori somewhat of what it had been like in college, although this time around, she was making friends more easily and didn't feel like the wall-flower she had once been.

When Ben finally finished reading, he looked up at her with an expression filled with concern. "Why are you just telling me about these dreams now, Tor?" he asked quietly.

Tori shrugged her shoulders innocently and replied, "There really wasn't much to tell until now! Honest! I had no idea what significance the dreams had until this last one."

Ben searched her eyes and found nothing but sincerity in them. Taking her hand in his, he replied, "Okay, but seriously, don't do that anymore. I want to know what's going on with you – no matter how unimportant you think it is. I know we haven't had that much time to spend together lately and I'll take my share of the blame in that. We need to make a point of keeping the line of communication open between us.

"I think I underestimated how busy we were going to be when we got here. I seriously miss you being first person I see every morning when I wake up and the last person I see before I go to sleep, even if it was from separate bedrooms."

Tori smiled at Ben tenderly and replied, "I know. I miss that too, Ben."

"So what's next? Have you talked with Agent Hunter about what he thinks these dreams mean?" Ben asked.

"That's what he, Agent Sullivan and I were talking about in the library earlier this morning," Tori replied. "I got the impression that they know more about my dream than they're telling me. Agent Hunter sent me a text asking me to join him in the forensics lab after our next class. Maybe I'll find out more then."

Ben finished off the last bite of his sandwich, crumpled the wrapper into a ball and stuffed it into his chip bag. Doing the same with Tori's wrapper, he asked, "I don't have anything going on after class today. Do you think he would mind me tagging along?"

Tori considered the suggestion, shrugged her shoulders and replied, "I don't see why not. I wouldn't mind and it's not like there's nothing you aren't supposed to know."

"Cool. Then I'm coming with you," Ben said happily as he got up to throw their garbage into the trash can.

Extending his hand down to Tori, he added, "It's almost time for class. Are you ready to go?"

Tori slid her notebook into her backpack, placed her hand in his and replied, "Yep. Ready when you are."

He pulled Tori up and in one smooth movement, brought her closer into his arms. Gazing into her eyes and seeing the mirrored affection from his, he smiled at her and whispered, "Hi beautiful." As he kissed her tenderly on the lips, Tori sighed contentedly and leaned into the kiss, sliding her hands up, encircling them around the back of his neck.

"Get a room!" jeered a loud voice behind them.

Forced to end the kiss much sooner than he had hoped, Ben looked at Tori longingly and then pulled away from the embrace. He turned to the source of the interruption and complained, "Seriously, Logan? Your timing sucks."

As Logan and Piper joined them on the sidewalk, Logan chuckled, enjoying the look of frustration on Ben's face. "It's your timing that sucks, my friend. It's time for class," he replied.

Piper looked at Tori apologetically and said, "Sorry, sweetie."

Tori laughed and replied, "No worries. We were on our way to class anyway."

"How come you never kiss me like that?" Logan said to Ben, jokingly.

"Shut up, Logan," Ben laughed, punching his friend in the arm.

Tori and Piper both rolled their eyes at each other and began quietly walking away.

"See? Now look what you've done! I can't even walk my girl to class," Ben accused, pointing at the women as he and Logan began to follow.

"You can walk me to class, handsome! Here, carry my books," Logan teased, attempting to hand Ben his books.

"Seriously, dude!" Ben laughed again. "Knock it off!"

"I hate it when we fight like this," Logan pouted.

"Arghh!" Ben groaned. "Okay, now they're practically running away from us. That's just great. Thanks!"

"Anytime, buddy! That's what friends are for!" Logan chuckled, happily.

~~~~~~~~~~

The classroom was pretty full by the time Tori and the others arrived, so Tori and Piper took two seats in one row, while Ben and Logan found a couple of empty chairs in the row behind them.

The classroom itself was very loosely referenced as it was more similar to a lab with theatre seating. The 'backstage' wall was comprised of forensic refrigeration drawers, evidence drying cabinets, fuming chambers and a section dedicated completely to mass spectrometers and microscopes.

'Center Stage' was where their forensics instructor, Agent Jayco, educated her students on various subject matters which today, was focused on DNA analysis, a subject Tori had been looking forward to all week.

Agent Jayco stood patiently in front of a long table where she had placed several items in preparation for class, while everyone found a seat and the conversations around the room quieted down.

"Good afternoon, everyone," she began. "Today we are going to talk about the science of DNA analysis and how it is used to assist the FBI and other law enforcement agencies in solving crimes. I trust that everyone read through the homework assignment as we have a lot to cover. For those of you who did not do their homework, I wish you luck."

Agent Jayco paused and looked around the room as a quiet murmur of laughter ensued, along with one or two guilty faces of the unprepared.

"So," she continued. "As you read, the basic understanding from the Genome to the Proteome involves cells, proteins and DNA. Cells are the fundamental working units of every living system. All the instructions needed to direct their activities are contained within the chemical deoxyribonucleic acid, or as we more commonly know it, DNA. DNA is made up of the same chemical and physical components and its sequence is the particular side-by-side arrangement of bases along the DNA strand. This order spells out the exact instructions required to create a particular organism with its own unique traits.

"The genome is an organism's complete set of DNA. Genomes vary widely in size: the smallest known genome for a free-living organism, such as a bacterium, contains about six-hundred thousand DNA base pairs, while human and mouse genomes have around three billion. Except for mature red blood cells, all human cells contain a complete genome. A chromosome contains many genes which are the basic physical and functional units of heredity. Genes are specific sequences of bases that encode instructions on how to make proteins and comprise only about two percent of the human genome. Can anyone tell me what the remainder of the human genome consists of?"

Tori immediately raised her hand, along with a few others in the room.

Agent Jayco pointed to one student and said, "Yes, Mr. Arrant."

In a very loud voice, he replied, "The remainder of the human genome consists of Pseudo genes."

"I'm sorry, that is incorrect," replied Agent Jayco.

"That is most certainly correct! It was in the assignment you told us to read!" he objected.

Tori and Piper exchanged a side-long look at one another and exchanged a sarcastic smile. They had nicknamed their fellow classmate, Chet Arrant, 'Arrogant Arrant' as he always had an air of superiority and looked down upon everyone around him from his self-appointed throne.

"Pseudo genes are inactive copies of protein-coding genes, often generated by gene duplication, that have become nonfunctional through the accumulation of inactivating mutations," replied Agent Jayco firmly.   "Although the number of pseudo genes in the human genome is nearly the same as the number of functional protein-coding genes that was not the answer I was looking for. Would anyone else like to try?"

Tori eagerly raised her hand again, not noticing that she was the only remaining student willing to subject themselves to their instructor's criticism.

Agent Jayco pointed to Tori and said, "Miss Cooper."

"The remainder of the human genome consists of non-coding regions, whose functions provide chromosomal structural integrity and regulate where, when, and in what quantity proteins are made," Tori confidently replied.

"That is correct," Agent Jayco announced proudly, nodding at Tori in appreciation. "The proteins are what perform most life functions and make up the majority of our cellular structures. Proteins are large, complex molecules made up of smaller subunits called amino acids. Chemical properties that distinguish the different amino acids cause the protein chains to fold up into specific three-dimensional structures that define their particular functions in the cell."

Agent Jayco turned around to pick up a stack of papers on the table behind her and approached the student in the first row of seats. "Okay. Now we're going to apply some of that background to the lab portion of today's session.

"Please take one of these packets and pass them along to the rest of the class and then we're going to break off into groups of four and review several slides I've prepared on the table behind me. When your team has completed their packet, sign your names to one copy so I know who was in which group, and turn them in before you leave. Does anyone have any questions before we get started?"

Agent Jayco looked around the room expectantly for a moment and when no one raised their hand she said, "All right then, please get started."

Tori, Piper, Ben and Logan quickly assigned themselves to a group as the rest of the class formed their teams. As usual, Arrogant Arrant was one of the last students to find a team as the others in the class had already learned he was not someone they generally enjoyed working with.

Tori watched him scan the teams looking for an opening and quietly said, "I almost feel sorry for him."

"Well don't!" Piper quickly replied. "He deserves what he gets, the way he treats people. He was quick to try and discredit you the last time he challenged one of the answers you provided in class, remember? A dose of humility would do that guy some good. I hope that whatever team he's eventually assigned to is as far away from me as possible. Having to work with that guy every day would be excruciating."

"His latest roommate just requested being reassigned," Logan said in a quiet voice. "That makes three guys this session who have moved to other rooms within the first few weeks of sharing a room with him. I heard the last guy said Arrant is a control freak and has a melt-down if you touch his stuff or if he finds anything out of alignment. The guy definitely has OCD issues. I could seriously mess with his head, given the opportunity."

"Aw, don't do that. If he's really as bad as that, he's got enough to deal with without you messing with him," Tori said.

Ben gave Tori a one-armed hug around the shoulders and replied, "There's the soft-hearted side of my girl."

"Okay enough about him. Let's get to work," Piper said. "Forensics is not my strongest subject and we only have about twenty minutes of class time left."

Scanning through the few pages in the packet, Tori smiled, confidently and replied, "This shouldn't take us long. I've got this."

Hearing her last comment and unseen from a chair in the back of the room, Agent Hunter smiled.

Chapter 7

After class, while everyone was leaving the room, Tori noticed Agent Hunter seated in the back row.

"Agent Hunter!" she exclaimed in surprise. "How long have you been sitting there?"

Agent Hunter smiled at the warm greeting; rose from his chair and replied, "Only about fifteen minutes or so. I arrived a bit earlier than expected so I decided to quietly observe."

Looking beyond Tori to where Piper was standing, he added, "You must be Miss Cooper's roommate, Piper Stirling."

Piper, who was completely enthralled with the beautifully gold aura surrounding the Agent, smiled and extended her hand quickly. "That's correct. It's very nice to meet you, Agent Hunter. Tori speaks very highly of you."

"And she of you, Miss Stirling," he replied, shaking her hand. "It's very nice to meet you as well."

"Hello, Agent Hunter," Agent Jayco said as she approached the group. "It's good to see you again."

"Good to see you again as well, Agent Jayco," Agent Hunter replied, turning his focus away from Piper. "Is this still a good time for you for us to talk?"

"Absolutely! I've blocked off the remainder of my afternoon so I'm ready when you are," Agent Jayco said.

"Excellent," Agent Hunter replied. Turning to Tori he added, "Miss Cooper, would you mind joining us?"

Confused yet curious, Tori nodded her head and replied, "Of course, Agent Hunter. Is it okay if Ben joins us? He asked me earlier and I didn't see a problem with it, if you're okay with him staying."

"No problem at all," replied Agent Hunter. Turning back to Piper, he added, "It was very nice meeting you, Miss Stirling. I look forward to having an opportunity to talk to you again soon."

Realizing yet not caring that she had just been gently dismissed from the group, Piper smiled brightly at Agent Hunter and replied, "I'll look forward to that as well, sir. Thank you." Turning to Tori, she added, "See you later, Tor! Come on, Logan."

Tori waved and replied, "Bye guys!"

When all but the four of them were left in the room, Agent Jayco closed the doors to the classroom and began clearing the center table.

Meanwhile, Agent Hunter returned to where he had been sitting, picked up small cardboard box from the floor beneath the chair and brought the box to the table.

"So, what have you brought me? It's too early for my birthday and it's not gift wrapped so I'm guessing this isn't a present?" Agent Jayco teased.

Agent Hunter snorted a laugh and replied, "Ah, no. This is not the kind of gift you would want someone to give you. At least under the circumstances this particular gift was given." He removed the cover of the box revealing an object in a sealed plastic container and a brown envelope noted with an evidence case number.

Agent Jayco removed the plastic container from the box and held it up at eye level for a closer look. "It's a rose. Or at least it was a rose - now its potpourri." Narrowing her eyes and turning the container on its side, she added, "Hold on. This isn't your ordinary grocery-store variety. I've never seen a rose like this before. Where did you get it?"

Agent Hunter removed the envelope from the box and pulled out several pictures, handing them to Agent Jayco.

"This is what the flower looked like when it was found. We were fortunate to have a very thorough forensic technician working the scene who took the time to carefully photograph and document this particular piece of evidence."

Agent Jayco placed the container on the table and carefully reviewed each photograph. "This looks

72

somewhat like a Mister Lincoln, but at the same time, it has characteristics of...." Her voice trailed off as her mind went to work. "No, that can't be. I would have heard from my former colleagues if this kind of cross-genetics had been successful."

"What kind of cross-genetics, Agent Jayco?" Tori asked curiously, picking up the container to examine it herself.

"A successful genetic cross between a Mister Lincoln and an Ingrid Bergman," she replied with a furrowed brow.

"Sounds more like a cast to an old movie," Ben replied, looking over Tori's shoulder at the dried flower.

Agent Jayco set the photographs down on the table and asked Tori, "May I?" reaching for the container.

"Oh, right," Tori replied, handing it to her. "Sorry."

"Agent Hunter, may I remove the flower from the container, in order to examine it further?" Agent Jayco asked, looking at him for permission.

"Yes, of course," he replied. "That's why I brought it to you. I was hoping your background in genetic botany could help provide some insight as this is really the only evidence we seem to have from our latest killer."

Tori looked at Agent Jayco with surprise and said, "I didn't know you had a background in genetic botany! That is so cool!"

Agent Jayco smiled at Tori warmly and replied, "That was many years ago but at one time, genetics was my deepest passion. Then the area of forensic sciences became more sophisticated and science and technology blended together with law enforcement and before I knew it, I was a student at the academy, training to be an agent in forensic sciences."

"Just like me," Tori murmured with a smile.

"Just like you, my dear," Agent Jayco smiled back at her. "So, why don't we take advantage of the situation and make this a teaching opportunity for both you and Mr. Vincent?"

Agent Jayco gently removed the rose from the container and positioned one of the retractable lamps attached to the table over the flower. "Historically, genetic botanists focus on opportunities to genetically develop new varieties of certain flowers in order to achieve new fragrances, prolonged shelf-life and improved resistance to things like temperature, disease and drought.

"Unfortunately, It can take anywhere from ten to one-hundred thousand seedlings to come up with a new variety."

Tori looked more closely at the flower and asked, "Can other flowers be cross-bred with roses?"

Agent Jayco shook her head and replied, "No, the gene pool is limited to roses and any cross-breeding is random and highly unpredictable. It's difficult enough to breed a specific trait like fragrance much less to cross breed a new species to the genetic structure. The average length of time it takes from the initial cross to getting a new variety is about ten years. Not to mention each rose has approximately one-hundred thousand genes and each variety has a different combination of all of those genes."

"Agent Jayco, what kind of experience would someone need to have for that kind of expertise?" asked Agent Hunter.

Agent Jayco thought for a moment and replied, "A plant scientist or genetic botanist would be my first guess. At a minimum, he or she would need to be fluent in the areas of biology, chemistry, physics and mathematics."

"Wow. Well that narrows it down to – nothing at all what-so-ever," Ben replied shaking his head. "So, what about what you said about Mister Lincoln and Ingrid Bergman?"

"The Mister Lincoln rose was introduced in 1965. It was a long stemmed variety with a deep velvety red color and an outstanding strong fragrance. The Ingrid Bergman rose is also a very fragrant and velvety, has a long stem, and was designed to be a more disease resistant variety than its predecessors. It was introduced in 1984."

"So what would be the advantage to genetically blending the two flowers together?" Tori asked.

"Blending the best qualities of both varieties into a completely new species would provide numerous opportunities for its creator. Think of all the places you've seen selling flowers such as retail and wholesale florists, nurseries who cater to wedding planners, funeral homes and grocery stores. Not to mention the possibility of scientific funding to explore pharmaceutical uses.

"As I said, this flower could have taken its creator a minimum of ten years to achieve. Even in its dried state, you can still smell some of its wonderful fragrance. I can only imagine what it must have smelled like while it was still alive! Here, can you smell it?" Agent Jayco asked, handing the rose to Tori.

Tori reached out her hand to take the rose and immediately felt a jolt run through her body as an image of a man's face flashed in her head. "Oh!" she cried, dropping the rose onto the table and stepping backwards a few steps.

"What's wrong? Did you get stuck by a thorn?" Ben asked taking her hand to check her fingers.

Agent Jayco shook her head and said, "There are no thorns on that flower. That's another trait that is not common but seems to apply to this particular rose. Miss Cooper, what happened?"

Tori looked up at Agent Jayco, her face filled with confusion and stammered, "I-I-I-I'm not sure. Uh, I saw a man's face when I touched the flower and it startled me." Looking down at the flower she added, "Oh! Did I break it?"

Agent Jayco looked at the flower and replied, "No, it seems to be fine."

Agent Hunter came around to Tori's side of the table and looked at her, earnestly. "What do you mean you saw a man's face?"

Tori shook her head and replied, "It was just a flash – like someone taking a picture."

"Can you try it again? See if the same thing happens?" he urged.

Tori looked at the flower speculatively and replied, "Fine. But if I start seeing the spirits of dead flowers – I'm screwed.... and moving to the North Pole!"

"I'm sure they have green houses up there too, somewhere, Tor," Ben joked.

Tori scowled at Ben and spat, "You're not helping!"

"I'm just saying," he reasoned.

Ignoring him, Tori turned back to the flower on the table and tentatively reached out her hand. Pausing briefly, she muttered, "Here goes nothing," and picked it up.

As before, she felt the electric shock run from her fingers through the rest of her body, except this time she was prepared for the sensation. She saw the flash of the man's face again, along with several other images.

"He's Caucasian, dark brown hair, brown eyes," she began quietly.

Agent Hunter grabbed one of the extra assignment packets from the end of the table, turned it over, and as Tori continued, he began writing the details down.

"He's angry yet excited at the same time," she continued. "He's carrying the rose with him."

"Can you see where he is?" asked Agent Hunter.

Tori's expression changed to concentration as she tried to make out details of what she was seeing. "He's in a long hallway somewhere. The walls on either side are only about five feet apart and there's a room ahead of him at the end of the hall." She paused again as she continued to watch. "He just entered the room...it's a bedroom. There's someone sleeping in the bed. It's a woman with long blonde hair. What's that? He's got something in his other hand. It looks like a scalpel! Oh! What is he doing? He's....Oh no!"

Tori dropped the flower again and stumbled away from the table with a terrified expression on her face. "He killed her!" she cried out as her eyes began to fill with tears. "He took the scalpel and slit her throat! She woke up as it was happening and I could see the terror and confusion on her face! He was enjoying it! Oh, he's a monster!"

Ben ran forward and pulled Tori into his arms to comfort her and murmured, "It's okay, breathe, Tor."

"No! It's not okay," she argued, struggling in his arms.

Turning to glare at Agent Hunter she said, "Did you know where that flower came from? How could you do that to me without warning me!"

Trying not to register outwardly the shock he was feeling, Agent Hunter replied, "I had no idea any of this would happen, Miss Cooper. How could I have warned you when I, myself, didn't know?"

Taking a deep breath to calm herself, she replied, "You're right. I'm sorry. I'm just....I don't know what I am right now. What the heck is going on?"

"What else do you remember," Agent Hunter asked. "Can you describe anything else like what the killer was seeing, feeling or thinking?"

Tori shuddered as she thought back to what she had seen and replied, "I don't know....uh, caramel colored silk, a wall made out of glass, the sound of the ocean... Does any of that make sense?"

Agent Hunter and Tori stared silently and unblinking at one another for several seconds before Agent Jayco interrupted. "Gabriel? What's going on?"

Agent Hunter turned away from Tori to meet Agent Jayco's eyes. "Miss Cooper just described the crime scene where that rose was found."

"I, what?" Tori exclaimed in shock. "How could I have done that? I wasn't even there!"

"How is that possible?" Ben asked. "How could a dead flower give Tori all those details?"

Agent Jayco looked at the now ashen expression on Tori's face and replied firmly, "Mr. Vincent, would you be kind enough to get Miss Cooper a drink of water? In the meantime, why don't we all sit down?"

Tori allowed Agent Jayco to lead her to one of the chairs and sat down. A few moments later, Ben returned with a paper cup filled with cool water and gently placed it in Tori's hands.

"Here, sweetie, drink this," he urged.

Tori took a sip of the water and then looked up to find both Agent Jayco and Agent Hunter regarding one another quietly. "What's going on?" she asked.

This time, it was Agent Jayco to look away from the stare-down first, but not before both she and Agent Hunter exchanged a small nod that neither Tori nor Ben missed.

"Miss Cooper, what can you tell me about matter as it relates to energy?" she asked.

Tori thought for a moment and replied, "Well, I know Albert Einstein believed that all matter is capable of being converted to energy, and that a relatively small amount of matter can be converted to a large amount of energy, like matter being transformed into non-matter. And that he also believed that although matter can be created or destroyed, neither the quantity of the mass nor the energy changes during the process. But, that's all I know."

Agent Jayco blinked in surprise, smiled slyly and replied, "I'm impressed. That's more than most people know, Miss Cooper."

"My head is filled with a lot of seemingly random things," Tori admitted.

"What does that have to with what just happened?" Ben asked.

"Well," Agent Jayco began, "there are some people who believe that all living things possess an energy signature that is uniquely owned by that living thing. Very much like a fingerprint. They also believe that an energy signature remains with that living thing up until the time it dies at which time the energy is released into the atmosphere and either dissipates or transfers to the nearest living creature it encounters upon leaving its host."

"Like a spirit?" Tori asked, trying to understand.

"Possibly a spirit, yes," Agent Jayco reasoned.

"What about the other people? You said 'some people' believed that theory. What do the others believe?" Tori asked.

Agent Jayco sat in the chair beside Tori and turned to face her. "Others believe that sometimes, when either a strong emotional tie or a traumatic event occurs at the time of an organism's death, that energy signature remains with the organism."

"Which of those people are you, Agent Jayco?" Tori asked, watching her expression carefully.

Agent Jayco smiled at Tori and replied, "I've always found myself on the fence when it came to that argument, as I've had no solid proof one way or the other. Now, having seen first-hand what you just experienced, I would have to consider that perhaps both theories may be correct."

"So are you saying that flower has an energy signature that recorded the death of the woman Tori saw?" Ben asked, incredulously.

"For the moment, I would have to say, yes. Unless anyone else has any other plausible explanation," Agent Jayco replied, looking around the group.

Tori shook her head silently and then looked up at Agent Hunter. "What was her name?" she asked, quietly.

"Marsha Foster," he replied.

"She looked so scared," Tori added. "Did she have a family?"

"She was married but they had no children," Agent Hunter replied.

"Her husband must be devastated. Do you have any leads on who the killer is?" Tori asked.

With a grim expression, he replied, "We didn't until just a few minutes ago. At least now we have at least a partial physical description."

"Back up. You didn't know anything about him until just now? How many other women has he killed?" Tori exclaimed.

"Mrs. Foster was his fourth victim spanning a two-year period," Agent Hunter replied.

"And you've had no leads into the other murders either?" Tori asked.

"Unfortunately, no, we haven't. We've been waiting for him to make a mistake or perhaps be fortunate enough for a witness to step forward; however, thus far, neither has happened," Agent Hunter replied.

Tori and Agent Hunter stared at each other silently yet still communicating with their eyes as Tori began to ask, "Where are the other three flowe..."

"Hold on a minute!" Ben objected. "Are you actually thinking what I think you're thinking, Tori?"

Tori turned to Ben and replied, "Ben, I have to! Don't you see? If I don't at least try to help identify this man, no matter how small of a chance it may be, then why am I here? Training to be an agent? Trying to help stop people like him?"

Ben sighed and crouched down in front of her chair. "I know, babe, but you didn't see your face just now. You were horrified by what you saw, what you felt. Do you really want to go through that three more times?"

"I have to, Ben," she whispered. "Those women need justice and their families need closure."

"All right," Ben replied, locking eyes with hers. "If you're sure, then I'll support you."

"Thank you," she replied with a small smile. Looking back to Agent Hunter, she asked again, "Where are the other flowers and the women's bodies? Can I talk to them?"

"All four of the victims were released to their families, three of which were buried. I believe the fourth victim was cremated. If you're sure you're willing to do this, I'll contact Agent Hughes and Agent Nichols and ask if they can pull the case details and to meet us in the morning."

Agent Hunter paused, deliberating something else. "We're going to need a diversion to excuse you from your classes. Agent Jayco, do you think you could come up with a cover to excuse Miss Cooper from class for a couple of days?"

"I want to come with you!" objected Ben.

"I don't think that's a good idea," Agent Hunter argued. "It will draw less attention having you remain on campus, Mr. Vincent. You can join us after your last class of the day if you would like."

While Ben silently brooded Agent Hunter added, "Agent Jayco?"

Agent Jayco gave him a secretive smile and replied, "I believe I could do that, on one condition."

84

Agent Hunter raised his eyebrows in surprise and replied, "And what would that condition be?"

"That I be able to join you as well," she replied, hopefully.

Agent Hunter began to object but Agent Jayco stopped him in mid-breath by saying, "You're going to need someone with my expertise in genetic botany to determine if all four flowers are the same variety. Considering the delicate nature of the circumstances, my ability to do that discreetly will help reduce the number of people made aware of Miss Cooper's ability."

Agent Hunter closed his opened mouth and pondered her reasoning. Not being able to find an obvious objection, he replied, "All right. I can see your point. Then I guess we'll need you to come up with an excuse for you as well."

"Wonderful!" she replied happily. "I'll make the arrangements!"

Chapter 8

Later that afternoon, after Tori, Agent Jayco and Agent Hunter confirmed their plans for the following day, Agent Hunter and Tori walked back to her dormitory together.

"Sir," Tori began, deliberating her question carefully. "Are you sure Ben can't come with us tomorrow? He's going to feel left out."

Agent Hunter continued looking ahead as they walked and replied, "This isn't his quest, Miss Cooper. Mr. Vincent will bring value to our team in certain ways; however, for now, I think it' important for you focus on what you will bring to the team."

"Yes, sir," Tori replied, quietly. They walked in silence a few minutes more when Tori asked, "Sir?"

"Yes, Miss Cooper?" he replied.

"What was the nod you and Agent Jayco exchanged earlier when we were talking about the flower?" she asked.

He chuckled at her, impressed that she had picked up on the exchange and replied, "That was an acknowledgement to one another that we had just witnessed an evolvement of your initial ability."

Tori stopped walking and hissed in a loud whisper, "She knows too?"

Agent Hunter stopped beside her, looked around them to make sure no one was within earshot and replied, "I told you that some of your instructors would be made aware of your ability, Miss Cooper. This shouldn't come as a shock to you."

"But you never said whom," she exclaimed, pausing to think about all of her current instructors. "Remind me not to play poker with anyone on campus. I have no idea who knows and who doesn't. Who else knows?"

Agent Hunter laughed in response; turned and continued walking. "Just Agent Sullivan and Agent Jayco have been made aware of it. That's all."

Tori thought for a moment longer and then quickly caught up with him. "Uh, sir, do you think there would be any benefit having Agent Easton be made aware of my ability?"

Agent Hunter laughed again, knowing her reason for asking and replied, "Having trouble with your firearms training, Miss Cooper?"

Tori smiled sheepishly and replied, "It's not one of my strongest areas, sir. Perhaps he would go easier on me if he knew?"

"Yes, I've seen your training scores. Besides, I don't think him knowing would change anything," Agent Hunter replied, dryly.

"I had a feeling you would say that," Tori grumbled.

As they approached the dormitory building, Tori noticed Piper sitting on the steps, reading a book.

"Hey, Piper!" Tori called out, happily.

Piper looked up and immediately smiled. "Hey, Tori!" she replied. When she looked over at Agent Hunter, her smile broadened as she once again found herself enthralled in the golden glow surrounding him. "Hi, Agent Hunter!" she added.

"Good evening, Miss Stirling," he replied as they approached her. "Enjoying the fresh air?" he asked, pleasantly.

"Actually I came out here to watch the sunset," she replied. "The colors on the clouds as the sun went down gave them the most beautiful pinkish-orange glow. Did you see it?"

Agent Hunter smiled at her simple enjoyment of a sunset and replied, "No, unfortunately we missed it. What colors are you seeing right now, Miss Stirling?" he asked, humorously.

Piper looked at Tori quickly in surprise to which Tori returned her look with a small shake of her head.

"Don't worry, Miss Stirling," Agent Hunter chuckled. "Miss Cooper did not give your secret away. I'm fully aware of your ability to see the auras surrounding people. It's in your file."

"It is?" Piper replied in shock. "How, who put it there?"

"Part of our acceptance of cadets into the academy is to conduct personal interviews of certain friends and family members in order to assess your general temperament and personality. Your Aunt Skyler gave you quite a colorful recommendation, if you'll excuse my pun," he chuckled.

"And still, I was accepted," Piper marveled.

"You passed your psych evaluation and your marksmanship scores were quite impressive, both of which easily qualified you as an ideal candidate for the program. Being able to see auras was considered a side advantage we thought might prove to be of service to us, very much like Miss Cooper's ability."

"Huh," Piper replied. "Okay, I guess."

"So, what colors do you see now?" he asked again, curiously.

Piper gave him a wry smile and replied, "Tori's is a beautiful shade of green, like it is most of the time, and yours..." she paused as she looked at the air around him, "is the most incredible golden glow I have ever seen. In fact, I was trying to figure out what gold represented because I've never experienced it before. That's what I was reading when you both walked up," showing him the book in her hand.

"Hmmm," replied Agent Hunter, curiously. "May I?" he added, motioning to the book.

Piper opened the book to where she had been using her finger as a bookmark and handed it to Agent Hunter.

Taking a moment to scan the page, he began to read. "Gold is the color of enlightenment and divine protection. When seen within the aura, that the person is being divinely guided by their highest good, and someone who is charismatic, is a hard worker, possesses a position of high responsibility and someone who is patient and successful.

"That's very interesting. Where is green?" he asked himself, flipping back a few pages. "Ah, here it is. Green indicates someone who is peaceful, social, close to nature, harmonious, compassionate with people and animals and tends towards a career in public services. Green usually represents growth and balance, and most of all, something that leads to change. That's a very clear definition of Miss Cooper, I would have to say. Would you agree?" he paused, looking at Piper.

"I would say yes to both descriptions, actually. Wouldn't you, Tor?" Piper asked, smiling at Tori who smiled and nodded back at her.

Agent Hunter flipped through a couple more pages, read to himself and then laughed again. "Brown indicates one who is egotistical, selfish, emotional and self-centered. I think I saw someone in one of your classes today who fits that description. Do you tend to find these definitions generally accurate, Miss Stirling?" he asked as he handed the book back to Piper.

"Yes, I do sir," Piper replied.

"What did you mean when you said Miss Cooper's aura is green most of the time? When have you seen it otherwise?" he asked.

Piper glanced at Tori, and replied, "Well, the other night when Tori had her latest dream, I came home late from alley simulations, Tori was already asleep. As I was about to turn off the light on my side of the room, I noticed Tori's expression looked puzzled and her aura was swirling around her like a thunderstorm mixing with dark shades of grey and black. As I watched, it suddenly went to completely black and then a few moments later she cried out and woke up as her aura switched back to green. I had never seen anything like that before. It was creepy. Then when she told me about her dream, I realized what had happened."

Piper opened the book and flipped through it to a particular page and read out loud. "A black aura indicates a drawing or pulling of energy into it and in so doing transforms it, capturing and consuming light. It typically indicates a long-term un-forgiveness towards others or another being."

Piper looked over at Tori and said, "He was trying to pull you in and take away your light. If you hadn't been pulled away when you were, there's no telling what could have happened."

"What do you mean, 'pulled away,' Miss Stirling?" he asked, puzzled.

"We don't know for sure that's what happened," Tori quickly interjected, giving Piper a stern look.

"We don't know for sure that it's not!" Piper argued back.

"What are you both talking about?" Agent Hunter asked, now very confused.

When Tori refused to answer, Piper scowled at her and said, "Tori told me that when Satan lunged at her, she felt as if someone had wrapped their arms around her and pulled her away."

Agent Hunter looked at Tori's guarded expression and gazed at her thoughtfully for a moment. "I believe you left that part out of your notes, Miss Cooper." When Tori still didn't respond, he turned back to Piper and asked, "And what do you think she meant, Miss Stirling?"

"Well," she began, "it sounded to me like maybe someone was protecting her. Maybe someone else was in the garden with her, but she didn't see him. Maybe he was hiding, watching, and when he saw what was going to happen, maybe he came forward and saved her."

"Like whom, exactly?" he prodded.

"Like maybe a guardian angel," she stated firmly, jutting out her chin, challengingly.

"That's a lot of maybes," Agent Hunter replied, looking once again at Tori's expression. "And what do you think, Miss Cooper?"

Tori inhaled deeply, paused for a moment and then sighed in defeat. "I have no idea what it meant, sir, which is why I didn't write it down. Maybe writing it down meant that I might have to actually consider Piper could be right."

"Now she says it!" Piper exclaimed, dramatically.

Tori rolled her eyes at Piper and sighed, "I said you could be right, not that you are right, Piper."

Agent Hunter's gaze wandered to the center of campus as he deliberated a thought for a moment. Making his decision, he pulled his cell phone from his pocket, dialed a number and waited a few moments for the call to connect. "Kent? It's Gabe. Are you still in your office? I was wondering if Miss Cooper and I could stop by. Yes, now. All right, we'll be there shortly." Ending the call, Agent Hunter turned to Piper and Tori and said, "Miss Cooper, would you care to take a walk with me?"

"Why, where are we going?" Tori asked, curiously.

"We're going to pay Agent Sullivan a visit. He should know about the part of your dream you very conveniently left out," he replied.

"What about Piper?" Tori asked. "Can she come too?"

Agent Hunter looked at Piper and said, "If you wouldn't mind sitting this one out, Miss Stirling, I would appreciate it. For the moment I feel its best that we limit the number of people in our discussion."

"No problem, Agent Hunter, I understand," Piper replied. "We can continue our other conversation another time."

"I would like that very much, thank you. Miss Cooper, shall we?" he asked, motioning her to join him on the walkway.

"Okay," Tori said, getting up from the steps. "I'll see you later, Piper."

"See ya!" Piper called out as Tori and Agent Hunter walked away.

~~~~~~~~~~

"So why do you think it's so improbable that you could have a guardian angel, Miss Cooper?" Agent Sullivan asked curiously, having just heard the most recent version of her dream.

"Improbable isn't the word I would use, sir. More like impossible and borderline crazy!" Tori exclaimed, throwing her hands up in the air and pacing back and forth across the room. "If I really have a guardian angel, then why is he or she just now deciding to reveal themselves to me? Why not after my sister disappeared when I really needed it? Why not when I was kidnapped by a serial killer and almost killed?"

"How do you know he or she hasn't been there all along?" Agent Sullivan asked, reasonably.

Tori thought back for a moment and replied, "Because that was the first time I've ever felt someone else there with me. I can still feel the pressure of his arms surrounding me, like I was in a cocoon or something like a shell. I don't know," she sighed, shaking her head.

"What makes you think it's male?" Agent Sullivan asked.

Tori looked up at him, puzzled and asked, "What?"

"You said, 'his arms,'" he replied.

"I did?" she asked, looking at Agent Hunter for confirmation.

"Yes, you did," he replied quietly, meeting her gaze from across the room.

"Did you have a sense of anything else about him?" Agent Sullivan probed further.

Tori slid her heart charm along its chain absently as she thought back to that night, shook her head slowly and said, "Not so much about him directly, like a smell or a sound. It was more like an awareness of power, speed and movement."

Agent Sullivan cocked his head sideways and gave her a puzzled look, "What do you mean?" he asked.

Tori ran her hands through her hair distractedly and then sat down facing Agent Sullivan, "It's hard to explain and I was a bit distracted by Satan coming at me and all that. But I guess if I had to put it into words, I would say it was like I was inside of a bullet and someone had just fired me from a gun. One moment I was standing there having a conversation with the devil, and then it felt like something closed in around me and then I was pulled away so quickly that I felt like my breath was pulled right out of me. The next thing I remembered was sitting up in my bed gasping for air."

Agent Sullivan and Agent Hunter exchanged a look with one another as Agent Sullivan asked Tori, "Was the cocoon or closed in feeling something that was hard or confining?"

"No, it was more like something warm, soft and comforting," Tori replied.

"Like a pillow?" he asked, trying to understand.

"No," Tori replied in frustration, "more like ...." She stopped short as the realization came to her. She looked at Agent Sullivan, doubtfully and added, "No, that can't be right...."

"What can't be right?" he asked, quietly.

"I almost said feathers," she whispered.

Without registering an expression, he asked, "But did it feel like feathers, now that you think about it?"

Tori nodded her head slowly and then turned to see Agent Hunter's surprised expression. Looking back at Agent Sullivan, she asked, "Could it be 'him'?"

Agent Sullivan sat back in his chair and exhaled a deep sigh, "Anything is possible at this point."

"Which one is it?" Tori questioned.

Agent Hunter chuckled as he pushed himself away from the wall he had been leaning against and walked over to one of the empty chairs to sit down. "I told you she wouldn't forget."

Agent Sullivan chuckled with him and replied, "Yes you did." Smiling gently at Tori, he added, "To answer your first question, I don't know which one. As for the question that you were going to ask next, I too have found myself wondering about the apparent distinctions between the angels Ramiel and Remiel. I haven't been able to find any conclusive evidence to support whether there were actually two different angels or if there was only one and somewhere down the line his name and or meaning was distorted."

Seeing the look on her face turn to disappointment, he added, "I truly wish I could give you a definitive answer, Miss Cooper; however, I promise you that I haven't stopped looking. I love a good mystery and this one has proven to be a really good one. I'm even more intrigued now that I may have met one of his descendants."

Tori blinked in surprise and replied, "Me? I'm one of his descendants? How do you know?"

97

"If you'll be patient with me and Agent Hunter until tomorrow morning, I promise we will tell you what we know and what we believe to be answers to all of your questions. Can you do that, Miss Cooper? Trust us until then?"

Tori nodded her head and replied, "Yes. I can do that."

"Thank you," Agent Sullivan replied.

Tori scrunched up her nose as she deliberated another question, "Um, sir, may I ask one other question? It's something that's been bothering me but I didn't know how to bring it up."

"You can always ask me about what's on your mind, Miss Cooper, no matter how random or unrelated it may seem," he replied. "What is it you would like to know?"

"How did Satan know about the tree of knowledge and what it could do?" Tori asked, curiously. "Even back in the time of Adam and Eve, he taunted Eve into eating from the tree because he knew not only would she not die from eating its fruit, but doing so would also open her eyes and make her aware of all that God knew. How did Satan know? Did God cast the angels out of heaven after he created the heavens and the earth or before?"

Agent Sullivan smiled warmly at Tori and replied, "You are full of tough questions that are very difficult to answer, my dear!" When she gave him an apologetic smirk, he laughed and patted her shoulder, gently. "No, don't ever apologize for searching for the truth."

Taking a few moments to formulate his thoughts into words, he continued. "The story of Eve and the serpent has been the topic of many heated discussions not only in Christian communities, but other religious groups who have tried to use it to discredit the book of Genesis.

"Always try to keep in mind that the Bible was not written to be learned in chapters, like a traditional book. There are many overlapping areas in the Bible which were written by different prophets or authors, but told from differing perspectives. For example, in Genesis, after Adam and Eve ate from the tree of knowledge, they both died and yet did not die."

Tori started to object so Agent Sullivan quickly added, "Just hear me out. The eating of the fruit was symbolic in that they died spiritually and were removed from a place where they had direct contact with God. Once that happened, they could not go back. They did not experience immediate physical death, but they did eventually die. Many theologians believe it may be that the process of aging and decay started on the day Adam and Eve ate the fruit."

Tori thought for a moment and replied, "Okay. I agree that does sound plausible. But it doesn't answer my question. How did Satan know that would happen and was it before or after he was cast out of heaven?"

"Again, it depends on who you talk to," replied Agent Sullivan. "If you talk to someone from the Jewish community, they'll tell you the snake was just a talking snake and that it wasn't Satan. They believe that Satan was actually God's 'right hand man' for lack of a better term, as was written in the book of Job. He was noted as the accuser of men, very much like God's cop, not his enemy. What's always intrigued me was the irony of Satan appearing to Eve as a serpent, and then God cursing Satan in the form of a serpent due to him tempting and causing Eve to sin."

When Tori gave Agent Sullivan a confused look, he rose from his chair, walked over to his bookcase and pulled a Bible from one of the shelves. Sitting back down in the chair beside her, he opened the book and began reading, "This is from the book of Genesis, chapter three, verses fourteen and fifteen: 'And the Lord God said unto the serpent, "Because thou hast done this, thou art cursed above all cattle, and above every beast of the field; upon thy belly shalt thou go, and dust shalt thou eat all the days of thy life: And I will put enmity between thee and the woman, and between thy seed and her seed; it shall bruise thy head, and thou shalt bruise his heel."'"

"I'm getting confused," Tori sighed.

"I'm sorry, I got off track again and didn't answer your question," Agent Sullivan replied, once again rising from his chair, selecting a different book from his bookshelf and returning to the chair next to Tori. "Let me back up a bit and I am by no means a theologian so I'm giving you my opinion on what I believe based upon my research over the years so take from it what you will."

Opening the book to a marked chapter, he began to read. "Lucifer was said to be one of God's archangels, his name meaning 'Morning Star.' Before the fall he was called Lucifer and after the fall he became known as Satan."

"So when I called him Satan in my dream and he indicated that I properly called him by name, that makes sense that I was talking with the fallen angel," Tori mused.

"So it would seem," Agent Sullivan agreed as he continued reading. "Modern Hebrew translations indicate the passage in which the phrase 'Lucifer' or 'morning star' begins with the statement: 'On the day the Lord gives you relief from your suffering and turmoil and from the harsh labor forced on you, you will take up this taunt against the king of Babylon: How the oppressor has come to an end! How his fury has ended!' After describing the death of the king, the taunt continues: 'How you have fallen from heaven, morning star, son of the dawn! You have been cast down to the earth, you who once laid low the nations! You said in your heart, "I will ascend to the heavens; I will raise my throne above the stars of God; I will sit enthroned on the mount of assembly, on the utmost heights of Mount Zaphon. I will ascend above the tops of the clouds; I will make myself like the Most High."'"

"Sounds like someone got on a power trip," Tori declared, snidely.

"Indeed it does," replied Agent Sullivan.

"So going back to Miss Cooper's question, it's possible that the archangels had much of the same knowledge as the Christians believed God did, which would mean they too would have known about the tree of knowledge and what it could do," reasoned Agent Hunter.

"That is one possible argument, yes," replied Agent Sullivan. Turning to Tori he asked, "Does that help answer your question?"

"I think so. At least it gives me a place to start since it sounds like I have some homework ahead of me to prepare for my next encounter. Thank you Agent Sullivan. I appreciate your taking the time off hours to talk about this," Tori replied.

Agent Sullivan smiled and said, "My door is always open, Miss Cooper. I'm glad to help."

"I think this would be a good stopping point for the night. We have a lot to cover tomorrow. We'll see you in the morning, Agent Sullivan," said Agent Hunter, rising from his chair.

"Yes, I agree. I will see you both in the morning," replied Agent Sullivan as he too, rose from his chair.

Tori joined Agent Hunter at the door and turned to Agent Sullivan, "Thank you again, sir. Good night."

"Good night, Miss Cooper," he replied, pleasantly as he stood in the doorway for a few moments, watching her and Agent Hunter exit the building.

Reflecting back upon the past hour's conversation, he slowly shook his head back and forth, snorted a laugh and muttered, "It felt like feathers.....fascinating!"

Chapter 9

Early the next morning, Agent Hunter picked up Tori, Agent Jayco and Agent Sullivan, and they all drove together to the conference center on the edge of campus.

As they entered their meeting room, Tori smiled broadly when she saw Agent Nichols and Agent Hughes standing by the breakfast bar, talking.

"Hey, strangers!" called Tori, happily. "This is an added bonus seeing you both today!"

"Hi, Tori," replied Agent Nichols, smiling in greeting.

"Miss Cooper," replied Agent Hughes, pleasantly.

"Did you just arrive in town this morning?" Tori asked.

Agent Nichols stifled a yawn and replied, "Yep. We caught the red-eye flight in from New Jersey."

"New Jersey? What were you doing there?" Tori asked, as she began her ritual of finding the perfect mixture of sugar and milk in her coffee.

"We'll get to that once everyone else is here," Agent Nichols replied as she looked beyond Tori towards Agent Hunter, who was walking up to the group with Agent Jayco and Agent Sullivan. "Hello, sir."

"Good morning, Agent Nichols. You remember Agent Jayco and Agent Sullivan?" inquired Agent Hunter.

"Yes of course! It's a pleasure seeing you both again," Agent Nichols replied, extending her hand to each of them in turn.

"Likewise, Agent Nichols," replied Agent Jayco, shaking her hand.

"Good to see you again, Agent Nichols," replied Agent Sullivan.

Agent Hughes stepped forward and extended his hand as well, "Hello. I don't believe we've met. I'm Agent Hughes."

"Nice to meet you as well, Agent Hughes," replied Agent Jayco, shaking his hand.

"Likewise," repeated Agent Sullivan.

Tori looked at Agent Nichols, curiously and asked, "What did you mean 'when everyone else gets here,' Agent Nichols? Who else is joining us?"

"I believe she was referring to us, honey," sounded her mother's voice from the doorway.

Tori whipped around quickly, shocked to see her mother, sister, Meda, Karla and an older man standing in the doorway. "Mom? Bree? What on earth are you doing here?"

"Gee, you could least pretend to be happy to see us," Aubrey teased.

"Of course I'm glad to see you, just surprised! I had no idea you all would be here," Tori replied rushing up to hug her mother. "Look at you! You've got a sun tan, Mom! I can't remember the last time you looked so relaxed!"

Sarah laughed, set down Aubrey's bag, hugged Tori back and replied, "You can thank Meda, Karla and Tobias for that! They've been spoiling me and your sister ever since the day we arrived at their home."

Tori's eyes moved to Meda, Karla and Tobias and the rolling suitcase Meda was pulling. She smiled broadly and said, "You all look so happy together! I'm so very glad you've found a way to bring Tobias with you. It's very nice to finally meet you."

Tobias smiled warmly and replied, "It is a pleasure to meet you as well, Tori. I have heard so many wonderful things about you. I feel as if I already know you!"

"And I, you," replied Tori.

"Why don't we all take a few minutes to introduce ourselves to one another, get a cup of coffee and a bagel or a pastry and then let's all have a seat at the table," Agent Hunter paused, a bit embarrassed and added, "for those of us who are able to have a seat, my apologies to Agent Neviah, Miss Cooper and Mr. Ramirez."

"No offense taken Agent Hunter," Meda chuckled. "We'll just put their bags over there, against the wall."

Agent Hunter watched Sarah and Meda set the bags against the wall by the conference table and tried not to think about the partial skeletons they were concealing.

Fortunately, he had already briefed Agents Jayco and Sullivan of the special circumstances which required Sarah and Meda to transport their loved ones' bodies in suitcases so Agent Neviah, her father and Tori's sister could join them.

While everyone made introductions and got their coffee, he decided to take advantage of the few minutes to go through some of the folders Agent Nichols and Agent Hughes had brought with them. He scanned through them briefly and took a few of them with him to his seat at the head of the table.

"Thank you all for joining us today. We actually have a bit more to cover than we originally planned when I asked you all to join us, so I hope you will forgive me for the expanded agenda," Agent Hunter began, nodding to Meda and Sarah. "We've recently acquired some new information about a serial killer the FBI has been tracking for the past few years. His pattern thus far has been sporadic and very difficult to profile, so our team's involvement has been limited as we had no strong leads. That is until yesterday afternoon," he added, looking directly at Tori.

Tori looked around nervously being called out and her eyes stopped on Agent Hughes, who was regarding her intently. *'Still doing that creepy staring thing, aren't you, buddy?'* Tori thought to herself, humorously. Resisting the urge to cross her eyes and make a face, she turned back at Agent Hunter.

"I contacted Agent Nichols and Agent Hughes last night and asked them to bring the details of the open cases we had so far, in order to bring Miss Cooper, Agent Jayco and Agent Sullivan up to speed on our killer's background," Agent Hunter added.

Sarah looked at Tori curiously and then turned back to Agent Hunter. "I don't understand, Agent Hunter. Why would Tori be involved in this investigation?"

"It would appear that Miss Cooper has an added ability we were not aware of," replied Agent Hunter. "Actually, now that I think about it, if you and Mrs. Neviah would be willing to try something for me, it would be interesting to see if either of you possess the same ability."

Agent Hunter walked over to a box on the sidebar table and picked up four identically shaped, oblong plastic containers, each with an identification label noting its respective case file number. Setting all but one of the containers on the conference table, he approached Meda and Sarah and said, "Yesterday afternoon, I brought this flower to Agent Jayco, in hopes she could identify its origin. While we were talking, Miss Cooper touched the flower and immediately saw the face of the man we believe might be our killer. She was also able to describe specific details about the crime scene."

"That is so cool!" Aubrey exclaimed in fascination. "Mom you've got to try it!"

Sarah laughed at Aubrey's reaction but then turned to see the expression on Tori's face and said, "Aubrey thinks that's very cool. However, I can see from my other daughter's expression that she may disagree. Honey, what's on your mind?"

Tori's mouth was set in a firm line and her eyes were troubled. "Mom, what I saw and felt was horrible. I still can't get the image of the woman's terrified expression out of my head. I'm not sure you should do it."

"And after what you saw, you're still willing to help?" Sarah asked curiously.

"Yes, of course. I have to!" Tori exclaimed. "Those women deserve justice."

Sarah smiled at her and replied, "Then that would be the exact same reason why I would do it, honey." Turning back to Agent Hunter, Sarah said, "I'll try it, Agent Hunter."

"Thank you," he said as he removed the flower from the container and handed it to her.

Sarah took the flower gently from him and held her breath. A few seconds later, she looked up and met his eager eyes. "Nothing happened. Was it immediate?"

Agent Hunter sighed in disappointment and said, "Yes, as soon as she touched it."

"May I try?" Meda asked, beside Sarah. Sarah handed her the flower and she too held her breath anticipating a reaction. When nothing happened, she shook her head and looked at Sarah. "Nothing," she said.

"Hmmm....interesting," murmured Agent Hunter. He took the flower back, returned it to its container and walked back to his chair. Setting the container aside, he picked up the other three containers and turned to Tori. "Before I go into any details about the cases and set any preconceived ideas about the victims, I would like to see what you are able to pick up from these other three samples. Are you still willing to do that, Miss Cooper?" he asked.

Tori nodded her head and confidently replied, "Yes, I am. How would you like to approach this? Have me start with the first victim and go forward or the third victim and go backward?"

Agent Hunter deliberated for a moment, turned to Agent Hughes and asked, "Agent Hughes, would it be helpful in your profile for Miss Cooper to start with the first victim and move forward? That seems the logical approach to me. However, I'm curious if you would agree."

Agent Hughes rocked back and forth in his chair a few times, considering the suggestion and replied, "I would agree. Starting with the first victim may help identify the trigger we've been looking for. Miss Cooper, did you happen to pick up on any emotions or thoughts from the killer during your experience yesterday?"

Tori shuddered at the memory and replied, "Yes. I was able to feel his anger and his excitement as he was approaching Mrs. Foster as well as while he was.....uh, slitting her throat."

"Oh, my," replied Sarah, now understanding Tori's reason for not wanting her to see what she had seen.

"Ugh, not so cool after all," Aubrey added. "I'm sorry, Tor."

"It's okay, Bree," Tori replied. "I'm actually kind of glad neither Mom nor Meda were able to see anything. It was gross and very disturbing." Tori shuddered again at the memory then shook it off and said, "Okay Agent Hunter, let's start with flower number one."

Agent Hunter set the container from the first victim down in front of Tori and watched as she picked it up and removed the lid. Very gently, she tipped the container, allowing the flower to slide onto the top of the table and then she set the container aside. Stretching out her fingers as if she was about to play Beethoven's Fifth Symphony, she looked up at Agent Hunter and said, "Ready or not."

As soon as she touched the flower, she felt the charge travel from her fingertips to the rest of her body and she gasped out loud as she felt as if she was being physically taken to another place. While the images began to emerge, she spoke them out loud. "I see a woman with long blonde hair walking in front of me, pulling a wheeled suitcase. She's wearing a blue skirt and jacket. She's very pretty." Tori paused as another image filtered into view.

"There she is again, but this time, she's dressed more casually and she's surrounded by flowers. She's smiling at me, like she knows me." Tori paused again as her expression changed to confusion, trying to figure out what she was seeing now. "Huh. Now I'm in the dark, but moving forward. His heart racing and he's feeling...happy? That's weird."

Tori turned her head in the direction towards Sarah as if she was going to ask her a question, but then Sarah realized Tori's eyes were glazed over and she couldn't see her. "Tori?" she asked, nervously.

"I'm okay, Mom" Tori replied, calmly. "Just trying to see if I can figure out where I am. I can hear a sound of a horn off in the distance like a boat or a train. Okay, I think I'm in an apartment or condo. It's too small to be a house and it's not a master bedroom, more like a smaller guest room. I can see a shape in the bed like I did last time. It's the same woman who was rolling the suitcase. She's sleeping. Ugh.....he has the scalpel in his hand and he's approaching the bed."

"Tori, can you see anything reflective like a mirror or a picture frame where you might catch a better glimpse of his face?" asked Agent Hughes.

Tori hesitated for a moment while she tried to look around the woman's bedroom and replied, "No, there's nothing like that in this room. There's only a bed, a dresser and a nightstand with an alarm clock. It's 3:18 AM. He's standing right over her now and she's not waking up. He's...oh!" Tori cried out, still holding the flower as her breathing became quick and panicked.

"Deep breaths, Miss Cooper," interrupted Agent Hunter. "Remember you're not really there. Try to stay with the image as long as you can."

Tori nodded vaguely as she focused on her breathing and said, "Yes, okay." She sat in silence a few minutes longer taking in long steady breaths while she continued to watch. Then she laid the flower back on the table and shook her head a few times as her vision began to clear and the tingling left her fingers.

Taking in a deep breath and exhaling loudly, she said, "She didn't wake as he slit her throat, thank goodness. He held the scalpel in his right hand and after he positioned her body, he placed the flower in her right hand and whispered, 'I haven't forgotten'. That's all. After that, the image stopped."

Tori looked around the room at all the faces staring at her, taking in everyone's expressions. To her right, Sarah's and Meda's faces were those of concern. To her left, Agent Jayco's and Agent Sullivan's were those of fascination and across the horse-shoe table, Agent Nichols' and Agent Hughes' were those of disbelief. When her gaze stopped with Agent Hunter, his was a mask of guardedness.

'Always the poker player', she thought to herself. "How did I do this time?" she asked, quietly.

Agent Hunter opened one of the manila folders in his hands and began reading, "Taylor Kellogg, killed on February 13, 2011, single, twenty-eight years old, flight attendant from Brookfield, Wisconsin. She was staying at an apartment in Edison, New Jersey the airline leases for flight attendants and pilots during flight rotations. Miss Kellogg and two other women were in the apartment that weekend. The other two women were unharmed and didn't hear anyone break in during the night. They found Miss Kellogg the next morning and called the police. There were no signs of forced entry and the coroner estimated time of death between three and four AM. Her throat was slit from left to right, indicating her killer was right handed, and he placed a single red rose in her right hand."

"Kellogg, I remember that girl," Agent Neviah noted. "Remember Mom? You and I went to her funeral and crossed her over after everyone left."

Meda smiled sadly and replied, "Yes, Karla, I remember her. She was a very pretty girl as Tori mentioned."

"You and Karla met her?" Tori asked, curiously.

"Yes, I believe Karla and I probably crossed all three of the previous victims over but I'll wait until you have had an opportunity to get a reading from the other two flowers before saying anything more," replied Meda.

Agent Hughes leaned forward in his chair and asked, "Miss Cooper, are there any other details about the man that you can remember? Are there any other thoughts or images that might give us more clues?"

Tori gazed off into the distance as she thought back and replied, "I got a sense of him being a younger man, like maybe in his mid to late twenties. He enjoyed the anticipation of what he was about to do but I also felt like afterwards he was disappointed, especially when he made the comment about 'not forgetting'. The act of killing her didn't give him the satisfaction he was hoping for."

"Hmm…" Agent Hughes murmured out loud.

"What are you thinking, Agent Hughes?" asked Agent Hunter.

Agent Hughes got up from his chair, grabbed a dry erase marker from the table and approached one of the white boards on the wall. "Well," he stated as he began writing, "from what Miss Cooper has said and referencing the profile we began two years ago, we know that our killer is a white male, he's between twenty-five and forty-five years old, he has brown hair, brown eyes, and is right handed. We are theorizing that he either has a menial job or one where he doesn't feel as if he's respected or in control.

"His method of killing indicates that he had a dysfunctional relationship with his mother, who was more than likely unmarried, blonde, attractive, yet she was neither warm nor loving and made her son feel unwanted. We're also considering the possibility that the mother may have either died suddenly when the killer was young, like from a drug overdose, or that she abandoned him and he may have gone into foster care. As he grew up, he may have begun killing women who look like his mother, to get back at her. He leaves his victims posed in peaceful positions because even though he hates his mother, a part of him still loves her."

"That is so sad," Aubrey murmured, quietly.

Sarah nodded in agreement and replied, "Yes, it is sad, Aubrey. It's hard to imagine someone could be so horribly affected by their childhood that they become killers as adults."

"Agent Hunter, are there any pathology reports in those files from the flowers while they were still in a viable stage?" asked Agent Jayco, intently. "If so, I would like to look over that histology so I know what level of forensic analysis was done."

"Yes, we have all that information. I made sure that was included in the case detail Agent Hughes and I brought with us," interrupted Agent Nichols.

Agent Hunter gave the file to Agent Jayco and said, "Here you go. I also saw a box of slides in the box on the credenza so you'll have those available for your analysis as well." He turned to Tori and asked, "Are you ready for the next one, Miss Cooper?"

Tori set her face in determination and replied, "Let's keep going."

As before, Agent Hunter brought her the second container and set it down in front of her.

Repeating the steps she performed earlier, she took a deep breath and picked up the flower. "Okay. Wow, this guy definitely has a look that he's attracted to. This girl and the other two could easily all have been sisters. Ah, I'm at a counter and she's handing me a small folder with....card keys...I'm at a hotel. It's the Embassy Suites. I can see the hotel logo on the wall behind her."

"Can you see a room number on the envelope?" prodded Agent Hunter, hopefully.

Tori paused for a moment and shook her head. "Uh uh, there's nothing written on it but he is going into the elevator and......he pushed the button for the third floor. Dang, the image is changing. I didn't get a chance to see what room he went to. I see the woman again and like Taylor Kellogg, she's dressed more casually and is looking at a bunch of flowers. She's approaching where our guy is standing and is talking to him. He's handing her one of the roses and she's smiling back at him. Shoot!" she exclaimed with frustration.

"What is it?" asked Agent Hunter.

"The images keep changing before I can get enough detail of what's going on. I'm back in a dimly lit room again. He's entering what seems like a back door into a kitchen. There's a bud vase on the table with the flower he gave her. He's enjoying the irony that this time he got to give the woman the flower while she was still alive. He's taking the flower out of the vase and bringing it with him down the hallway to her bedroom. He just took the scalpel from his jacket pocket. He's standing over her now and....is calling out her name so she'll wake up and......"

"Breathe, Miss Cooper. Don't lose control," cautioned Agent Hunter.

Tori gulped in a few deep breaths and choked out, "I'm okay, I'm okay." Less than a minute later, she released the flower and her eyes regained their focus.

She wanted to get up from her chair but was afraid her trembling legs would give way beneath her. "Her name was Lydia and this time, he made sure to wake her up before slitting her throat because he wanted to see her reaction and watch her die." Tori buried her head in her hands and began to cry softly.

Sarah quickly leaned over, took Tori into her arms and soothed, "Oh honey, I'm so sorry you had to see that. That's enough. I don't want you to do this anymore."

"No, Mom, I have to keep going. I'll be okay, I promise," Tori argued, wiping the tears from her cheeks. She looked up at Agent Hunter and asked, hopefully, "Did I add anything new on that one?"

He regarded her carefully and asked, "Do you want to take a break?"

"Not yet. I want to wait until after we go over Lydia's case details. Am I right? Was her name Lydia?" Tori asked.

Agent Hunter opened the file and read, "Lydia Moore, killed on July 30, 2011, single, thirty years old, Concierge at the Embassy Suites in Norman, Oklahoma. The door you mentioned was the back entrance of her townhouse. The back panel window pane on the door had been cut and removed allowing her killer to turn the deadbolt and unlock the door. When she didn't arrive for work or call in the next morning, her manager became worried, called the police and they found her body. Same MO as the other women, throat slit from left to right and a single red rose was placed in her right hand. None of her neighbors saw or heard anything and there was no physical evidence found at the scene."

Tori's mouth formed into disappointed pout and she muttered, "I'm not helping very much am I? Those are details you already had."

"Actually, you're helping out quite a bit, Miss Cooper," Agent Hughes noted as he rose from his chair and went back to the whiteboard. He took the marker and divided one section of the board into four columns, noting three of the four sections with each victim's name. "You picked up pieces of the puzzle we didn't have until now.

"For example," he stated as he began writing under Taylor Kellogg's column, "you saw Miss Kellogg as she was walking away from the killer pulling her suitcase indicating that he may have been on her last flight of the day or flew from somewhere if he was in the airport beyond security. We can pull flight history for all men who traveled into that airport the few days before she was killed and start filtering through physical descriptions and age ranges to see if we can narrow down the list which obviously would be several hundred men."

Tori's eyes widened in surprise and she exclaimed, "That could take days to go through!"

Agent Hughes chuckled and said, "A lot of times, that's all we have to go on and our only option is to weed through the details. However, this time, you also picked up a very vital clue from Miss Moore's case." Under Lydia Moore's column, he wrote two entries and read them out loud. "We've learned that the killer booked a room at the

Embassy Suites in Oklahoma and pushed the third floor button in the elevator. We can cross reference all the names from the reservations for the hotel for the days before Miss Moore's death, against the names of the men from the airport list around the time of Miss Kellogg's death and see if we get any hits."

"What's the connection with both women being around flowers?" Agent Nichols asked. "Is our guy a florist or a delivery driver?"

"I was wondering the same thing," remarked Agent Sullivan.

Agent Jayco shook her head in objection and replied, "I don't think we're looking for someone that typical. These flowers he's giving the women are not your run of the mill roses. These are a hybrid, genetically engineered specimen that hasn't hit the market yet." She referred to an entry in Taylor Kellogg's case file and began typing something on her laptop.

"What are you thinking, Agent Jayco?" asked Agent Hunter, curiously.

As she continued typing, she replied, "Taylor Kellogg was killed on February 13, 2011. The New Jersey Flower & Garden Show was held at the New Jersey Convention Center, Edison, NJ February 11 through the 13 in 2011. When did you say Lydia Moore was killed?"

Agent Hunter looked back at the page of the file in his hand and replied, "July 30, 2011."

Agent Jayco began typing again and after a few moments replied, "The Oklahoma State Florist Association held a flower show at the Embassy Suites in Norman, OK, the weekend of July 29 through the 31 in 2011."

"Interesting," noted Agent Hunter as he began sifting through the files, looking for something in particular.

"Very interesting indeed!" marveled Agent Hughes, adding those details under each victim's column on the board. "Okay, now we're getting somewhere!"

"I don't remember seeing anything like that yesterday when I held the flower left with Marsha Foster," Tori objected. "Shouldn't I have picked up on something like that with her?"

"Not necessarily," Agent Hughes replied.

"Ah, here it is!" announced Agent Hunter, reviewing the contents of the folder. "Marsha Foster was a florist. That's our connection."

"When was she killed?" Agent Jayco asked.

"August 4th of this year," replied Agent Hunter.

Agent Jayco queried another search on her laptop and read out loud, "Jacksonville, North Carolina held their Annual Florists Convention the weekend of August 2nd through the 4th, 2013." She sat back in her chair and added, "That ties three of the four victims together."

"Perhaps now would be a good time to take a break" Sarah suggested, worried about the strained look on her daughter's face.

"No, I want to keep going," Tori insisted. "Now that we have some leads, I want to see what more I can find with the other flower."

"Okay, if you're sure you're all right, we'll keep going," replied Agent Hunter.

"I'm sure," Tori confirmed.

Agent Hunter placed the third container in front of Tori and said "Here is flower number three."

Tori immediately opened the container and tipped the flower into her right hand. A few moments later she said, "I'm at a restaurant and I can see boats on the water outside the window where I'm sitting. The waitress serving him is blonde and very pretty. She just served his food and brought another mug of beer."

"What makes you say 'another mug of beer,'" probed Agent Hughes.

"Because I already have an empty glass in front of me," Tori replied, distractedly, confusing herself with the image of the killer. "I-I-I mean he has an empty glass in front of him."

"Is it bright outside or dark?" Agent Hughes probed again.

"What? Why?" she asked, impatiently.

"Something to give us an idea of what time of day it is," he reasoned.

"Oh, got it. Sorry, Agent Hughes," Tori murmured, trying to focus more on what was around her. "Um, the sun is pretty bright outside so I'm thinking it might be lunch time." Tori sat quietly for a couple of minutes and then she said, "The image is changing. I'm following her on the street."

"He's following her, remember you're just watching, Miss Cooper," Agent Hughes warned.

"Right, he's following her," she muttered, quietly. "It's dark now and she's wearing her uniform so she must have just left the restaurant. She doesn't seem to realize I'm...I mean he's following her."

Agent Hunter and Agent Hughes exchanged a look of concern across the table. When she didn't say anything for a few minutes, Agent Hunter asked, "What's happening now, Miss Cooper?"

"We're inside her house, watching her sleep on the couch," she replied.

"Why are you watching her sleep?" he asked in confusion.

"I can't kill her on the couch!" she snapped. "It has to be done on the bed like I did with the others!"

The awkward silence in the room and the mirrored look of shock on everyone's faces, prompted Agent Hunter into action. He immediately walked over to Tori and pulled the flower out of her hand. "Miss Cooper?" he asked, watching her carefully.

As Tori's eyes regained their focus, she cried out, "Why did you do that? We weren't done yet!"

"We, who, honey?" Sarah asked, gently.

"Wh-what?" Tori stammered.

"I think now would be a good time for a break," Agent Hunter announced. Pondering a thought, he looked at his watch and said, "Let's pick this back up again in thirty minutes. Please excuse me." With that, he turned and strode from the room.

"Come on, Tori. Let's go take a walk," Sarah urged.

"What was that all about?" Agent Nichols whispered to Agent Hughes as they watched Tori and Sarah leave the room.

"It seemed like Miss Cooper was having difficulty seeing herself apart from the killer," he murmured. "I've never witnessed anything like that before."

"Nor have I. Where do you think Agent Hunter ran off to so quickly?" she asked.

"I don't know," he replied, curiously. "I guess we'll find out in thirty minutes."

Chapter 10

Thirty minutes later, as everyone was returning to their seats, Agent Hunter arrived, accompanied by Piper.

"Everyone, this is Piper Stirling, Miss Cooper's roommate." Pointing to everyone in turn he said, "Miss Stirling, this is Agent Nichols, Agent Hughes, Meda Neviah, Sarah Cooper and you know Agent Sullivan and Agent Jayco."

"Hi everyone," Piper waved around the table nervously, trying to remember everyone's names.

"Why don't you sit on the other side of Miss Cooper, Miss Stirling," he directed.

Tori looked at Piper curiously and asked, "Not that I'm not happy to see you Piper, but what are you doing here?"

"Agent Hunter called me about a half hour ago and said he needed my help. When he said it concerned you and that you needed me, I immediately said yes so here I am!" Piper exclaimed.

"I don't understand," Tori replied. "What kind of help?"

"Based upon the last conversation we had with Miss Stirling outside the dormitory yesterday afternoon, as well your reaction to the third flower earlier, I have a suspicion that Miss Stirling will pick up on some changes when you hold the flower again," advised Agent Hunter.

Tori gasped in surprise, turned to Piper and said, "Are you sure you're ready for this, Piper?"

"Ready for what, exactly?" interrupted Agent Hughes. "Sir, what's going on?"

Agent Hunter opened his mouth to say something, closed it again and then decided, "I believe it would be easier to show you rather than trying to explain it. Miss Stirling, are you ready for what we discussed?"

Piper nodded her head confidently and replied, "Yes, sir. Ready when you are."

"Very well," he said as he once again placed the container with the third rose in front of Tori. "Miss Cooper, would you try again please?"

"Are you sure that's such a good idea, Agent Hunter?" Sarah inquired. "We all saw how confused Tori became earlier."

"We're almost finished with the readings, Mrs. Cooper. Once we know we have all the information available to us, I won't ask your daughter to do this anymore."

"It will be okay, Mom," Tori said. "I agree that we need to get this over with."

Not fully convinced, Sarah shrugged her shoulders and said, "All right. I'll have to trust that you know what you're doing."

"Well, I wouldn't go that far, Mom" Aubrey interjected. "It doesn't sound like anyone knows what they're doing right now."

"I heard that, Bree," Tori chided.

"I said it loud enough so you would, Tor," Aubrey taunted.

"Girls, please," Sarah sighed.

"Your sister is here too?" Piper marveled, looking around the room. "That is so very cool."

"Tori can introduce the two of you later. In the meantime, let's continue," interrupted Agent Hunter.

"Yes, sir," Tori replied as she opened the container and took out the flower. She was silent for a few moments as she reconnected her mind to the images. Piper, held her breath and was amazed as Agent Hunter predicted, Tori's aura began to change.

"Where are you, Miss Cooper?" Agent Hunter asked, cautiously.

"Back in the living room," she replied, quietly. "He's frustrated because she fell asleep on the couch instead of in her bed. He enjoys the feeling of invading their homes and taking his time before going into their bedrooms so he's confused and doesn't know what to do."

"So he needs his pattern of events in order to feel like he's in control," Agent Hughes thought out loud.

"Miss Stirling?" Agent Hunter inquired, noticing the concerned look on her face.

"It's definitely affecting her, sir. Her normally bright clear green has become dark and muddy," replied Piper.

"And what does the dark, muddy green represent?" Agent Hunter asked.

"It usually represents jealousy and resentment along with the feeling like that person is a victim of the world. They blame others for causing their behavior and are sensitive to perceived rejection or criticism from others around them," Piper advised.

"Are you actually reading Miss Cooper's aura?" Agent Hughes exclaimed in fascination.

Piper glanced away from Tori briefly towards Agent Hughes and anxiously answered, "Um, yes?"

Agent Hughes's look of surprise made Agent Hunter laugh and he joked, "Don't worry, Miss Stirling. Agent Hughes isn't mocking you. I believe this is the first time I've ever seen him caught off guard by someone."

Agent Hughes smiled in embarrassment and said, "I've never met a true reader. What I do is really more like first impression character assessment. But what you can do – that's amazing!"

"Uh, thanks," Piper replied, feeling a little more comfortable. She was still watching Tori carefully and suddenly saw the color around her friend changing. "Something is happening!"

Agent Hunter looked at Tori and asked, "Miss Cooper? What's going on?"

"We have the scalpel in our hand and we're walking around the couch," she answered in a monotone voice.

"He's walking around the couch, Miss Cooper. Remember you're just an observer," warned Agent Hunter.

Ignoring him, she continued, "I'm shaking her so she'll wake up. So she'll see my face and recognize who I am. So she knows I haven't forgotten what she did to me!"

"Agent Hunter," cautioned Piper, fearfully. "It's totally black now."

Tori's breathing became labored and the glazed look in her eyes became wild and frantic.

"Tori?" asked Sarah, quietly. When Tori didn't respond she called more loudly, "Tori!"

"I'm okay!" Tori choked out, struggling to breathe.

Everyone watched in stunned silence as they listened to her fight for control. A few minutes later, she opened her trembling hand and let the flower land on the table with a whispered thud. Slowly, her eyes regained their focus and her body relaxed in the chair.

"She's back to bright, clear green," Piper announced, quietly, placing a glass of water in front of Tori.

"Honey?" asked Sarah, gently touching Tori's shoulder.

A bit dazed, Tori looked at Sarah and replied, "I'm all right Mom. I just need a minute."

"Do you want to take another break?" her mother asked.

Tori shook her head and replied, "No, we need to go over the details before any of it starts to fade."

"What happened?" asked Agent Hunter.

Noticing the water, Tori took a drink and looked around the room, seeing everyone's concerned faces. "Well based upon what you all look like, I guess I didn't have as much control over the situation as I thought I did."

"Your aura turned to black again, Tor," Piper advised.

"And you began speaking first person again as if you were the killer," Agent Hughes advised.

"I did?" Tori whispered. "I don't remember doing that."

"What do you remember?" Agent Hunter asked.

Tori ran her hands through her hair carelessly and said, "This time was different from the others. He wasn't just mad that she was sleeping on the couch – he was out of control furious. I've never experienced that kind of rage before. This is a game to him. He sees himself as a hunter and when he finds a woman that looks like 'her,' it's like he's cleansing his spirit or exorcising demons. He didn't get to feel that with this woman because his pattern was disrupted."

"So there's some significance to the woman being on the bed," Agent Hughes reflected, looking at the information written on the whiteboard.

"Could his mother have been a prostitute?" asked Agent Jayco.

"We can't rule that out, but that's not the impression I'm getting from the crime scene details. There's no sexual intent thus far which makes it seem more emotional than physical," mused, Agent Hughes.

"You mentioned earlier that your initial profile of the killer suggests that he had a dysfunctional relationship with his mother, who may not have been a warm, loving parent," noted Agent Sullivan. "If you'll humor me for a moment, this sounds very familiar to a patient I once had who came to me for counseling who's mother was a drug addict and treated her son in the same manner. She felt her getting pregnant with him ruined her life and used him as her emotional punching bag."

"That poor man," Meda exclaimed. "Why not give the baby up to foster care where he would have been treated better? Why ruin his life as well?"

Agent Sullivan smiled sadly in agreement and replied, "That is one of those questions virtually impossible to answer, Mrs. Neviah. People do things for reasons we never understand."

"What happened?" Tori asked, curiously.

"As I mentioned, the mother was a drug addict," advised Agent Sullivan. "She never showed affection to her son when she was sober so he would wait until she would pass out in her bed and then he would sneak into bed with her in order to be close to her. Then before she would wake in the morning, he would sneak back out."

"Oh that is so sad," Sarah whispered. "Did the mother ever realize what he was doing?"

Agent Sullivan exhaled a deep sigh, reliving the details of the case and hoarsely replied, "The last time he did it he was thirteen years old. It was winter and the rented room they were staying in didn't have any heat. He woke up during the night because he was cold. When he tried to get closer to his mother for warmth, her body was cold. She had overdosed and died in her sleep."

"Oh, that's horrible," Meda murmured, shaking her head, sadly. "Where is that man today? Do you know?"

Agent Sullivan shook his head and said, "No. He stopped coming to see me. I tried to find him but he gave me a false address and phone number. That was more than twenty years ago and I was only a few years out of college into my own practice. I didn't know what else to do. A few months later, I decided I wanted to do something more with my professional career and help people before they became victims so I joined the academy."

"You know, I think you may be onto something," said Agent Hughes. "There's definitely a pattern between the control issues of our killer has, his relationship to his mother and the significance of the victims needing to be in their beds asleep," noting the details on the whiteboard.

Agent Hunter paused for a moment to study the points on the board and said, "So let's back up for a moment. We know our killer is triggered by women with delicate facial features, long blond hair, athletic builds, slits their throats while they are sleeping in their beds, and tells them he hasn't forgotten what 'she' did. What exactly did 'she' do?"

"She left him alone," Tori answered, quietly. "I keep getting this feeling that he doesn't live a lonely life but he has this deep-seated sense of loneliness within him. He's looking for something to fill that void and nothing's working. He's lost...lost and very angry."

"What else do you remember, Miss Cooper?" urged Agent Hunter.

"When he was shaking her awake, he was calling out the name Ava. It was very important for him to have her to see his face. For a moment, I actually think I saw the reflection of his face in her eyes. He had a wild, crazed look," Tori recalled.

"Do you remember any more details about him specifically?" he urged further.

Tori reflected back for a moment and replied, "Same image of his face. He had dark brown hair, dark brown eyes, clean shaven face, kind of average. He would blend in easily in a crowd."

"What about any birthmarks or scars?" inquired Agent Neviah.

Tori's face lit up suddenly and she exclaimed, "Wait! He has a tattoo on the inside of his right wrist!" Tori jumped out of her chair and strode up to the whiteboard. "Agent Hughes, may I borrow that marker, please?" Taking the marker from him, Tori quickly drew the image on the board. "I know my drawing abilities aren't the best, but this is the closest I can get to what I saw," said Tori.

Agent Nichols began typing on her laptop and a few moments later, approached Tori with it and asked her, "Is that what it looked like?"

Tori looked at the image on the screen and exclaimed, "Yes! That's it! What does it mean?"

Agent Nichols scrolled down the page and read to the group, "The traditional symbol of the Chinese dragon represents luck and good fortune. The downward facing dragon like what Tori drew, is considered bad luck as it is seen as disrespectful to place a dragon in such manner that it cannot ascend to the sky. It also symbolizes strength and power, especially in some criminal organizations where dragons hold a meaning of someone being fierce and strong enough, hence earning the right to wear the dragon on his skin, lest his luck be consumed by the dragons."

"So is our killer part of a gang?" asked Agent Jayco.

"It's possible that he either was at one time or he just liked the symbolism of what it represented," reasoned Agent Hughes while he added the notation of the tattoo to the board. "Something else we may have to consider in our profile."

"Hmm....," murmured Agent Sullivan, reading something from his own laptop.

"What is it, Agent Sullivan?" asked Agent Hunter.

"Well, there's another possibility to the symbolism associated with that tattoo, depending on the cultural definition. Sometimes, they are a symbol of hope and purity, and sometimes...jealousy, miserliness and fierce rage. The origin of the word 'dragon' has been traced to a Greek word, 'derkein,' meaning 'sharp-sighted one,' which appears to describe a snake, so when it was converted to Latin, the word became 'draco,' or 'giant snake,'" added Agent Sullivan, looking over to meet Tori's eyes.

Tori's expression became grim as the realization of what he meant sank in. "Are you suggesting what I think you're suggesting?" she asked him.

"I'm merely pointing out that we should consider the possibility of a darker power here," he replied.

"What are you both talking about?" asked Agent Nichols, looking between the two of them.

"We'll get to that in a moment," Agent Hunter interjected, quickly, trying to keep everyone from veering off onto another subject. "Let's review the details of Miss Cooper's last reading against the case file and see if there's another tie into a florist or convention as the other three victims."

He opened the fourth file and began reading out loud while Agent Hughes filled in the last empty column on the board. "Ava Ronin, killed on March 13, 2012, single, twenty-eight years old, waitress at McClaren's Pub in Chicago, Illinois. She was found on her couch as Miss Cooper said, and not only was her throat slit, she was stabbed several times in the chest by the same type blade the coroner indicated was similar to a surgical instrument. As with the other victims, the killer placed a single red rose in her right hand and despite the violent nature of her death, he took the time to pose her afterwards with her hands resting on her chest."

Sarah looked at Tori critically and said, "You didn't mention anything about the additional stabbing, Tori. Why?"

"I don't want to talk about it," Tori snapped as she stood up abruptly, grabbed the empty glass in front of her and walked over to the water pitcher further down the table.

With a trembling hand, she refilled her glass and took a long drink. Without turning around to face her mother, she said, "I'm sorry for snapping, Mom. Please don't ask me to talk about that."

"All right, honey," Sarah replied, quietly.

Meanwhile, Agent Jayco was looking up the date Agent Hunter mentioned. After the search completed, she announced, "The Chicago Flower and Garden show was held at Navy Pier between March 9 through the 17, 2012 which places our killer in Chicago that same week."

Agent Hughes wrote the additional details under Ava Ronin's column on the board and stepped back to review it.

Deep in thought, he crossed his arms over his chest and tapped the marker gently against his chin. "Okay, so we have a mutual connection to floral conventions during the same time span each woman was murdered. There doesn't appear to be any connection between the women other than their similar physical appearances, yet somehow he seems to get them to come to him at these shows. Miss Cooper, would you consider the killer an attractive man?"

Tori scrunched up her face in concentration as she recalled the image of the man's face. "I guess to some women he might be, but he wouldn't be someone I would go out with."

Aubrey laughed and joked, "That's because he doesn't look like Ben. You've never even gone out on a date with anyone other than him."

"I didn't want to date anyone before Ben, Bree!" Tori exclaimed in annoyance.

Sarah sighed and said, "Girls, please."

"That is so wickedly cool!" Piper breathed in amazement, looking around the room.

"Let's try to stay on subject, shall we?" interrupted Agent Hunter. "What else do we have? What about the weapon? What significance would a scalpel have to someone who cultivates flowers?"

"Gene splicing," Tori and Agent Jayco, both announced in unison.

Both women laughed and Agent Jayco and said, "Well done, Miss Cooper! You are correct." Turning to the others she continued to explain, "The use of the scalpel would be to provide a clean angled cut on a flower stem and then the two stems of differing species are fitted together, bound to keep the pieces in place and then placed in a special greenhouse where certain light conditions, soil, fertilizer, moisture control, temperature and nutritional supplements are administered until the specimen produces the desired results."

"And that's the part that can take as long as ten years?" asked Agent Hunter.

"Yes. A genetic botanist may attempt several hundred of those genetic splice fusions before they see any progress in their research," she replied.

"So would you say we're looking for a man who is highly educated in the field of genetic botany or related sciences?" Agent Hunter asked her.

"I think it would be safe to assume so," replied Agent Jayco.

"Then wouldn't that kind of experience and knowledge warrant someone who is older than our profiled age range?" asked Agent Hughes.

Agent Jayco paused for a moment considering the question and shrugged her shoulders. "I wouldn't even being to assume if that's probable."

"He could be a student," suggested Agent Nichols.

"I'm still thinking florist delivery driver," commented Agent Sullivan.

"Or an apprentice," added Agent Hughes.

"Is this what your job was like while you were working with these people, Karla? They seem to have more questions than answers," Tobias noted, curiously.

Karla turned to her father and replied, "Yes, Dad. Quite often, the police and FBI don't have many clues from a crime scene and much of what they do is trying to fit pieces of a puzzle together until the pieces form a picture."

Tori half-listened to both conversations in the room, as a nagging question began to build in her subconscious that she couldn't quite grasp.

A few moments later, there was a knock on the conference room door and everyone abruptly stopped talking.

Agent Hunter noticed everyone's surprised faces, looked at his watch and said, "That will be our lunch." He then walked over to the door and allowed the delivery man entry into the room.

Tori absently watched as the man wheeled a cart by her towards the buffet, where the remainder of their breakfast from earlier that morning still remained. The cart was laden with trays of sandwiches, fruit, soft drinks, bottles of water and a carafe that Tori surmised, contained fresh coffee, because she smelled it as he walked by.

'Coffee grounds...,' she thought to herself.

Within a few minutes, the man switched out the food and beverages, and pushed the cart towards the door, passing Tori again on his way.

'Compost....,' she thought, staring at the remaining food on the plates.

As Agent Hunter held the door, thanking the man for his service, Tori suddenly announced, "He's not a delivery man!"

Alarmed, Agent Hunter placed his hand on the gun holster on his belt, stopped the man at the door, and said, "Hold on a moment!"

Startled, the man looked at Agent Hunter and the others in the room in confusion.

"No, not that guy!" exclaimed Tori, shaking her head adamantly while gesturing towards the man, "Our guy!"

Embarrassed, Agent Hunter removed his hand from his side and said, "My apologies for the confusion, young man; you're free to go."

Agent Hunter closed the door behind him and added, "Well that was a bit awkward."

He walked back to the table and asked, "What makes you feel certain our guy isn't a delivery driver, Miss Cooper?"

Tori stood up from her chair, began pacing back and forth in front of the white board and said, "I don't have a clear picture in my head yet, which is really ticking me off right now because it's right here, I just can't seem to reach it!" she exclaimed in frustration placing both hands on her temples. "While that guy was taking away our remaining breakfast plates, I caught the smell of the stale coffee and saw the partially eaten food and heard 'coffee grounds' and 'compost' in my head."

"Now you're hearing the voices of dead food?" Aubrey asked, sarcastically.

"Not funny, Bree, and no I am not hearing the voices of dead food!" Tori sighed in frustration.

Sarah turned to Aubrey and whispered, "Honey, please."

"Okay, fine! I'm just trying to lighten the mood! Geez!" Aubrey whined.

Turning back to Tori, Sarah urged, "Go ahead, sweetheart. What were you saying?"

"I was saying that both the smell of the coffee and left over food seem familiar, like they were part of the visions I was seeing earlier holding the flowers. I think the guy we're looking for either handles or is around those items on a daily basis."

"Well, compost from food and natural acids like you would find in coffee grounds are often used by people in the horticultural industry as soil additives," admitted Agent Jayco.

"Which isn't something a commercial florist would need as almost all of their flowers are probably already cut and stemmed or purchased pre-planted from local nurseries," added Agent Nichols.

The room became silent as everyone stared at the whiteboard, unable to come up with any other ideas.

Realizing that they had possibly come as far as they could for the moment, Agent Hunter cleared his throat and announced, "Let's table this conversation for the moment and allow the information we have to sink in. How about we take a quick break for anyone needing to stretch their legs or use the facilities, and then we'll have some lunch and begin talking about our other agenda item for today? Sound good?"

Everyone quickly agreed that a break would be good, rose from their chairs and filed out of the room.

While they were gone, Agent Neviah, Aubrey and Tobias approached the whiteboard and reviewed the notations made by Agent Hughes.

"So, Karla, any ideas?" her father asked curiously.

Karla mentally compared the notations from each column and said, "I remember the details of the first three victims pretty clearly. Those were the trips Mom and I took together the past couple of years when we crossed each woman over. Thinking back now, it's too bad we did that because we could have asked them questions specific to this guy Tori keeps seeing."

"Well they still have the fourth victim that nobody has crossed over yet, don't they?" Aubrey asked, innocently.

Instinctively, Karla's hand shot out, slapped Aubrey on the shoulder and she exclaimed, "Holy cow! I didn't even think of that! You're a genius, Aubrey!"

"Ouch, that hurt!" Aubrey cried out, rubbing her shoulder. "What did I say?"

"Whoops, sorry about that," Karla winced, apologetically. "I've got to go find Mom and Sarah. They need to tell the others that we may have another lead!"

Watching Karla run off to find her mother, Tobias chuckled proudly, wrapped his arm around Aubrey's shoulders in a fatherly manner and said, "That's my Karla, always the investigator!"

Chapter 11

After lunch was over, Agent Hunter cleared his throat, calling everyone's attention back to the conference table and said, "Everyone please return to your seats."

He waited patiently while the room quieted down and his audience was once again seated. "We've temporarily tabled our earlier discussion as both Miss Aubrey Cooper and Agent Neviah reminded us that we may still have a witness to interview." Aubrey and Karla smiled at one another, pleased that their contribution had been mentioned.

"We'll determine how we'll proceed once Agent Neviah and her mother have had an opportunity to arrange a meeting with Mrs. Foster. Hopefully she will be able to provide some new information regarding the details surrounding her death," added Agent Hunter.

"Agent Jayco said she wanted to begin working on the sample analysis from the flowers so she went back to her office. She said she will let us know if she finds anything noteworthy. Agent Sullivan, would you like to lead off our next discussion?" Agent Hunter asked.

Agent Sullivan nodded and replied, "Yes, thank you, Agent Hunter." Agent Sullivan looked at Sarah, Meda and Tori in turn and explained, "Our original intention in bringing you all together today was to assist Miss Cooper regarding a series of dreams she's been having." He paused, looked directly at Meda and added, "One dream in particular that I'm hoping perhaps your daughter can also share some of her prior experiences, Mrs. Neviah."

"What is it you would like to know, Agent Sullivan?" Meda asked, curiously.

Agent Sullivan stood up from his chair, walked around the table, picked up a small stack of papers on the table in front of him and replied, "Miss Cooper was kind enough to give me permission to copy and share the details of one of her dreams with everyone, which will help explain what I mean."

He walked around the table, handing everyone but Tori, a copy and said, "Both Agent Hunter and I believe this dream is the beginning of a period in Miss Cooper's life where she will encounter situations where both her special gifts and her faith will be tested. Situations where she may need others to help her."

Startled by his comment, Tori exclaimed, "Hold on a second! Why didn't this come up last night when you, Agent Hunter and I were talking? What kind of 'situations' are you talking about?"

Agent Hunter looked at Tori and replied, "Remember when we asked you to be patient and that we would explain everything today?"

Tori gave him a resolved nod and admitted, "Yes, I remember. Okay, fine. Please continue, Agent Sullivan."

"All right, then. I'll give everyone a few minutes to read through what I've handed out and we'll go from there," Agent Sullivan replied.

As the others were reading, Agent Sullivan walked over to a stack of boxes on one of the tables against the wall and brought a very old looking document back with him to the table. When he looked around the room at everyone's faces to see if they were finished, he noticed that Meda and Sarah were exchanging a worried look.

"Mrs. Cooper? Mrs. Neviah? Do the details of Miss Cooper's dream sound at all like the dreams Agent Neviah was having before her death?" he asked.

Sarah turned to Karla, noticing she too had a worried look on her face and asked, "Karla?"

Karla shook her head back and forth slowly as she scanned the information and replied, "This is way more elaborate than anything I ever dreamed. I never got further than the tree and the bench that both you and Mom saw. And I certainly never had a conversation with Satan!"

Tori looked sharply at her mother and asked, "What does Karla mean about the tree and the bench both you and Mrs. Neviah saw, Mom? You both had the dream too?"

Agent Sullivan blinked in surprise and asked, "What? You both had this same dream as well, Mrs. Cooper? When was that?"

Sarah sighed, shrugged her shoulders and replied, "I guess neither Meda nor I thought it was important to tell Tori, not to mention it just happened a couple of nights ago. Both Meda and I fell asleep on the couch. There was so little to tell I honestly forgot all about it."

"What exactly did you see, Mom?" Tori asked.

"Well," her mother began, "Like I said, there's not much to tell, except that I dreamt that I was standing on a dirt path in front of a very large tree, and at the base of the tree there was a wooden bench. Meda was sitting on one end of it so I walked over and sat down on the bench beside her."

"Then what happened?" asked Agent Sullivan, expectantly.

Sarah looked at Meda and said, "Then I asked Meda, 'What's going on?'"

"And I said, 'I have no idea'," Meda replied.

"Then we both woke up, staring at each other in confusion from opposite ends of the couch," Sarah added, turning back to Agent Sullivan.

"That was it?" he asked. "Neither one of you had any other dreams like that before?"

Sarah gave Agent Sullivan a puzzled look and replied, "No, nothing like that has ever happened before. Why do you ask?"

Agent Sullivan paused and thought inwardly for a moment. *'How can I best phrase this without sounding like a lunatic?'*

Taking a deep breath, he walked to the center of the area in front of the table and looked around the group seeing only patient expressions. "I would appreciate it, if everyone would please allow me a bit of leeway for a few moments. I would like to tell you a story. It is very important that you know, this story is based upon historically documented events and is not science fiction as to some of you it may sound."

When he saw Agent Hughes give him a speculative smirk, Agent Sullivan added, "I'm quite serious and Agent Hunter will back me up on this one."

Everyone turned to look at Agent Hunter and he immediately replied, "Yes, that is correct. I assure you all that what you are about to hear is factual."

"Okay," Agent Sullivan said as he clapped his hands together and rubbed them back and forth a few times, preparing his narrative. "A very long time ago, we're not exactly sure of the date in time, several of God's archangels fell from heaven's grace. There are many conflicting opinions as to the reasons which caused their fall, however the resulting fact being is that they did in fact fall from Grace.

"After the fall, some of those angels found favor with mortal women on the earth and produced offspring of those, um, unions – for lack of a better term," he

147

murmured, embarrassed at the imagery his story provided.

"Anyway, those offspring, or 'Nephilim' were the 'sons of God' and the 'daughters of men' according to Genesis 6:4. They were described in many different forms. Some thought the meaning meant they were giants, other translations indicate the word is derived from a Hebrew root meaning 'fallen' or 'those that cause others to fall down'. It has also been recorded that the Nephilim often times possessed certain abilities that mortal children did not."

"Abilities like communicating with spirits?" Piper asked, excitedly.

Agent Sullivan smiled wryly at her and replied, "Among many others, yes, however that does bring us to where I was going in our story, specifically to one particular archangel and his descendants, Ramiel."

"But we talk...," Tori began to say.

"I know we did," interrupted Agent Sullivan. "But for now, let's not get caught up in details as to whether there were one or two angles similarly named, or the spelling of his name and whether we're talking about the 'Thunder of God' or 'The Mercy of God,' let's just try to focus on the angel, not the name."

Tori sat back in her chair, crossing her arms over her chest and replied, "Okay, fine."

"You could always just ask him the next time you see him," Piper offered, humorously.

"Wait, what?" Agent Nichols asked, scanning the page again for something she must have missed.

Tori gave Piper a stern look and uttered through gritted teeth, "Seriously, Piper?"

Piper stared back at Tori innocently with doe eyes and replied, "What?"

Agent Sullivan quickly intervened, and said, "Oh, right. My apologies, there were a few details that were left out of Miss Cooper's notes, however we can talk about those in a few minutes. Let's stay on track with the story for a bit, shall we? Now, where was I? Oh, yes, Ramiel. From as far back as I've been able to uncover, the descendants of Ramiel have always been reported to be prophets, seers and spiritual guides. Since in those times, people did not have last names, they were usually known by their patrilineage, for example Miss Cooper would have been known as 'Tori, daughter of Ramiel'. As times progressed, people began using their first names with their patrilineage which then became 'Tori Ramiel'."

Meda gave Agent Sullivan a puzzled look and inquired, "If that's true, then why did my ancestors change their name from 'Ramiel' to 'Neviah'?"

"What does the translation of 'Neviah' mean, Mrs. Neviah?" he asked.

"It means, 'Prophetess, seer into the future'," she replied.

"Correct. Let's hang on to that for a moment. I promise what I'm about to tell you will help clear up some of these questions. Okay, ah....yes, descendant names. Originally, there was only one line of descendants from Ramiel and they all were known by the name 'Ramiel'.

"Because Ramiel had fallen from Grace, he was no longer able to guide the souls of the faithful into heaven. So still having some powers of his own, he passed that ability onto his descendants by giving them the ability to communicate with spirits and be their spiritual guides. Since his descendants were half human, they had limitations as mortals so he channeled his divinity and formed it into two objects representing his power."

"The statue and the amulet!" Tori exclaimed.

"Precisely," Agent Sullivan replied.

Sarah and Meda looked at one another in surprise, searching each other's face. "So somewhere back in our ancestry, Meda and I are really related?" Sarah asked.

"We believe so, yes," replied Agent Sullivan. Seeing everyone's expressions morph into confusion, he quickly added, "Stay with me, everyone. Let me continue."

Turning around, he picked up the document he had placed on the table earlier and said, "These pages are from an ancient Hebrew writing from a man named Baruch, who was the scribe and devoted friend of the Biblical prophet Jeremiah."

Sarah turned to Meda excitedly and reminded her, "Remember that letter I showed you? The one you have, where a man named Baruch wrote a letter to the nine and a half tribes about an angel named 'Remiel'?"

Meda nodded her head and replied, "Yes I remember! But I don't recall there being a mention of the statue or the amulet." Meda turned to Agent Sullivan and asked, "Is what you have there, the same letter, Agent Sullivan?"

Agent Sullivan glanced at Agent Hunter a bit nervously and looked back at Meda. "Ah, well, I believe the two may be the same letter, however what I have here is actually the complete letter. I believe you only have a portion of that letter, Mrs. Neviah."

Meda gasped in surprise and accused, "How can you know that, Agent Sullivan? My family has kept very careful record of our history for hundreds of years for the very purpose of honoring our ancestors and being aware of exactly who we are!"

"Mom, calm down," Karla said, anxiously.

Agent Sullivan approached Meda and quietly asked, "Does the letter you have mention anything about the statue or the amulet and the power they possess when used together?"

The room became eerily silent as everyone around the table registered surprise.

Meda's eyes widened and she shook her head back and forth very slowly. "No. It doesn't," she whispered.

"What do you mean by 'power' when the two objects are used together, Agent Sullivan?" asked Sarah.

He looked at each woman thoughtfully for a moment and said, "Mrs. Neviah, Mrs. Cooper, did you both bring the statue and amulet with you today?"

Both women nodded in reply and said, "Yes."

"Would you please get them and place them on the table in front of you?" he asked, politely.

Meda reached up and gently grasped a thin cord of leather from around her neck and pulled out a small amulet from within her blouse. She looped the cord over her head and gently placed it on the table. Meanwhile, Sarah rose from her chair and recovered a small wooden box from within her bag that she had placed by the wall earlier. She returned to her chair and placed the box on the table in front of her.

"Thank you," Agent Sullivan replied. "As I was saying, the letter I'm holding was written by a scribe named Baruch. The carbon dating of the paper indicates that it was written around the time of the late first century AD. The letter itself is a recording of events when the elders of the Ramiel clan agreed to split the clan into two families and break ties with one another. The Ramiel family was to retain the statue and the Neviah family to retain the amulet."

Agent Sullivan quickly raised his hands in front of him, as he felt the wall of shock from everyone head towards him. "Please let me continue before anyone asks me any questions. To answer everyone's first question, yes. Mrs. Neviah, Mrs. Cooper and Miss Cooper are blood relatives. Uh, as are Agent Neviah's daughter and Mrs. Cooper's other daughter...my apologies. I keep forgetting that they are here as well."

"Out of sight, out of mind," Aubrey noted, sarcastically.

Karla snorted a laugh in response as Tobias gently patted her on the shoulder, comfortingly.

"Aubrey," Sarah warned.

"Sorry, Mom," she replied.

Tori shook her head in frustration and murmured, "Seriously?"

Agent Sullivan laughed nervously not knowing what had been said and replied, "Yes. Anyway, to answer what would most likely be the second question, why, involves the amulet and the statue. The amulet that Mrs. Neviah's family has used to guide spirits and the statue that Mrs. Cooper's family has used to guide spirits were originally used together by one individual. They were not only used to guide spirits into heaven, but were also used to see into one's future."

"So you're saying the original family members were actually seers, guides and prophets?" Agent Nichols exclaimed. She then winced, apologetically and added, "Sorry....not supposed to ask questions. I forgot."

Agent Sullivan chuckled and replied, "I can tell from everyone's expressions that they were all thinking the same question, Agent Nichols. And you are correct. The original family was known as possessing the gifts of sight, spiritual guidance and prophecy."

Tori frowned in confusion and asked, "Then why split the family and the powers? What happened that made the elders decide that was needed?"

Agent Sullivan smiled at Tori and asked her, "Remember when I told you to prepare yourself for an encounter with a very old soul?"

Tori nodded her head and replied, "The day we talked about my dream, yes."

"That very old soul has had an interest in your family for a very long time. Probably as far back as when Ramiel fell from Grace," noted Agent Sullivan, patiently waiting for her to make the connection.

Tori thought for a moment and suddenly understood. '*Click.*' "He tried to corrupt the owner of the amulet and the statue, didn't he?"

Proud of Tori for figuring it out so quickly, Agent Sullivan nodded and replied, "That is exactly what happened."

Turning back to the others he held up the letter in his hand again and said, "The story written here indicates that throughout many generations of the Ramiel family history, Satan would visit the women in their dreams and tempt them with the idea that he could give them more power than they already possessed, trying to gain access to the amulet and the statue. He was unsuccessful until about the time this letter was written, when one particular young woman became tempted by the thought of having more power than any of her ancestors."

"What happened?" Tori asked, curiously.

Agent Sullivan looked at Tori and replied, "She began passing judgment on those she was meant to guide and began sending some of them to hell."

"Oh no!" Tori cried out. "What happened to those souls?"

"They were lost and could not be recovered," Agent Sullivan replied, quietly.

"Oh my goodness," murmured Sarah, sadly.

"I can see why our ancestors made the decision to split the family," Meda added.

"What happened to the young woman?" Agent Hughes asked.

"She was cast out from her family and stoned to death as was the proper form of punishment at the time," replied Agent Sullivan.

"That's horrible!" Piper called out, indignantly.

Agent Sullivan returned to the stack of material he had placed on the table, set the letter in his hand aside and picked up a Bible. Locating the passage he needed, he read "This is from the book of Deuteronomy, chapter thirteen, verse ten. 'And thou shalt stone him with stones, that he die; because he hath sought to thrust thee away from the LORD thy God, which brought thee out of the land of Egypt, from the house of bondage.' I know it sounds brutal, Miss Stirling, however stoning people to death for their crimes was common in those days. And since the crime which the young woman committed was one directly against God, it seems justified."

"I guess that explains the missing family history, Mom," Karla stated firmly.

"Yes it does," replied Meda, quietly.

The sound of Agent Hunter's cell phone buzzing against the conference table broke the silence as everyone's heads turned in that direction.

Looking down at the caller identified on the screen, he said, "If you would all please excuse me, I need to take this call. Let's take a quick fifteen minute break."

Chapter 12

While everyone returned from the break, Agent Sullivan resumed his place in front of the table, patiently waiting until everyone was seated. "Before I continue with the story, does anyone have any questions on what we've already covered?" he asked.

Tori immediately spoke up and replied, "I do, Agent Sullivan."

"All right, Miss Cooper, go ahead," he replied.

"What happened to the young woman who was stoned to death?" Tori asked.

Agent Sullivan replied, "That is one piece of information I have not been able to verify, unfortunately. According to the Mosaic law, also called Law of Moses, burning was reserved, either for the living who had been found guilty of unnatural sins, or for those who died under a curse. For example the case of a man named Achan. He and his family were burned by fire after they were stoned to death. I would assume that is more than likely what happened to the young woman."

Tori inhaled a surprised breath and exclaimed, "So it's possible that her spirit is still here on earth, after all these years?"

"It's quite possible, yes," he replied.

"Remember when Agent Nichols and I took you to that cemetery, Miss Cooper?" Agent Hunter asked. "There were spirits there that day as well. There will always be souls who remain here on earth until judgment day."

"Yes, I remember," Tori replied, annoyed. "It just seems so cold-hearted that she made one mistake by being tempted and it cost her, her life! At least Eve got to live and have a family! She was tempted too and God didn't kill her! It doesn't seem fair!"

"The gifts your family was given were an act of divine trust," advised Agent Sullivan. "There's no room for anything but obedience with that trust, Miss Cooper. This is especially important for you to understand as you are the only remaining heir left in your family. The responsibility of those gifts, now lie solely upon you."

"What?" Tori and Sarah both exclaimed in unison.

"Oh my," Meda murmured, seeing what Agent Sullivan meant.

"Ouch, he should have softened that blow a bit more," noted Karla.

"Yeah, that was kind of harsh," added Aubrey.

Agent Sullivan gave Agent Hunter a pained look and said, "This is too much too soon, Gabriel."

"She needs to know, Kent," Agent Hunter replied, unwaveringly. "She's already had the dream. They've already made contact with her! It's only a matter of time until she's forced to make her choice!"

"What are you both talking about?" Tori shouted above their voices as she stood abruptly from the table, her chair falling backwards behind her. "Make my choice about what!"

As she stood there trembling in frustration, everyone's gaze was immediately redirected when they noticed the deep Turquoise of Meda's amulet being to faintly glow and pulse like a heartbeat. Once, twice and then it stopped.

"What was that?" Agent Nichols asked as she rose from her chair and walked over to the amulet.

"I've never seen it do that before," murmured Meda in confusion. "What's going on?"

Agent Sullivan gazed upon the amulet a few moments longer and then quietly asked, "Mrs. Cooper, would you please remove the statue from the box and place it next to the amulet?"

Sarah's worried eyes met his briefly and then she nodded and whispered, "Yes."

Sarah picked up the box, pushed her finger against the side of one of the carved images and a small drawer slid open, revealing a very old key. She slid the key into the lock on the front of the box and slowly opened the lid.

When the lid was opened to a certain point, everyone began to hear a muted 'humming' sound coming from inside. "That's strange," Sarah said, quietly. "I've never heard it do that before." As she reached into the box to remove the statue, she gasped quietly and pulled her hand back. "Oh!"

"What's wrong, Mom?" Tori asked, quickly coming to her mother's side.

Sarah looked at Tori and said, "It's not cold like it usually is. It's warm, like it's been in the sun."

"Please place the statue on the table beside the amulet, Mrs. Cooper," Agent Hunter said firmly.

Sarah immediately obeyed and reached into the box, gently removing the statue. She set the box aside and carefully placed the statue beside the amulet. As she did, the humming from the statue became louder, as if it was singing, and the amulet began to glow again.

"Oh," Tori, Sarah and Meda breathed in unison.

"Are they talking to one another?" Agent Nichols asked, curiously.

Agent Sullivan turned to Agent Hunter and the two men regarded each other silently.

Not getting a response to her question, Agent Nichols turned to Agent Sullivan and noticed the exchange between the two men. She looked at Agent Hughes, who was also witness to the moment and he returned Agent Nichols' look of concern.

"Sir, I believe an explanation is in order," demanded Agent Hughes. "What did you mean earlier when you said 'they've already made contact with her' and why are the amulet and the statue reacting in this way? We've been around them together before when we were all in Denver and they didn't react this way. What's going on?"

Agent Sullivan broke the stare-down with Agent Hunter and took a long surveyed look at everyone at the table, stopping with Tori, whose face was a mixture of confusion and fascination. He raised one eyebrow at her and asked, "So, do you want the abridged 'punch in the gut' version or the warm and fuzzy 'fairy tale' version?"

Tori smiled faintly back at him and said, "A punch in the gut might be what I need right about now."

"All-righty then," he said, taking in a deep breath. "The prophecy states that there will be a daughter born from the lineage of Ramiel, who will be pure of heart, strong in spirit, unwavering in her faith and gifted beyond all others before her. When the daughter has been named, the statue and the amulet will call out to her in a celebration of light and song, ending the darkness and singing out in praise. This time will be known as 'The Enlightenment'.

"Upon that revelation, a great battle will ensue between the forces of darkness and the grace of heaven, in order to control the chosen one and the power she possesses. If grace prevails as the victor, the faithful will continue to rightfully be guided into heaven. If darkness overcomes her, those souls will unmercifully be cast into hell, and remain there until judgment day."

"Ugh," Tori choked out, stepping back a few steps, feeling nauseous. "Maybe I should have said fairy tale."

She wavered uncertainly a few moments until Piper picked up Tori's chair and slid it gently behind her. "Here, sit down, Tor."

Tori sat down obediently and stared at the glowing amulet while the song from the statue gently soothed her.

"Ending the darkness and singing out in praise," she murmured, quietly. "That's what they're doing aren't they? The amulet's glowing has ended the darkness and the humming of the statue is singing out in praise."

After a few moments she met Agent Sullivan's patient eyes and asked, "So that was Ramiel who rescued me from Satan, wasn't it? I really did feel feathers, didn't I?"

Silently, he nodded in response.

"You've met him?" Karla asked, amazed.

Tori turned towards Karla and looked at her fascinated, semi-transparent face. Suddenly, Tori realized that Karla had the dream about the garden before she did. "You were the original prophecy, weren't you? You were meant to be the chosen one. Before you were killed, the dream came to you first."

Karla shook her head and argued, "Nobody can know that for sure, Tori. My dream never got as far as yours has. Maybe mine was a test and for some reason I didn't pass it so the dream came to you instead."

"Or you were killed in order to prevent your part of the prophecy from coming true!" Tori exclaimed, in shock.

She whipped her head around and glared at Agent Hunter. "Is that possible? Was Agent Neviah the intended chosen one and 'he' influenced a mortal to kill her? Is that what's in store for me as well?"

Agent Hunter regarded Tori silently for a moment and asked, "Have you ever asked yourself why you went into private investigation, Miss Cooper? What drove you in that direction?"

"I don't need to ask myself that question! I did it so I could find my sister! I've known that was my destiny since I was fifteen years old!" Tori replied, indignantly.

"Are you sure that was the only reason?" he asked, calmly. "Don't you think it's a bit coincidental that you found your sister as well as her killer? Do you know what the odds are that you would have actually found your sister, ten years after she disappeared? Even the most seasoned investigator rarely has that kind of luck. Have you ever asked yourself how that all came about? Whether you had any assistance from anywhere else?"

Tori continued to glare at him while a multitude of questions bombarded her subconscious. *'Could he be right? Is it possible that I was guided to that warehouse by someone other than Laurel Meadows? Is that why I'm here, training to be an FBI agent? Preparing me for an eventual fight against evil?'* She shook her head to quiet her mind and calmly answered, "Honestly, no. I haven't, Agent Hunter, and you still haven't answered my question."

"That's because I have no answer for you," he replied, directly.

They continued to stare at one another as the others in the room became aware of the awkward silence that ensued.

"So what do we do now?" Agent Nichols interrupted. "Do we just sit and wait for the impending tug of war to begin or is there something we can do to help Miss Cooper prepare for what's about to happen? We can't just let her go at this alone!"

Agent Sullivan looked at Agent Nichols with a compassionate smile and replied, "Forgive me, Agent Nichols, but this isn't your battle to fight."

"Well forgive me, Agent Sullivan, but that's a load of crap!" Agent Nichols threw back, looking at him and then everyone else in the room. "And if any of you here think I'm about to sit here and watch the show from the peanut gallery, then you're sadly mistaken! I already lost one friend and colleague, I'm not about to let that happen again."

"Same here," chimed in Piper, standing behind Tori, placing her hands firmly on Tori's shoulders.

"Same here," added Karla, joining Piper and Agent Nichols.

"Me too, even though most of you can't hear me!" Aubrey exclaimed, standing beside her sister.

Meda and Sarah both quietly rose from their chairs and stood on either side of Tori, placing their hands on top of Piper's.

"Aubrey and I agree as well," Sarah stated firmly, challenging the rest of the group.

"As do Karla and..." Meda began to say, but paused briefly to look beside her. Smiling fondly, she re-stated, "As do Karla, Tobias and I."

Attempting to play the role of mediator, Agent Hughes rose from his chair, walked over to stand between the opposing sides and reasoned, "Hey, let's not forget that we're all on the same side here. If you want to talk about evil gaining home field advantage, then this was a pretty scary start to the game! I don't believe either Agent Hunter or Agent Sullivan is saying that we throw Miss Cooper to the wolves, or in this case the wolf. So far, the encounters have occurred while Miss Cooper has been sleeping which means, none of us can physically help her."

"Perhaps some of us can!" exclaimed Sarah, quickly meeting Meda's eyes. "Remember in our dream? We were both there and we were able to communicate with each other!"

Meda smiled, victoriously, nodded her head and replied, "So maybe you and I can be with Tori and the three of us can band together! After all, we are all daughters of Ramiel!"

"And I can be with her and monitor her aura to make sure nothing happens while she's sleeping!" chimed in Piper.

Tori turned around to look at Piper and asked, "And when are you going to sleep, Piper? I can't ask you to do that when we have no idea when or how often my dreams will happen. You'll never get any sleep and you have classes to attend!"

"Then we'll take shifts! Between me, your mom and Mrs. Neviah, we'll have someone with you at all times so nobody loses sleep," Piper replied.

"At least let us try, honey," Sarah urged.

Tori deliberated for a moment, sighed and shrugged her shoulders in defeat. "All right, I'm willing to give it a shot."

Tori turned to Agent Hunter with an agreeable expression and asked, "Will that be okay with you?"

A bit bewildered that all of that had just been decided without his involvement, Agent Hunter laughed and replied, "It doesn't sound like I have a choice, does it?"

"Excellent!" Sarah replied, happily, smiling at Tori. "And Agent Hunter arranged for me, Meda, Karla, Tobias and Aubrey to stay in one of the guest apartments here on base so you and Piper can stay with us at night and still attend your classes during the day!"

"Okay. I'm game if the rest of you are," Tori agreed, turning back to stare at the pulsating amulet. Hesitantly, she reached out her hand and gently touched the surface of the stone, causing the light to glow brighter. She then picked up the necklace, holding the amulet in the palm of her hand and the pulsating turned to a steady glow.

Meda sat down in the chair next to Tori and quietly said, "It has claimed you as its new owner, my child."

Tori looked at Meda with concern and said, "It doesn't seem fair. This necklace has been in your family since the beginning! It belongs to you!"

Meda smiled at Tori, gently cupped Tori's cheek in her palm and replied, "It is our family, yours and mine. And the amulet now belongs to you. Let's see how it looks on."

As Meda took the necklace from Tori to place the cord over Tori's head, the stone's glow dimmed. Once the stone made contact with Tori again, the glow returned. Meda then leaned back to look at the necklace around Tori's neck and smiled. "It suits you. Don't you think so, Sarah?"

Meda and Sarah exchanged a smile and Sarah replied, "It looks beautiful and very content."

Tori speculatively looked at the statue on the table and asked, "Agent Sullivan, does the prophecy say anything about what happens when both items are held at the same time?"

Agent Sullivan shook his head slowly and replied, "Other than the owner having 'great power' no, I'm afraid not. I'm not even sure what 'great power' would equate to in modern terms."

"Huh," Tori muttered, considering her next move. She looked up at her mother, meeting her eyes and gave her a questioning look.

Sarah shrugged in response and asked, "Why not?"

Tori looked back at the statue and set her mouth firmly in determination. Placing one hand around the amulet, she reached out her other hand and picked up the statue. As her hand encircled the warm marble, she felt herself being whisked away.

Chapter 13

The sensation of movement slowed and then stopped.

Tori looked around her and realized in amazement that she was no longer sitting at the conference table back in Virginia. Instead, she was standing in the middle of a sunlit field, surrounded by fragrant wildflowers.

The sound of voices drew her eyes to a spot a few yards away, where two men were facing each other in a heated argument. Oblivious to Tori's presence, she saw that the men were standing over something on the ground at their feet. At first she couldn't tell what it was, but then she quickly realized it was the form of a young woman. Tori peered closer and gasped in shock when she saw how badly beaten the woman was.

"Oh!" she cried out.

As both men turned to look at her, Tori immediately recognized the polished, exquisitely dressed figure from her dream. Meeting her eyes, he sneered, villainously and crooned, "Ah, look who's here! Hello, Tori, my dear. What a nice surprise! Long time no see!"

Tori's gaze darted over to the other man's unfamiliar face and saw kindness, compassion and concern reflected in his grey eyes. His weathered face looked reminiscent of someone she couldn't place, however she felt certain that she had seen him before.

"What? You can't say hello to an old friend? What about a hug?" Satan jeered as he turned to face her and began to walk slowly towards her.

"No! Leave her alone, Luc!" the other man warned, sternly. He reached out his arm to block Satan's approach, turned to Tori and ordered, "Go back, now, Tori! Release the statue!"

Instinctively, Tori opened the hand where she held the statue and she immediately felt herself being propelled forward until once again the movement stopped and she was back in the conference room.

"Whoa. What the heck was that?" she murmured to herself, staring at her tingling hand. When she looked up at the others in the room, she noticed everyone was looking at her.

"What was what?" asked Agent Hunter.

"Um, how long was I gone just now?" she asked, curiously, rubbing her fingers together.

"Gone? You never left your chair. What do you mean?" Agent Sullivan inquired.

Tori looked at everyone's faces again and exclaimed, "I mean just now! One second I was here sitting in this room, then the next I'm standing in the middle of a field with Satan and some other guy and then I'm back here again! How long was I gone?"

Sarah touched Tori's shoulder gently and calmly replied, "Honey, you never went anywhere. We were just talking about what would happen if you touched both the amulet and the statue so you picked up the statue and a few seconds later, you placed it back on the table."

Tori turned to her mother in confusion and said, "I don't understand. What was it I just saw then?"

"Tell us what you think you saw, Miss Cooper" urged Agent Sullivan.

Tori looked back down at the statue in front of her and then at the glowing amulet in her hand. She gently laid the amulet against her shirt and then rubbed both palms against her jeans. "Well," she began. "As soon as I picked up the statue, I felt myself being pulled backwards. Like one of those roller coasters that makes you think the ride is over but then it pulls you backwards in reverse.

"Then I was standing in the middle of a field and there were two men arguing, a few feet away. There was something on the ground at their feet. At first I couldn't tell what it was. Then I recognized that it was a woman who appeared to have been beaten to death. At least I think she was dead, she wasn't moving.

"Anyway, I guess I made a sound because the men stopped arguing and noticed me standing there. One of the men was Satan but I'm not sure who the other guy was. He looked familiar, but I can't remember where I might have seen him before."

"What did he look like?" Agent Sullivan asked, curiously.

Tori took in a deep breath and exhaled a groan of frustration. "Ah, okay, let's see. He was about the same height and body size as Satan; not thin but not brawny either. He had long grey hair that was pulled back in a ponytail, his face was weathered like he'd been in the sun a lot during his life and he had light grey eyes. He was wearing a leather jacket, a faded graphic t-shirt of some kind; I couldn't read what it said, worn-out jeans and a pair of boots."

"Satan was arguing with a biker?" asked Piper.

"Did he speak to you?" Agent Sullivan asked.

Tori thought back for a moment and replied, "Yes, he did! He said, 'Go back, Tori,' and he told me to release the statue. So I did, which brought me back here."

"Fascinating!" murmured Agent Sullivan, as he began to pace the room deep in thought.

"What are you thinking, Kent?" asked Agent Hunter.

"I'm wondering if the statue and the amulet took Miss Cooper to the last place they were used together," replied Agent Sullivan, still pacing the room.

"What would be the significance of that?" asked Agent Hughes.

"I don't know yet," replied Agent Sullivan.

"What about the other man Miss Cooper described, the one she hadn't seen before?" asked Agent Nichols.

"Do you think it was him?" Agent Hunter asked, watching Agent Sullivan, closely.

Agent Sullivan stopped pacing and looked at Agent Hunter, thoughtfully, "Don't you? Who else could it have been? They've both made contact with Miss Cooper and the statue and amulet took her to the place where they were both together."

"What about the woman at their feet?" Agent Hunter asked.

Agent Sullivan paused for a moment and replied, "It could have been the Ramiel descendant that Satan coerced who was stoned to death."

When Agent Hunter reacted in surprise, Agent Sullivan added, "It makes sense. After she was killed by her family, the statue and the amulet were split up, thus dividing the power that Ramiel originally created. He and Satan were more than likely arguing over the death of the woman which is when Miss Cooper showed up."

"Why would the statue and the amulet have taken Miss Cooper to that moment in time?" asked Agent Hughes.

"To take me back to the beginning," Tori said, quietly, mesmerized by the glow from the amulet. "To show me what happened and to remind me what would happen if I make the wrong choice." As if confirming her summation, the amulet pulsated brighter and the statue hummed more loudly.

"Do you remember anything else about where you were, Miss Cooper?" Agent Sullivan asked.

Tori shook her head slowly and replied, "No, I don't recall anything else."

"So what's our next step?" asked Agent Hughes.

Breaking her trance from the amulet, Tori looked around the room, placed her hands on the arm rests of her chair and pushed herself onto her feet. "I don't know about the rest of you, but I'm done experimenting for today! I need time to allow all of this," she said waving her hands over the table in front of her, "stuff, to soak in, and there's only one thing that will allow me to do that."

Turning to look at Sarah, she asked, "Mom, does that apartment Agent Hunter set you up in have a full kitchen?"

Sarah smiled, knowingly at her daughter and replied, "Yes, honey, it does. And it's fully equipped."

"Sweet!" exclaimed Tori, happily. "Then I need that address and a couple hours to go do some shopping. Dinner is on me tonight!"

Chapter 14

A few hours later, Tori found herself surrounded by a mountain of groceries that covered every inch of available counter space. Donning an apron and securing her long auburn hair into a ponytail, she pressed the play button on her iPod, turned up the volume on the apartment's stereo speakers to a disrespectable level, poured herself a glass of her favorite zinfandel, and began contentedly chopping and staging ingredients for her menu.

Meanwhile, Sarah and Meda lounged on the patio, enjoying the music, they too having a glass of wine, allowing Tori her time of self-therapy.

"Is that normal?" Aubrey asked, motioning to the open doorway.

"It is for your sister," Sarah replied. "I'm afraid she picked up her cooking-therapy from me, although I have to admit it has its advantages. Your father has never gone hungry."

"Shouldn't we offer to help?" Meda asked, politely.

Sarah shook her head firmly and replied, "No. We need to allow her some time as she asked. Seriously, Meda, she's having fun in there."

Karla chuckled as she came back out to the patio from inside and added, "She's fine! I just peeked in on her and she is totally in the zone. I sure wish I could still eat food because dinner is going to be awesome! By the way, Tori's phone has been buzzing. She left it in on the table right inside the door so I figured maybe she did that on purpose. Should we tell her?"

Sarah got up from her chair and stepped through the doorway to look at Tori's phone. As she did, it immediately began to register an incoming call. Smiling to herself, she picked it up and answered it. "Hello, Ben!"

"Sarah?" He replied in confusion. "Why are you answering Tori's phone? Is she all right? Did something happen?"

"Calm down, sweetheart. She's fine! We all arrived in town earlier today and now we're relaxing on the patio while Tori is making dinner," Sarah replied.

"Huh. Tori didn't mention you were....uh, oh...I hear Little River Band, don't I? That only means one thing – cooking therapy. What happened today?" he asked, cautiously.

"She didn't know we were coming and she had a bit of a rough day today, Ben. It's too much to go over on the phone. Would you like to come over and join us?" she asked.

"That depends," he replied. "Has she made it to 'Cool Change' yet and is she singing along?"

Sarah chuckled lightly and replied, "The second chorus just started and yes, she's singing."

"Then give me that address. I'll be right over," Ben replied.

~~~~~~~~~~

Thirty minutes later, Ben stood in the doorway of the kitchen, watching Tori cook, listening to her sing along to 'Reminiscing.' Her back was turned to him so she wasn't aware that he was there, until she felt his arms gently circle her waist and he began quietly singing along with her, pulling her body against his.

She smiled at his touch, placed the spoon on the spoon-rest and circled her arms around his, leaning backwards into the hug. They swayed back and forth to the music and sang the chorus in perfect harmony, until Ben spun her around and smoothly took her into his arms.

"Hi, beautiful," he murmured, kissing her tenderly on the lips. "Rough day?"

Tori sighed, leaned her head on his shoulder and replied, "Honestly, I haven't decided what kind of day I've had. I can say that I've never had one quite like it, nor do I expect I will ever again! I guess you talked to Mom?"

"She answered your phone earlier and suggested I come over for dinner which by the looks of it, you're going to have more than enough for everyone! Did you leave any food for the rest of the people in town?" He laughed as he surveyed all the groceries surrounding them. "And what is it about bacon that nearly brings a man to his knees, just by its smell? Good Lord, what are you making?"

Laughing with him, Tori turned to the counter where she had several trays lined out and pointed them out. "Those are bacon-wrapped, cream cheese stuffed cherry peppers; those are Gruyère cheese Gougères; that is a sweet chipotle dressing that I'll toss with a chopped salad already chilling in the fridge; and that pan will eventually be steamed mussels with bacon, bourbon and jalapeños. Oh, and I also baked some bread to soak up the broth from the mussels."

Ben blinked several times in surprise and looked at her in bewilderment, "Wow! You even baked your own bread. You have had an interesting day, haven't you? What can I do for you? May I help?"

"You," Tori replied, "may refill my wine, pour yourself a glass and go visit with Mom and Meda. The first course should be ready in about fifteen minutes so I'll let you know when I'm ready."

Knowing Tori as well as he did, he knew better than to argue. Kissing her on the lips one more time, he said, "Okay! I will leave you to your work, Mademoiselle!"

He refilled her glass, poured one for himself and quietly left the room.

Distractedly, Tori turned back to the stove and muttered, "Now, where was I?"

As Ben emerged through the doorway to the patio, Sarah looked at him expectantly and asked, "So?"

He smiled, sat down at the table with Sarah and Meda and replied, "She's fine, Sarah. She politely pushed me out of the room so she could focus but I think she's okay. What went on today anyway? How come she didn't know you were coming?"

Sarah took a sip of her wine, savoring the nuances of the deep blackberry and chocolaty toasted oak. "Well," she began, glancing briefly at Meda, whose face intentionally held no expression, "it has to do with Tori's dreams, Ben."

Ben looked back and forth, warily, between Sarah and Meda and asked, "What about her dreams? Why do they involve the two of you?"

"This should be interesting," murmured Aubrey, sarcastically.

Ignoring the comment, Sarah looked at Ben and replied, "Ben, what I'm about to say will sound very surreal. It's important that you try to keep an open mind, okay?"

Ben looked at Sarah, snorted a laugh and said, "Surreal as in my girlfriend talks to spirits and sometimes dreams about the devil? Something like that?"

Sarah chuckled and quietly replied, "Touché." She took in a deep breath and said, "Okay then. The reason Tori's dreams involve me and Meda is because today we all learned that the Ramiel and the Neviah families are in fact actually one family."

Sarah looked at Karla, Aubrey and Meda and added, "We are all the descendants of the archangel Ramiel."

Ben's eyes widened in surprise and he carefully set down his glass on the table. "How do you know that for sure? What proof do you have?"

"Agent Sullivan has a collection of documents, recording the Ramiel family history," Sarah replied.

"So why don't either of you have that information? Why is it that an instructor at the FBI academy does and you don't?" Ben asked, puzzled.

Sarah and Meda exchanged another look and this time Meda replied, "It appears that in the beginning, the amulet and the statue were used by one chosen member of the family. The combined powers from both items gave their owner an incredible amount of power. It seems as though over time, Satan repeatedly attempted to tempt the chosen ones and eventually, one woman succumbed to his charm and used the power for evil. When the family discovered what she had done, they stoned her to death.

"The family then decided the combined power was too tempting for one mortal to have, so the objects and the family were divided. One family was to continue using the amulet to guide spirits and the other family to continue using the statue. The families were never to make contact with one another again in fear of history repeating itself."

"I don't understand," Ben said. "If the families have been successfully using their abilities to guide spirits up until now, why is it so important for everyone to find out that both families were once one?"

Sarah smiled worriedly at Ben, placed her hand on his and replied, "Because, Tori is now the sole survivor of the original family. Once she dies, the line of Ramiel will die with her. She has no choice but to claim her place in the line of the descendants of Ramiel and to assume ownership of both the amulet and the statue."

"But what about what happened before with the last owner of both objects?" Ben asked, now understanding Sarah's concern.

"We're still trying to figure all of that out, Ben. In the meantime, we need to support Tori however we can and give her time to figure some of it out on her own," Sarah replied.

"Here we are!" Tori announced, happily, emerging onto the patio, carrying two serving dishes heaped with food.

"Honey, that looks wonderful," Sarah replied, quickly putting a smile on her face while helping Tori arrange the plates onto the table.

"Here, let me help!" Ben chimed in, mirroring Sarah's smile. He popped one of the bacon wrapped peppers into his mouth and sighed, "Oh, bacon, I've missed you!"

Meda laughed at Ben's reaction and asked, "What is all this?"

"These are Tori's bacon-wrapped cream cheese stuffed cherry peppers and they're amazing!" Ben mumbled as he tried to both chew and talk at the same time. He looked at Tori, admiringly and added, "Oh, and you added chopped jalapeños to the cheese so there's just the right amount of heat. Honey, these are wonderful!"

Tori laughed, pleased at Ben's reaction and replied, "Thank you, Ben."

She sat down at the remaining empty chair at the table and said to Sarah and Meda, "Eat up, please! I have a few minutes to relax before I start the next course."

Meda placed a sampling of the peppers on her plate and looked at the other dish, curiously. "What are those? Is that bread?"

Tori grinned and replied, "Those are called Gougères but you may have also heard them called 'Pâté à Choux.' They're like a pastry but they're more on the savory side. I added shredded Gruyère cheese to give them a little creaminess."

Meda bit into one of the Gougères, chewed and then looked at the remaining half of the pastry still in her hand with a surprised look on her face. "Oh my goodness! I don't think I've ever had anything like this before. It's so light and airy and yet creamy like you said. It's wonderful!"

"See? I was right! Man, I wish I could try one of those!" Karla said, wistfully as she watched her mother eat the remainder of the Gougères in her hand.

182

Tori placed a couple of each appetizer on a plate and began nibbling on one of the Gougères. "So, what were you guys talking about before I came out?"

"We were catching Ben up to what went on today," Sarah replied.

Tori regarded Ben thoughtfully for a moment and said, "Well you don't have a panic stricken look in your eyes yet like you're ready to bolt. They must not have gotten very far."

Ben smiled his crooked smile and replied, "You were already one peanut shy of being a box full of Cracker-Jack crazy, Tor, and that wasn't even enough to scare me away. It's going to take a lot more than this to make me change how I feel about you."

"Ha, famous last words!" Tori snorted.

"Hey, everyone!" Piper announced as she emerged through the doorway of the patio.

"Hi, Piper!" Tori replied. "Perfect timing, I just brought out the first course! Have a seat, I need to get back in the kitchen," she added rising from her chair.

"Well I don't want to kick you out of your chair, Tor! Why don't you relax for a few more minutes, I'm okay," Piper argued.

"No, seriously, I need to get back in there. Did you find all my toiletries?" Tori asked, hopefully.

Piper nodded her head, affirmatively and replied, "Yep. I've got your overnight bag with all your clothes and personal stuff in the living room with mine. If there's anything I missed, we can swing by our dorm room between classes tomorrow and get it."

"Thanks for doing that! I needed to clear my head after everything that went on today and shopping for groceries always seems to do the trick," Tori said.

"Wait, how did you end up in the meeting today?" Ben asked Piper.

Piper looked around the table quickly at everyone's faces and asked, "Did I say something I wasn't supposed to?"

Sarah smiled at Piper, understandably and replied, "No, sweetheart. You're fine. We haven't told Ben about that part of today yet."

Sarah looked at Tori and said, "We can fill Ben in, honey, if you want to get back to your cooking."

Relishing the opportunity to escape and avoid hashing out the events of the day again, Tori jumped up out of her chair and replied, "Thanks, Mom! Eat up everyone! The second course will be out shortly."

Waiting for Tori to go back inside and get out of immediate ear shot, Sarah said, "Pour yourself a glass of wine and have a seat, Piper. We have a lot to cover in a short amount of time until Tori comes back."

"Okay, you don't have to tell me twice," Piper replied happily as she reached over to pour a glass while checking to make sure everyone else's glasses were filled to acceptable levels in the process.

As she settled into the chair Tori vacated, she took a sip of the wine and eyed the platters in front of her, hungrily. "Wow! I didn't realize how hungry I was until just now. Okay, go ahead, I'm set!"

While Piper filled her plate, Sarah turned to Ben and said, "Okay. We don't have a lot of time so here's the abridged version of our day…."

~~~~~~~~~~

Fifteen minutes later, Ben was staring at Piper with his mouth hanging open in surprise. "What?" he uttered in disbelief.

Smirking back at him, Piper picked up one of the bacon wrapped peppers from her plate and shoved it into Ben's open mouth. "Here, do something useful with that gaping hole before a bug flies in. Besides, didn't anyone ever tell you it's not polite to stare?"

Ben chewed, contemplatively while he reasoned in his mind what he had just learned. He swallowed and curiously asked, "So what, now you and Tor are like the Wonder Twins or something? Is that why you were paired up together?"

Piper laughed and replied, "Well, Agent Hunter did admit that he knew about my ability the whole time. My aunt,

Sky, was one of the family members the FBI interviewed prior to accepting my application and she apparently told them everything. Not that I was really hiding it or anything like that. I've just learned to be careful who I share my ability with."

"How long has Tori known?" Ben asked, hurt that he was being left out of a lot of secrets lately.

Piper quickly shook her head and answered, "She didn't know, Ben. I promise. She just found out a couple days ago and I made her promise not to tell anyone. Please don't blame her. She was being a good friend. This is all still a bit weird knowing the FBI is aware of my ability. I've never really known how to react to people once they find out. I don't have any other siblings and never really had any close girlfriends while I was growing up so Tori has become like a sister to me. I don't want that to change."

"She already has a sister," grumbled Aubrey from the other side of the patio.

Sarah smiled at Aubrey and quietly said, "She didn't mean anything by that, honey."

Piper quickly turned to Sarah and then looked around the patio. "Oh, I'm so sorry, Aubrey! I really didn't mean anything by that! I'm making things worse aren't I?"

Sarah patted Piper's hand, gently and said, "You're okay, honey. We're all figuring things out as we go so we all need to do our best not to take offense to what someone says."

"Hot stuff, coming through!" Tori announced, once again emerging through the doorway, carrying a large stock pot with a plate of bread balanced on top.

Ben chuckled and quickly jumped up to take the pot from her and said, "Nice double-entendre, Tor. Here, let me help."

Tori smiled and replied, "Thank you! I have one more thing to grab from the kitchen and we'll be all set!"

While Tori went back into the kitchen, Ben went inside to get a side chair from the living room and placed it beside his. Tori returned a few moments later carrying a large salad bowl and a stack of several smaller bowls, plates and utensils.

"Here, Tor, you can sit here," Ben suggested.

"Thank you!" she replied, placing the items on the table and sitting down beside him. She looked around at everyone and said, "Bon appétit, everyone!"

"Now what have you made?" Meda marveled, pleased that she hadn't overdone the appetizer round.

Tori pointed to each container and replied, "That is a chopped salad with a sweet chipotle dressing, that is home-made rustic multi-grain bread, and in the stock-pot I have prepared my own special recipe of steamed mussels with bacon, bourbon and jalapeños."

"Oh...It's been ages since you've made that! Yum, more bacon," Ben breathed in contentment.

Tori laughed and replied, "I think that's what I've missed most since we joined the academy. Not having a kitchen. This is nice and it was exactly what I needed after today. Thank you, everyone, for indulging me and giving me time to do all this."

"Are you kidding?" Piper exclaimed. "We're the ones getting the better end of the deal here, Tor. This all looks absolutely amazing! Your aura has the happiest, healthiest green glow right now. It's beautiful!"

Tori smiled at Piper and replied, "Thanks, Piper!"

"Yum, I had forgotten how much I enjoy your cooking, honey," Sarah remarked. "The smokiness in the salad dressing pairs with the spiciness of the mussels perfectly! And this bread is just the right vehicle for soaking up the broth! This is divine!"

"I second that!" Meda chimed in. "Once again, you've allowed me to experience something I've never had before and it is wonderful!"

Tori smiled in contentment and replied, "Thank you! Okay! Less talking and more eating!"

~~~~~~~~~~

Later that evening, after the evidence of dinner had long since been cleared away and Ben bid them all a good night, the group migrated to the living room. Sarah, Meda, Tori and Piper relaxed on the chairs and couches, while Aubrey, Karla and Tobias stood nearby.

"Oh! I'm so stuffed right now, I can barely move," Piper groaned, rubbing her stomach. "You need a warning label on you, Tori! You are a menace in the kitchen. Thank you for not making a dessert. I think I would have literally exploded if you had."

Tori chuckled with her eyes closed and replied, "There was no spell cast over the food, my friend. You consumed at your own risk."

"I know, I know. It was just so good!" Piper sighed, her eyelids suddenly feeling very heavy.

"I hate to say it, but I'm actually jealous right now," Karla said to Aubrey and Tobias. "I don't think I've ever missed food until tonight. Look at them all! They're literally in food comas!"

Meda giggled and replied, "Don't forget the wine, my dear!"

Tobias chuckled and added, "Perhaps your new friends are a bad influence on you, plying you with both food and alcohol!"

Sarah and Tori laughed in response and Sarah replied, "Don't worry, Tobias. We'll take good care of her. In a very indirect way, Meda and I are sisters."

Tori eyed the women speculatively and said, "You know, I hadn't thought about that! That's actually pretty cool! I have an Aunt! I realize the three of us are the remaining children of Ramiel that we know of, but you're right, Mom."

Meda smiled at Sarah fondly, and said, "Sisters. I like that!"

Piper yawned loudly and asked, "So what are the sleeping arrangements going to be, because I'm not going to be able to stay awake much longer."

"I'm comfortable right here on the couch," Tori yawned in response.

"This chair is very comfortable. I don't want to get up yet," Sarah sighed, reclining further backwards and closing her eyes.

"I agree. I like being able to put my feet up! I'm going to have to buy one of these when I get home," Meda muttered.

A few minutes later, all four women were asleep.

"Great! Now what do we do?" Aubrey sighed.

"What we always do. Wait." Karla shrugged and sighed in response.

Chapter 15

Hearing the sound of gently stirring leaves through tree branches, Tori opened her eyes and realized she was back in the garden at the path in front of the tree.

"Great," she sighed in frustration. "Of course I would end up here after the day I've had. All right, where are you this time?" she asked, looking around her, impatiently.

Completing a full circle, she returned to facing the tree and saw Satan standing a few feet away, smiling at her. He was wearing a different suit than earlier that afternoon, although its cut was still expensive looking and very tailored. The deep garnet necktie chosen to accompany the black suit was a sharp contrast against the crisp white dress shirt beneath the jacket.

"Somebody should put a bell on you," Tori grumbled in irritation. "What now? And to answer your earlier question, no, you do not get a hug."

Satan's smile broadened and he replied, "Oh well. You can't blame a guy for trying!" He chuckled at his joke and added, "You know you should make more of an effort to stay on my good side, Tori. It would be in your best interest not to upset me."

Tori gave him a sarcastic smile in response and asked, "Why? Are you going to tell me that I might hurt your feelings?"

"Would that be so hard to believe?" he asked, innocently.

Tori furrowed her brow in confusion and replied, "Could I actually do that?"

"Well of course not! Don't be ridiculous!" he laughed, shaking his head and rolling his eyes, dramatically.

Tori frowned at him asked, "Seriously. I had a really stressful day today and I need to get some sleep. So unless you had something particular in mind that you wanted to talk about, I would appreciate it if you would send me back."

"You know what I want to talk about, Tori," he murmured, menacingly.

She eyed him suspiciously and replied, "I'm not sure that I do."

Playing along with her he added, "Did you enjoy the power you experienced earlier today?"

Tori stuck out her chin defiantly and replied, "I am not going to talk to you about the amulet and the statue, so if that's why you brought me he.."

"That's not what I'm talking about and you know it," he interrupted with a sly smile, cutting her off mid-sentence.

She looked at him with a confused expression until suddenly, it dawned on her what he meant. "Is that why you brought me here? To talk about that...about him and what he did to those women?" she gasped.

He continued to smile slyly at her, his eyes defiantly glaring at her to contradict him.

Tori shook her head vehemently and said, "Uh, uh. We are so not having this conversation." She turned around sharply and began walking away from the tree down the path, trying to find a way out of her dream. "How do I get out of here!" she cried.

~~~~~~~~~~

"What was that?" Karla exclaimed, looking into the corner of the room.

"What was what?" Aubrey asked, looking in the same direction.

"I saw something dark move over there in my peripheral vision," Karla replied.

"See?" Aubrey said, excitedly. "Now you saw it too! Remember that shadow I saw the other night when Mom and Meda were asleep? Right before they woke up? You said you didn't see it but I did!"

"Okay, okay, now I believe you," Karla replied, quietly, walking around the room, trying to find the shadowy image.

"I don't see anything!" Tobias said, joining her.

"It was just a flash, like something running by," Karla replied, still looking around her.

"What's going on?" Sarah said quietly, waking.

"Mom!" Aubrey exclaimed. "We saw the shadow again. Well, at least Karla saw it this time!"

Now suddenly very awake, Sarah sat up in her chair, looked around the room and asked, "Do you see it now? Where is it?"

Karla shook her head and replied, "I don't see it anymore. It was just a flash, over there in the corner behind the couch."

Sarah looked over at the couch where Piper and Tori were sleeping on opposite ends. "Over there?" she asked, pointing behind Piper.

"No, behind Tori," Karla replied, firmly.

"Do you think the shadow is Satan? Is that what we keep seeing?" Aubrey asked.

Sarah got up from her chair and walked over to the couch beside her daughter. She noticed that Tori's breathing was short and rapid and that her face was troubled. She went over to Piper and gently shook Piper's shoulder, "Piper," she whispered.

"Wha?" Piper uttered, opening her eyes and sitting up. "What's going on?"

"Something's going on with Tori. Can you see anything around her? Karla said she saw a shadow but we can't see it anymore," Sarah whispered.

Piper looked over at Tori in confusion and suddenly her eyes widened. "Oh! Her aura has gone completely black again. Look how fast she's breathing. She's with him! What do we do? Should we wake her up?"

"Wait! Isn't it dangerous to wake someone when their dreaming?" Aubrey asked.

"No, honey," Sarah replied, calmly. "That's when someone is sleepwalking."

"Oh, right. Never mind," Aubrey said, rolling her eyes. "Then I say wake her up."

"What's going on?" Meda asked, having been woken by the sound of voices.

Sarah looked at her fearfully and replied, "Tori's having a bad dream and Piper said her aura has turned black again. We think Tori's with Satan. Should we wake her up?"

~~~~~~~~~~

195

"I need to leave! How do I go back?" Tori said in frustration, now running down the path away from the tree. She stopped suddenly as Satan materialized on the path before her.

"I wasn't finished talking with you yet," he said quietly with a calm expression.

"Well I am!" she replied, firmly. "I would like to leave now, please."

He shook his head slowly, walking towards her and replied, "I will tell you when you can leave."

As Tori's eyes began to fill with tears, she heard a deep, drawled voice beside her say, "I believe the lady said please, Luc."

Tori turned to the sound of the voice and saw the other man from her vision earlier that day, smiling, tenderly down at her. His light grey eyes were troubled, yet patient. "Come on," he said, taking her by the hand. "Let's go."

As Tori felt her body being pulled away, she heard Satan yell furiously after them, "I said I wasn't finished yet!"

~~~~~~~~~~

"Wait!" Piper called out, extending her hands towards Sarah, who was about to wake Tori. "Her aura is changing again! It's back to green. Well, mostly green. Huh. Now it looks like it's...what is that?" she murmured, leaning forward, squinting her eyes at Tori.

"What?" Sarah asked, confused at Piper's reaction.

"Her aura looks like its sparkling! Like it's glittering with diamonds! It's...well, beautiful! What the heck does a sparkling aura mean?" Piper asked to no one in particular.

"Is she still in danger?" Sarah asked, still prepared to wake her daughter.

Piper shook her head and replied, "No, I don't think so. Look at her face. It's calm and she's no longer breathing heavy. I think she's okay. Let's wait a little longer."

~~~~~~~~~~~~

Tori looked around her and realized that she was in a place she knew well, almost by heart. "You brought me to Lonesome Mountain," she whispered in disbelief.

She smiled as she felt the warmth of the sun on her face and couldn't resist closing her eyes and breathing in the fragrance of the wild flowers and clean mountain air.

Exhaling a loud sigh, she turned to the man beside her and asked, "How did you know to bring me here?"

"Isn't this where you usually go when you need to clear your head?" he asked with concern, fearing that he had misjudged the location.

Tori grinned and replied, "There's no place I would rather be right now, than right here! What I meant was how did you know it was where I would want to be?"

He smiled, warmly at her and said, "Tori, I know just about everything there is to know about you, maybe even a few things you don't know about yourself."

Tori cocked her head to one side and eyed him questionably. "Like what?" she asked.

He gave her a secretive smile and replied, "Well, for example, you found this place by accident one day when you went hiking in the Beartooth Mountains a few years after your sister disappeared. You sat on that boulder right over there and stayed there until the sun set."

Tori stared at him with a shocked expression and whispered, "That's exactly what happened."

"And over the years, you've come back here and camped, sometimes bringing your friend, Ben, with you. This is the one place you've always felt safe and at peace. That's why I brought you here. It's my responsibility to watch out for you," he said.

Tori walked over to 'her boulder' and gently ran her fingers over the sun-warmed, rough stone. "Your responsibility?" she questioned, turning back to him. "How long have I been 'your responsibility'?"

"Your entire life," he said, quietly.

Tori gasped and asked, "My entire life? How is that possible?"

"You do you know who I am, don't you, Tori?" he asked, curiously.

Tori opened her mouth to respond but then hesitated a moment as she realized she hadn't even questioned the idea that this was Ramiel. *'Or is it Remiel?'* she thought, inwardly.

Pursing her lips and squinting at him speculatively, she replied, "Well I'm pretty sure I know who you are, but I guess you know what I'm going to ask next, don't you?"

He laughed at her expression and said, "My brothers and I have been called many things throughout the years, some of them not so favorable. I suspect, however you're referencing whether I am the 'Thunder of God' or the 'Mercy of God.' Is that what you mean?"

Tori winced, guiltily and whined, "Well….."

He laughed again and said, "Both of which being one in the same."

Tori's eyes widened and she exclaimed, "So there never were two angels? It's just you?"

"Nope, just me," he confirmed, firmly.

"So what's with all the mystery over the years? Do you have multiple personalities or something? Like Dr. Jekyll and Mr. Hyde? Maybe you have an evil twin!" she challenged.

He scowled at her insult and replied, "What? No, it's nothing like that! My goodness, the things you come up with sometimes! I have no idea when or who made the mistake. I know who I am and who I have always been!"

"Huh," Tori said, taking a seat on the boulder. "Well, that should make my mom and Agent Sullivan happy," she surmised. "So what should I call you?"

"You can call me Remy," he replied, bowing graciously in front of her.

"Remy," Tori murmured quietly as the sound of his name on her lips suddenly triggered a long forgotten memory. She drew in a deep breath as the entire memory returned to her and she looked up sharply at Remy's expectant face.

"I knew you looked familiar to me when I first saw you!" she exclaimed. "I've seen you before! You were the man who gave me hot chocolate and sat with me in the police station the night my sister disappeared! That was you, wasn't it?"

Remy grimly set his mouth, nodded his head and replied, "Yes, that was me."

"How is that possible?" Tori asked, puzzled at the possibility that Remy could have been there that night.

Remy sighed and rubbed his chin thoughtfully, knowing where this conversation would lead them. "Under certain circumstances, I have the ability to appear in physical form to mortals. And before you ask or accuse me of anything, no, I could not have stopped what happened to your sister that night. I didn't know what was going to happen to her. I'm not 'in the know' to certain pieces of information if you know what I mean."

Tori stared at Remy while she thought back to that night and replied, "You sat with me the entire time until my parents came to take me home. When I looked back to say goodbye, you were gone. I asked my mom where the nice man went who had been sitting with me, and she said I was sitting by myself. There wasn't anyone there. Was I the only one who saw you that night?"

Remy nodded and gruffly replied, "Yeah."

Tori continued to reflect back upon that night while Remy patiently waited for her next question. "So let me make sure I understand you correctly," she began, speculatively. "On occasion, you can appear to mortals – humans?"

"That is correct," he replied.

"And you cannot prevent events from happening to other people," she asked.

"Also, correct," he replied.

"And you don't know what's going to happen to someone, no matter how wonderful or tragic it may be. You are only made aware of the event, after the fact along with everyone else," she probed.

"Yep," he quipped, rocking back and forth on the heels of his boots.

"Why?" Tori asked, point blank.

Remy cocked his head to one side and gave Tori a puzzled look. "Why, what?"

Tori sighed in frustration and asked, "Why are you only allowed to know what we know? Why don't you know what's going to happen?"

Remy raised his eyebrows in surprise and exclaimed, "Because only God can do that, Tori! Come on! I'm surprised that you even asked me that question!"

"But you were one of God's special angels!" Tori argued back. "Do you mean to tell me that you and your 'brothers' as you called them earlier, never knew ANYTHING about what was going to happen here on earth?"

"That wasn't our job!" Remy argued back. "Or at least it wasn't mine! My job was to guide the souls of the faithful into heaven and to enlighten mortals of God's grace through visions. He didn't want me to know anything other than that!"

Tori glared at Remy and asked, "Really? If you were fine with that, then what happened? What made you fall out of His grace and end up here on earth? And what were you and Satan arguing about back in that meadow? And why did you tell me to let go of the statue? What didn't you want me to hear?"

Remy groaned and rubbed his hands over his face in frustration, muttering, "Sweet Father in heaven you ask a lot of questions!"

"Well if you've been watching me my entire life, you already knew that!" Tori replied in defense. "So?"

"So it's a long story for another time," Remy sighed. "I promise I'll tell you one day but you're not ready to know all of it yet."

Tori looked at Remy, suspiciously and asked, "How do you know that?"

Remy met her eyes, readily and answered, "Because He told me."

Tori took in a sharp breath in surprise and asked, "He still talks to you? Even though....?"

Remy smiled and replied, "Yes, even though, He still talks to me. They call it 'Amazing Grace' for a reason, Tori."

"So there's still a chance for redemption, even after all this time?" she asked, fascinated.

"Through the Lord's mercies we are not consumed, because His compassions fail not," Remy reverently quoted from Lamentations.

Tori grinned at Remy, quietly.

"What?" he asked, suspiciously.

"That makes me happy!" she exclaimed.

"Well good, it's supposed to," Remy replied, thankful for the change in subject. "What's your next question?"

Tori scrutinized Remy carefully and asked, "Is this how you look all the time?"

Remy placed his hands on his hips and scowled at her again. "What's wrong with the way I look?" he asked.

Tori's cheeks flared red in embarrassment and she stammered, "Nothing! I...I...I was just wondering..."

"You want to know where my wings are?" he probed, humorously.

"Well...." She paused.

Remy flashed Tori a mischievous grin and barely moving a muscle, extended two massive white wings from behind his shoulder blades.

Tori's jaw dropped in amazement and her eyes filled with tears as she choked out, "Oh, they are the most beautiful things I've ever seen."

"Oh! For heaven's sake! I didn't mean to make you cry!" Remy drawled, guiltily as he began to retract his wings.

"No! Please don't do that," Tori quickly replied, jumping up from the boulder, walking towards him with her hands outstretched. She swiped at her tears, hastily and said, "These are tears of joy, not sadness, Remy. Have you never seen anyone react to your wings like that before?"

Remy looked down, dug the toe of his boot in the dirt and quietly replied, "It's been so long, I've forgotten what it feels like to have someone see me for who I really am."

Tori hesitantly touched Remy's shoulder in comfort and asked, "How long has it been, Remy?"

He looked down into her searching eyes and hoarsely replied, "It feels like it's been forever."

Without saying another word, Tori slid her arms around Remy's waist and pulled him against her into a gentle hug.

He hesitated for a moment, not knowing what to do but when he realized just how much he missed the feeling of human contact, he wrapped his arms around Tori in response and slowly brought his wings forward and closed them around her. They stood quietly, holding one another for a several minutes until Remy sighed and quietly said, "Yes, Father. I know."

When Remy pulled away from the hug, Tori looked into his eyes, questioning him without asking and he sadly replied, "It's time for you to go."

Chapter 16

Tori opened her eyes and was startled to see everyone standing, crowded around her. She immediately sat up, looking around her and asked, "What's going on? Why are you all staring at me like that?"

"Why don't you tell us, 'sparkles,'" Aubrey asked, dramatically.

"Sparkles?" Tori asked, scowling back at her sister. "Where did that come from?"

"Apparently, it came from all around you!" her sister laughed.

Tori looked at Piper with a quizzical look and asked, "Seriously, what's going on? What is Bree talking about?"

Piper briefly glanced at Sarah and Meda, then back to Tori. "Your aura was doing some pretty strange things earlier, Tor. It was black one minute, then it went back to your normal green, and then it began to sparkle, like diamonds. What the heck were you dreaming about?"

Tori rubbed her hands over her eyes, wearily and looked at the curious faces surrounding her. She chuckled quietly and said, "Well, you all might as well have a seat and get comfortable. This is going to take a while."

Picking up on the seriousness in her daughter's tone, Sarah quickly said, "Ah, I think I'm going to go make some coffee."

Tori smiled, wanly at her mother as Sarah headed for the kitchen and called out after her, "That's a great idea, thanks Mom."

<center>~~~~~~~~~~</center>

An hour later, Tori sipped her coffee and looked at all the dumbfounded faces surrounding her. Even after re-telling her dream to the others, she had to admit that it sounded like a chapter right out of a science fiction novel.

"He came to me," Aubrey murmured, quietly.

Tori looked, quickly at Aubrey and asked, "What?"

"Remy. He came to me the night I died," Aubrey replied, looking at her sister.

"Why didn't you say anything about it until now?" Tori asked with a puzzled look.

Aubrey shook her head and replied, "I didn't remember until you said his name. Then all of a sudden, it all came back to me. It was right after I fell off my bike, before I died. He was crouched down beside me, his face filled with sadness. He said, 'don't worry, Aubrey, I will send her to you. Be patient. She'll find you.' He meant you, didn't he? He was going to send you."

"Who didn't say what until now?" Piper asked, lost in the conversation.

"Bree said that Remy came to her the night she died and he told her that he would send 'her' to find her," Tori replied, miming air quotes.

"He came to me too," Karla added with a grim expression. "The night I died at that farmhouse." She looked at Tori and added, "He said the exact same thing to me. To be patient and that he would send 'her' to me. He meant that he would be sending you."

"He came to Karla too the night she died," Tori repeated, deep in thought. Suddenly, it all made sense. "My dreams," she realized.

"Divine visions," Meda whispered in amazement.

"Why now?" Piper asked, looking at Tori, curiously.

Tori looked at Piper and frowned. "Why 'what' now?"

"Haven't you ever wondered why all this just started happening to you in the last year or so? Why you haven't had things like this happen before now?" Piper asked.

Tori stared into her coffee cup, thinking about Piper's question and quietly answered, "I don't know. I didn't think to ask."

"I think I do," Sarah said, as she sat down on the couch beside Tori and began to gently rub her back. "And part of the reason is my fault, I would guess."

Piper looked at Sarah oddly and Sarah continued, "I knew of my family history ever since my mother decided I was old enough to learn about it. I didn't embrace my gift the way Tori has, I was afraid of it."

"Afraid? Why?" Piper asked, curiously.

Sarah smiled sadly at Piper and said, "I don't know. After my mother died, I locked it and the statue away and tried to live out a normal life. I avoided places like hospitals and cemeteries, to keep the girls from seeing the spirits. Tanner and I moved to a very small town where I knew there would be little chance of us coming across anything unexpected.

"After Aubrey disappeared, we all 'shut down' a bit inside, Tori more than I. If it wasn't for Ben, she would never have left her room other than going to school. She surrounded herself in a fortress made out of wiring from the internet and pillars of books." Sarah gently cupped Tori's face in the palm of her hand and said, "She blocked out as much human contact as she possibly could."

Tori blinked back tears as she quietly whispered to her mother, "I'm sorry I did that to you, Mom. I never meant to hurt you."

Sarah smiled, tenderly at Tori and replied, "I know. I'm sorry too, honey." Turning back to Piper, Sarah said, "I think the pivotal moment was the day Tori and Ben accepted the case to find Laurel Meadows, the daughter of one of my husband's colleagues. Somehow, that decision either woke something that was sleeping inside of Tori or perhaps tore down a wall of that fortress and allowed Remy the opportunity to find his way in."

"So he never appeared to you, Mom? Not even when Grandma died?" Aubrey asked.

"No, sweetheart, he never did," Sarah replied. "He may have tried, but I was probably too closed off if he did."

"What about you, Mom?" Karla asked, curiously. "Did he ever come to you?"

Meda shook her head and replied, "No, I don't recall ever seeing anyone that looked like the man Tori described."

Tori looked at the clock on the mantle and sighed. "Well, this night is shot. We've only got a couple hours until sunrise and I need to record all the details from my dream for Agent Hunter before Piper and I leave for class."

"And I need to pack for our trip out to North Carolina," Meda chimed in. "Karla and I will be leaving this morning to talk with Marsha Foster, the final victim." Turning to Sarah, she added, "Would you like to come with us, Sarah?"

Sarah smiled at Meda and replied, "Actually, if there's room on the plane for me and Aubrey, I think I would like that. That is as long as Tori and Piper don't mind us leaving them for a couple of days. Would that be okay, Tori?"

Tori shrugged her shoulders and replied, "Sure, that's fine. Piper and I can go back to our dorm room until you all get back."

Tobias chucked, heartily and replied, "What man would argue the opportunity to be in the company of such beautiful women?"

"Take it easy, Dad," Karla warned, laughing at her father. Tobias winked at Karla, good-naturedly and said, "I'm just teasing."

"All right, I guess I better get started," Tori declared, getting up from the couch to retrieve her laptop from her backpack.

"I guess I better go pack!" Sarah replied, as she retrieved the empty coffee pot and cups and headed for the kitchen.

Chapter 17

"This doesn't make any sense!" declared Agent Jayco in frustration as she hunched over her microscope. She was analyzing the last slide from the rose stains she prepared earlier that evening and still didn't have any answers.

She sat back in her chair and stared off into the corner of her office, rubbing her strained shoulders, trying to recall why this particular cellular structure looked so familiar to her. *'I know I've seen this same pattern before, but from where?'* she thought, wearily. "I've been staring at these slides for hours and I can't quite put my finger on it."

Suddenly, the realization hit her. "Philly cheese-steak sandwiches - Andrew!" she exclaimed loudly, snapping her fingers. She laughed in a crazed, sleep-depraved haze as she jumped from her chair and rushed to her credenza to find her old college yearbook. Finding the book which she sought, she plopped down into her desk chair and began hastily flipping through the pages until she found the face she was looking for. "Andrew Porter!" she cried out, happily, pleased that her memory had not failed her.

Swiveling her chair around to face her laptop, Agent Jayco opened a web browser and searched for her former colleague's name. "Oh my," she muttered, grimly. "There are a lot more Dr. Andrew Porters out there than I expected." Glancing at the time she added, "And it's too early to start making calls."

Realizing there was little she could do at that hour, she groaned, sat back in her chair and attempted to blink away the grainy, sand-like dryness caused by the hours of staring into the lens of her microscope. Finding it easier to simply close her eyes, she sank deeper into her chair and quickly drifted off to sleep.

~~~~~~~~~~~

"I don't get it, she's never missed a class," Tori said, looking anxiously at the entryway of the classroom door.

"Maybe she's running late?" offered Piper, optimistically.

"You know if she's more than fifteen minutes late, we get to leave and not be considered absent! That would be two days in a row that she's missed class!" announced Arrogant Arrant in his know-it-all, boastful tone.

"Feel free to leave now. We won't stop you," replied Piper, glaring at him in annoyance.

"Speaking of which, you weren't in class yesterday either. Where were you and Tori yesterday, anyway?" he challenged back.

"We were working on a special assignment with Agent Jayco called 'Noneya,'" Piper quipped in response.

"What?" he argued.

"Noneya. As in none-ya-business," Piper taunted.

"I don't believe you! If there was an opportunity for a special assignment, the entire class should have been given the chance to participate. What makes you and Tori so special that you were chosen and excused from class?" Arrant asked.

"Maybe you're not as special as you think you are?" Piper teased.

"Enough!" Tori exclaimed, loudly which made everyone around them suddenly stop talking and stare at her. "No one is more or less special than anyone else. As for why we weren't in class yesterday, that's none of your business, Chet." Tori turned to Ben and said, "It's been almost twenty-five minutes. I'm getting worried."

"What is there to be worried about, Tor?" Ben asked.

"I don't know, but something doesn't feel right. I'm going to go look for her." Without waiting for a response, Tori grabbed her backpack and began walking towards the door.

"Wait! I'm coming with you," Piper called after her, picking up her bag, hurrying to catch up.

Ben deliberated for a moment and then decided to follow. "Hang on, I'm coming too!"

"If she shows up, I'll tell her you all left together! You'll be counted absent!" Arrant called out as they left.

~~~~~~~~~~

Two hours later, Tori, Piper, Ben, Agent Hunter and Agent Sullivan were in Agent Jayco's office, searching for any clues to help explain why no one could reach her.

"Did you try her cell again?" Tori asked Agent Hunter, anxiously.

"I've tried a half a dozen times in the past two hours, Miss Cooper. The calls go directly to voice-mail so she must have her phone turned off," replied Agent Hunter, calmly. He looked at the array of glass slides beside Agent Jayco's microscope and asked, "What do you think all these slides are?"

Tori walked up beside him and surveyed the arrangement carefully. She looked at the last slide Agent Jayco had left on the microscope's specimen holder, made a quick visual comparison to the other slides on the table and said, "These look like they could be samples from the roses you gave her yesterday afternoon. Didn't she say she was going to analyze them when she left? Did she give you any information on what she found?"

Agent Hunter shook his head slowly and replied, "No, she didn't contact me." Turning to Agent Sullivan he asked, "Did she happen to contact you, Kent?"

Agent Sullivan also shook his head and replied, "No, she didn't."

Tori turned around towards Agent Jayco's desk and noticed the college yearbook lying beside the computer. She saw the year printed on the spine and did a quick mental calculation between the years. Picking up the book and shuffling through the pages, she found Agent Jayco's picture. "Agent Jayco's first name is Iris? That's beautiful! And funny when you think about how she originally started out in genetic botany. I wonder why she recently looked at her college yearbook."

"What makes you think it was recent?" Ben asked, taking the book from her to look at the picture.

"Look at the top of her desk. There's paper and folders everywhere and this book was on top, right next to her computer. If she was in her office most of yesterday afternoon into last night, anything she looked at would be on top. So she must have looked at this book. The question is, why?"

"What about looking at the browser history on her computer?" Piper offered. "Maybe she was trying to find an old classmate?"

Tori gave Piper an appraising look and replied, "Piper, that's brilliant! I can't believe I didn't think of that!" Tori sat down in Agent Jayco's chair, powered up the computer and waited a few moments while the browser page opened. In just few clicks, she had her answer. "She was looking for someone named Andrew Porter."

Ben quickly flipped through the pages of the yearbook until he found the picture. "Here he is! You were right, Piper. He was one of her classmates. There's a notation written next to his picture that says, 'To one day being THE President'. What do you think that means? Does that mean President as in the United States?"

"I don't know," Tori murmured as she continued searching through Agent Jayco's history. "They both attended Temple University in Philadelphia, but I don't see any Andrew Porter's listed in that city or surrounding area."

"How many Andrew Porters are there?" Agent Sullivan asked, curiously.

"Fifteen total from what I see, but only two are within our Andrew Porter's age range," Tori replied, scowling at the screen.

"What?" Ben asked, noticing her expression.

"Well there's one listing in Dover, Delaware for a Dr. Andrew Porter and another one in Gatlinburg, Tennessee. I'm trying to find out what kind of doctors they both are. Ah, here we go! Dr. Delaware has a PhD in Horticultural Science, and Dr. Tennessee has a PhD in Agriculture. Huh, well that doesn't help us much, does it?"

"Are there any other possible candidates we need to look at?"Agent Hunter asked while making notes of both names in a pocket notepad.

Tori shook her head firmly and replied, "No, those are the only two I'm seeing that fit the age range of Agent Jayco's classmate."

Agent Hunter deliberated a moment, trying to decide what the next course of action should be. Both Agent Nichols and Agent Hughes accompanied Agent Neviah and her mother to North Carolina where Marsha Foster's remains were located, and they weren't due to return until later that week.

"Will you please email me the details of those two individuals, Miss Cooper?" he asked, politely.

"Sure. What are you going to do, sir?" Tori asked.

"Well, both Agent Nichols and Agent Hughes are with Agent Neviah and her mother, so it looks like for now, I'm going to have to arrange a couple of trips to Dover and Gatlinburg."

"Can we help?" Tori asked, hopefully. "I'm not going to be able to focus on anything going on here, worrying that something might have happened to Agent Jayco."

Agent Hunter reasoned the limited options available to him and replied, "You three should stay here and attend your classes as normal. You've already missed enough of your classes this week. I'll contact both Dr. Porters and find out if either of them knew or have had recent contact with Agent Jayco. Agent Sullivan, please let me know if you hear from her in the meantime and I'll do likewise. Agreed?"

"Agreed," they all replied in unison.

"Good. I need to get going so I can make my travel arrangements. Agent Sullivan, please contact facilities and instruct them to lock this office and not do any custodial clean up until they've heard from me. Until we know for sure where Agent Jayco is, her office could hold more clues that we'll need to come back and look for," Agent Hunter instructed.

"I'll take care of it," replied Agent Sullivan.

Agent Hunter took one last look around the room and said, "All right, I think that should do it for now." Pointing to Tori, Ben and Piper, he added, "The three of you need to get going to your next class. I'll let you know what I find out."

"Yes, sir," replied Tori, Piper and Ben, begrudgingly.

Chapter 18

Agent Jayco looked down at the address on the piece of paper in her hand and compared it to the number on the brownstone in front of her. "This looks like the place," she said to herself. Taking in a deep breath, she straightened her shoulders, walked up the stairs and rang the doorbell.

While she waited for someone to respond, she looked down at the planters flanking both sides of the front door, and smiled, knowingly. Although they weren't the exact same specimens she had looked at through the lens of her microscope earlier that morning, she recognized that these roses were not the standard nursery variety.

A few minutes later, a woman opened the door and greeted her, pleasantly, "Hello."

Agent Jayco smiled, warmly and replied, "Hello. My name is Iris Jayco. Is this is the residence of Dr. Andrew Porter?"

The woman nodded her head and replied, "Yes, it is. I'm Elaine Porter, his wife. May I help you?"

"I'm sorry for showing up unannounced", said Agent Jayco, apologetically. "I left a message for your husband earlier this morning, but I'm afraid the battery on my phone died and I forgot to bring my charger with me. Is he in? May I speak with him, please?"

Elaine paused for a moment, uncertain as to whether or not she should allow the stranger into her home.

Reading into the woman's hesitation, Agent Jayco removed her badge from her pocket, held it out for Elaine to see and said, "Your husband and I both attended Temple University. After I graduated, I joined the FBI and am currently an instructor in forensic sciences. I remember Andrew was working on botanical cross genetics so I'm hoping he might be able to answer a few questions for me regarding a case I'm working on."

"Oh! Well I'm sure Andrew would be more than happy to help out an old friend!" Elaine replied. "Please come in. He's out back in the greenhouse. I'll show you the way."

"Thank you so much," Agent Jayco replied following the woman down the hallway.

"It must be exciting working with the FBI! I don't recall Andrew ever mentioning that one of his former classmates became an agent," Elaine commented, casually as they walked.

"Well, I'm ashamed to say that I haven't been very good about keeping in touch. Andrew and I kept in contact a few years after graduation, but after a while, our lives took different directions," replied Agent Jayco.

Elaine laughed, lightly and said, "Well, if Andrew was anything then like he is today, I can see how that may have happened. Once he goes into the greenhouse, I've learned not to expect to see him for hours afterwards. Once he gets into the zone, the outside world falls away. Watch your step coming through the door."

Making note to follow the woman's advice, Agent Jayco carefully stepped over the threshold into the greenhouse, and instantly felt the temperature change as the warm humid air washed over her. Once she was sure of her footing, she looked up and froze in amazement.

Everywhere she looked, there was color. Color so bold and brilliant, it was as if somehow, someone had captured a rainbow and locked it inside the room. There were planters of flowers of every kind and every color both on raised platforms set up like isles in the center of the room, and hanging pots suspended from cords secured along metal beams from the ceiling.

"Oh my, I've never seen anything this beautiful before!" Agent Jayco exclaimed as she caught movement out of the corner of her eye. When she turned towards the movement, the color was fluttering in front of her face. "You have butterflies!" she laughed, as she slowly held out her hand and watched as the insect gracefully lighted upon her finger.

Elaine smiled, at Agent Jayco's enraptured response and said, "Aren't they lovely? The butterflies were my idea! They help with the cross pollination of the plants. We have another round of cocoons incubating in our nursery which should hatch in the next few weeks."

Agent Jayco looked at Elaine's proud, motherly face and smiled. "You're an entomologist, aren't you?"

Elaine laughed in response and replied, "You're a quick study! Most people don't figure that out so quickly. I can see why the FBI made you one of their agents! Oh, there's Andrew now. Andrew!" she called out in a raised voice, in the direction of her husband.

The man turned in response, looked at his wife, questioningly and then saw that she had someone with her. He looked at Agent Jayco with a blank expression for a brief moment and then his face lit up with recognition. "Iris?" he asked, hesitantly.

"Hello, Andrew," Agent Jayco replied, smiling warmly.

"My goodness, how long has it been?" he asked as he walked towards her.

"I'm not sure exactly. Maybe eighteen years? Twenty?" she asked.

"That's horrible if you're right. Much too long! You look wonderful!" he replied as he embraced her in a warm hug.

"As do you!" she replied, hugging him back.

He pulled away from the hug and smiled. "What a wonderful surprise. And you've met my wife, Elaine!" he added, turning to his wife. He laughed gently as he noticed two small butterflies resting comfortably on her arm. "Two of your children are saying hello, my dear," he said, affectionately. "Remember to check before you leave."

Elaine looked down to where he was indicating and she laughed with him. She looked up to see Agent Jayco's curious expression and said, "Every time I come into the greenhouse, my babies come to visit me. I need to be careful I don't take anyone out with me when I leave. It's too cool outside this time of year for them."

Agent Jayco looked back and forth between Andrew and his wife and said, "A genetic botanist and an entomologist. It's like a match made in science heaven! Where did you two meet?"

"Why don't we go back into the house and I'll make some coffee so we can talk more comfortably," Elaine said, gently nudging the butterflies off her arm into flight. She spun around in a circle in front of Andrew and asked, "Are there any others?"

He looked his wife over as she spun and replied, "No, you're clear."

"Thank you, my dear! Now, let's get out of this sauna and back into the house. If we stay in this humidity any longer, Agent Jayco will start to melt!" she said, motioning Agent Jayco towards the door.

Appreciating Elaine's observation that she was already starting to feel the dampening of her shirt on her skin under her wool suit, Agent Jayco followed her lead and replied, "That would be lovely, thank you. And please, call me Iris."

~~~~~~~~~~

A short time later, Iris, Andrew and Elaine were seated at the kitchen table, drinking coffee and catching up.

"Wait a second, do you seriously expect me to believe that you met while digging through a dumpster behind a hotel?" Iris exclaimed, incredulously.

Andrew and Elaine looked at one another and laughed fondly at the memory. "I'm afraid Andrew is telling the truth," Elaine replied. "I was standing in the middle of the dumpster, picking through the bags of garbage, looking for discarded fruit to feed my butterflies, when all of a sudden, I heard this strange voice. I looked up and saw him staring down at me."

Iris looked over at Andrew and asked, "What did you say to her?"

Andrew laughed and replied, "I told her it was a misdemeanor to remove trash from a dumpster and she could be changed with petty theft and thrown in jail."

Iris's eyes widened in surprise as she exclaimed, "You did not!"

Andrew laughed again and said, "I did. I was afraid she was going to take all the food waste that I wanted for compost to feed my roses! I had been using that dumpster for months for my fertilizer and all of a sudden, here was this girl in bright yellow wading boots, blue-jean overalls and a faded 'Save the Earth' baseball cap, picking through my garbage!"

"Your garbage," Elaine chuckled. "It was no more mine than yours. Besides, I got there first!"

Iris shook her head back and forth slowly, admiring the comfortable way the two of them interacted. "Then what happened?" she asked.

"Then," Andrew said, "She decided that we should work together and share what we found."

"We decided!" Elaine argued.

Andrew shook his head and said, "No, I'm pretty sure you decided but that was okay with me. Once I saw you standing in the middle of the dumpster, surrounded in garbage, I didn't care. You looked up at me with those big brown eyes with freckles splashed all over your cheeks and I was a goner."

"We were married a year later," Elaine said, proudly.

Iris smiled at them both and said, "That's a wonderful story. Do you have any children?"

Andrew and Iris exchanged a small smile and Andrew answered, "We tried for a few years but we were never able to conceive. We had all but given up hope of having a family until someone from our church, told us about a seven year old boy who had been abandoned by his mother. The Social Services office was trying to find a foster family until they could get the court to relinquish the mother's rights of custody. Elaine and I met with the boy and immediately fell in love with him. He was so pale, thin and scared. For months we had to keep the lights on at night because he was terrified of the dark. Once the court ruled there was no family member to care for him, we adopted him as our son."

"I'm happy for you both. It's amazing that what we think we want in life so badly often times ends up not being what we get, and can be better than we imagined," Iris said.

"What about you?" Andrew asked. "Did you ever marry?"

"Sadly, no, I didn't." Iris replied. "After we graduated, I worked with a couple organizations who where developing new technologies around cross-breeding certain grains to be more drought resistant for third-world countries. Those organizations were partnering with government organizations, which is primarily where the funding was coming from. That's where I first learned about forensic sciences and how seemingly well our genetic research blended that science and technology together with law enforcement.

"Before I knew it, I was a student at the academy, training to be an agent in forensic sciences. Several years later, I decided that academia was really where my heart was so I become an instructor and am now teaching at the academy."

Andrew laughed and said, "Wow, I never would have thought your path would have taken you to the FBI."

Iris laughed with him and replied, "Believe me, nor would I have!"

"So, what brings you here today?" Andrew asked, curiously. "Elaine said you were working on a case where you thought I could help answer some questions? Do FBI instructors work active cases?"

Iris shook her head and replied, "Generally, no. This is a special circumstance. And yes, I'm hoping you can help. But before I show you what I brought with me, please understand that its evidence and part of a working FBI investigation. Our conversation needs to remain strictly between us. Do you understand?"

"Oh, should I leave?" Elaine asked, anxiously.

Iris shook her head again and said, "No, that won't be necessary. You already know why I'm here and considering your background is in a similar area of genetic sciences that Andrew and I studied, perhaps your insight could be helpful. Do you both agree that this conversation stays within this room?"

Both Elaine and Andrew looked at one another for confirmation, nodded their heads in agreement and replied, "Yes," in unison.

"Thank you," replied Iris, appreciatively. She reached down for the satchel that she had with her and carefully removed four plastic containers marked with identification numbers.

"These flowers were found in four different crime scenes and the FBI feels certain that they were all left by the same person." Taking the first container, she opened the lid and gently removed one of the dried roses from inside. She laid the flower on the table in front of Andrew and waited.

Andrew looked down at the flower in front of him, curiously and then his eyes widened as he recognized what it was. "What is…..how did you……where did this come from!" he exclaimed, angrily, glaring at Iris.

Somewhat surprised by his reaction, Iris asked, "Do you recognize what that is?"

"Andrew, what's going on?" Elaine asked in confusion.

Andrew picked up the flower and held it in his hands like it was an injured bird. His eyes filled with questions, he looked up at Iris and quietly said, "I don't understand. What's going on?"

"Is it one of yours, Andrew? Is it one of 'The Presidents' you were once working on?" she asked.

"It's not the exact specimen I remember, however it's very similar, too similar. This particular flower has been completely re-engineered," Andrew replied, carefully examining the flower.

"What do you mean by re-engineered?" Iris asked, intently.

"Well, the stamens of my particular specimen this flower was originated from wouldn't mature properly. I had to discard the entire lot and start over."

When Iris didn't respond immediately, he said, "You know that the stamen is the pollen-producing reproductive organ of a flower. If the stamen cannot properly support the filament and the anther, then the flower cannot reproduce!"

"What do you mean by your comment that you discarded the entire lot?" Iris asked, patiently.

"I threw them away! They were of no use to me! I've spent my entire career focused on only one thing and that is to engineer the perfect breed of rose. You remember, don't you, Iris? All the hours we spent in the science lab, absolutely certain that one day we would create a species that would be applauded in both the botanical world as well as to be used for pharmaceutical purposes to help people! Do you remember?" he asked, pleadingly, nearly distraught.

Iris gently laid her hand on his arm and replied, "I remember, Andrew. I didn't come here to accuse you of anything, I promise. I knew at one time you were working on a cross genetic specimen of the President Lincoln and the Ingrid Bergman. That's why I'm here. I was hoping maybe you would recognize the flower and help me figure out where it came from and who is using them as a calling card to murder women."

"Murder?" Elaine whispered, quietly, looking at her husband. "Andrew?"

Andrew locked eyes with Iris and said, "I honestly don't know who that person could be. I spend all my time in my greenhouse, working. Elaine can attest to that! I stopped using this specimen of flower years ago. I threw them all in the trash myself!"

Iris's expression slowly morphed into a sarcastic smirk as she considered the possibility of a very ironic question. "Is it possible someone knew of your work and could have um....removed those flowers from your garbage for their own use?"

Andrew's face fell as he considered the possibility and looked at Elaine who saw what he was sure was his mirrored expression. "Well that would irony, wouldn't it?" he replied, dryly.

Suddenly, they were interrupted by the sound of the front door opening and closing and a male voice calling out down the hallway, "Mom, Dad?"

"Back here, in the kitchen, sweetheart," Elaine called out in reply. "That's our son, Mattox," she explained to Iris who had turned towards the open doorway.

The sound of approaching footsteps revealed the origin of the male voice, paused in the entry way, regarding Iris, curiously. "Hello," he said, politely.

"Good morning," she replied, tipping her head forward slightly while she attempted to discreetly cover the exposed flower with a napkin.

"Hello, my boy!" Andrew said, heartily, standing up and walking over to his son. He patted the young man on the shoulder and said, "This is an old friend of mine from college, Iris Jayco. Iris, this is my son, Mattox."

"Pleased to meet you, Iris," Mattox said, pleasantly, extending his hand in greeting.

"Nice to meet you as well, Mattox," Iris replied, shaking his hand.

"Come join us! Have a cup of coffee! Are you hungry?" Elaine asked, getting up from her chair, preparing to fix her son something to eat.

"No. Thanks, Mom. I don't have time today. I just came by to see if Dad had another batch of compost ready yet for me to take out to the other greenhouse," Mattox replied.

"Yes, I do. Thank you for saving me the trip! I had an idea that I wanted to try today with the next series of rose fusions so not having to drive out there would be wonderful. It's such a far drive for me and I really don't like going out there," Andrew replied.

"Yeah, I know. It's been months since you saw the place. No worries though. I'm taking good care of it. So, what's your idea?" Mattox asked, showing interest in his father's comment.

Andrew shook his head and said, "I don't want to say anything until I've had a chance to prove out some of my theory. But I'll let you know when I have something to share."

The look of disappointment on Mattox's face told Iris more than as if he had spoken his thoughts out loud. She got the impression that this conversation was exchanged frequently between father and son and that Andrew had no clue that his son felt him shutting him out of his work.

Mattox felt Iris's eyes on him and he turned to meet her gaze. They regarded each other silently for a moment until Mattox asked, "So, Iris, what brings you to Dover?"

"I had some business to take care of and decided to look up your father while I was here," she lied, casually.

Mattox's eyes glanced over to the napkin on the table and saw the dried stem of the flower sticking out from the edge. Before Iris could stop him, he reached out and removed the napkin, revealing the entire flower.

"What's that?" he asked, looking back to meet her frozen expression. He then looked over at his mother and father and noticed their nervous glances towards Iris.

Iris laughed, lightly, picked up the flower and quickly placed it in the container saying, "Oh it's just an experiment I'm working on that I wanted to discuss with your father. It's nothing really."

Mattox looked back at his father as Andrew's eyes shifted quickly from Iris's to his and he said, "Yeah, well good luck with that. Dad's pretty close to the belt when it comes to discussing what he's working on."

Seeing Andrew's eyes darken with disagreement, Iris quickly interjected before an argument could ensue, "Oh, I would never ask him to reveal anything he's currently working on. I know Andrew well enough to know that he doesn't share trade secrets. I was more interested in his professional opinion as a colleague."

Mattox shrugged his shoulders and replied, "Yeah, like I said good luck with that. Anyway, I better get going. I've got a lot to do. It was nice to meet you, Iris. Mom, Dad, I'll see you later."

"Are you sure I can't get you something before you go, honey?" Elaine asked, tenderly.

"No, thanks anyway," replied Mattox as he waved and headed for the doorway to the greenhouse.

After they were all sure he was gone and out of earshot, Andrew sat down heavily in his chair and looked at Iris, apologetically. "I'm sorry about that. Lately it seems as if there's nothing I can do to make him happy. He just seems so angry at me all the time."

"Have you ever tried to bring him into your world and share your work with him?" Iris asked, gently.

Andrew nodded his head and replied, "For years, he was like my shadow. I taught him everything I knew. He was like a sponge and couldn't learn fast enough. He's very smart and quite gifted when it comes to anything involving science or chemistry."

"What happened?" Iris asked, curiously.

"Puberty, I think," Andrew laughed as Elaine gently patted her husband on the shoulder. "When he was a boy, he used to get so excited about traveling around the country with me to all the flower shows. He would spend hours looking at all the flowers and talking to all the exhibitors about what kind of soils or fertilizer they used. You could almost see his brain taking it all in. As he's gotten older, he still comes with me to the shows, but we don't spend as much time together. He disappears for hours at a time. I guess it's no longer cool to hang out with his Dad."

Iris gave him a knowing smile and said, "Ah, I get it. You mean the fight for the role of alpha-male. I get a few of those in my classroom every year. I wish I could help you out but have to admit, I tend to bite my tongue and pray that the semester goes quickly when I have one of those students in my class."

"Well unfortunately, he was one of those students. Mattox has the intelligence and capability to have done well in school, however he lacks the social skills on how to effectively deal with people. I can't tell you the number of times we were called into school because of Mattox's fighting. Eventually, he was kicked out and Elaine helped him complete his GED by home-schooling him," said Andrew.

"He didn't go to college?" Iris probed.

"He wanted to go to Temple University, like his dad, but unfortunately his high school transcript sealed his fate," replied Elaine, sadly.

"I'm so sorry," Iris said, looking at them both.

"Thank you," replied Andrew. "Well, enough of all that. You didn't come here to talk about our family drama. Let's get back to what we were discussing earlier. What are you going to do now?"

Iris picked up the containers and returned them to her satchel, "Well, I guess first, I need to call my colleagues and let them know that we now know where the flowers originated. Next we need to find out where they went from your dumpster to where they are now. Do you have any enemies, Andrew? Is there anyone in your field who would know how re-engineer flowers who might have a bone to pick with you?"

"Not off-hand, no," Andrew replied, going through all the names in his head of people he knew. "But I'll let you if anyone comes to mind."

Iris picked up her satchel and rose from her chair. "I would appreciate that. Thank you both so much for taking the time to speak with me. I wish it were under different circumstances."

Andrew gave Iris a quick hug and replied, "As do I. I'll call you if I come up with anything."

"Thank you." Iris replied. She turned to Elaine and added, "It was so nice meeting you, Elaine. Thank you so much for your hospitality."

"It was very nice meeting you as well, Iris," Elaine replied. "I'll walk you out."

"Thank you. Bye, Andrew. We'll talk soon," Iris said, giving him a quick wave.

"Yes, goodbye," Andrew replied, returning the wave.

~~~~~~~~~~~

A few minutes later, Agent Jayco gave her final wave goodbye and began walking towards her car that she parked around the corner earlier that morning. She instinctively pulled her phone from her pocket, planning to call Agent Hunter with her news, until she remembered that the battery was dead. "Dang it," she mumbled as she slid the phone back in her pocket and turned the corner. "I guess it can wait until I get back to Quantico."

Suddenly, she saw a shape of a human shadow on the sidewalk standing directly in her path. She looked up, stopped abruptly, and caught her breath in surprise.

"You're not going anywhere, Iris," the shadow's owner growled as he covered her mouth with one hand before she could scream, while grabbing her arm with the other. "It's time for us to have a little chat."

Chapter 19

Tori pressed the end call button on her cell phone, growled in frustration and fell back against the pillows on her bed. "Grrrr....I feel so totally helpless."

"What did Agent Hunter say?" Ben asked, sitting on the bed beside her.

"Gatlinburg was a bust so he flew to Dover this afternoon and met with the other Dr. Andrew Porter and his wife Elaine. So at least we have confirmation that the Dr. Porter in Dover is the former college friend. He said Agent Jayco was there earlier this morning and that she said she was going to call her colleagues to let them know what she, Dr. Porter and his wife discussed," Tori replied.

"So if she never called Agent Hunter, something happened to Agent Jayco right after leaving his house," Piper speculated. "What about her car? Didn't she drive her car there?"

"Yes she did and so far they haven't found it." Tori said.

"Did Agent Hunter mention what the doctor and his wife discussed with Agent Jayco?" Ben asked.

"He said he couldn't go into any details over the phone and that he would let us know if he found anything," Tori replied. She looked at Ben with worried eyes and added, "Ben, what if something terrible has happened to her? What if something that I found out about those flowers ends up getting her killed?"

"Tor, you don't have any control over that," Ben consoled, pulling her into his arms. "Agent Jayco is a field trained agent. Until we have any concrete details on what's going on, we have to trust that she's okay."

"You know, Dover is less than two hours from here and we don't have any classes scheduled tomorrow," Piper chimed in, looking down at the screen on her laptop. "I'm looking at the driving directions and it wouldn't take us long to get there."

"And do what, exactly?" Tori asked, sitting up to look at Piper. "You heard Agent Hunter yesterday before he left. He gave us explicit instructions not to leave campus."

"No, he didn't," Piper said, emphatically. "I believe his exact words were, 'You three should stay here and attend your classes as normal,' which we did. Tomorrow is a no class day so technically, we're not disobeying his orders."

Ben looked at the expression on Tori's face and knew she was seriously debating Piper's point. He scowled, gave Piper a disapproving look and said, "You're walking a fine line there, Piper. We would be taking a big risk doing this. We could get expelled."

Tori looked at Ben and said, "You don't have to go if you don't want to. I understand how much being here means to you. I'm sorry but I can't just sit here, Ben. If it means the possibility of finding Agent Jayco, then it would be worth it to me to risk getting kicked out."

"Same here," said Piper. "We have to at least try."

Playing the devil's advocate, Ben reasoned, "We don't even know yet if she's really missing! Say we go and we find this Dr. Porter and talk to him. What exactly do we do then? We don't have any more information than Agent Hunter does at this point and he's been doing this job a heck of a lot longer than we have! Finding people is his life! He's got all the resources of the FBI behind him. Just humor me for a moment and ask yourself, 'what do I think I can do better that Agent Hunter isn't already doing?'"

Tori smiled tenderly at Ben, patted his cheek and said, "Ben, it's okay. Like I said, you don't have to go."

He stared into her determined sea-green eyes and knew the battle was already lost. "You know, this mental manipulation of yours is totally unfair," he grumbled.

Tori smiled and kissed him tenderly on the lips. "I love you too," she replied.

He sighed in defeat, turned to Piper and asked, "So, what time in the morning do we leave?"

~~~~~~~~~~~~

Later that night, after finalizing their plans for the following morning, Ben left the girls so they could all get a few hours sleep before they drove to Dover.

Tori climbed into bed and reached over to turn off the lamp on her night stand, when she noticed Piper was still working on her laptop. "Aren't you going to bed?" she asked Piper, curiously.

Piper looked up briefly at Tori and replied, "I will in a bit. I have a couple things I want to finish up here before shutting down."

"Okay. Goodnight, Piper," Tori yawned as she clicked off the light and snuggled down under her covers.

"Night, Tor," Piper replied, quietly.

Piper continued to quietly 'work' on her laptop which was really her mindlessly scrolling through news articles and web postings, biding her time like she did every night now until Tori went to sleep. Since that first night, when she witnessed Tori's reaction to her dream with Satan, it had become Piper's routine to stay up and watch Tori sleep.

Fifteen minutes later, Piper heard the slow deep breaths from the other side of the room and knew it was time. She powered off her laptop, crossed her legs on top of her covers, leaned back against the wall and began watching the colors change.

~~~~~~~~~~

Tori swung her legs casually back and forth and looked around her, waiting. She wasn't surprised this time when she found herself sitting on the bench under the massive tree. It was starting to become familiar to her, good or bad. As she was waiting, a piece of fruit from above dropped from its branch and gently landed on the ground at her feet. She smiled, sarcastically and called out, "Very funny."

Satan materialized instantly in front of her and laughed, amicably. "You know me so well, already. I find that humorous."

"You would," Tori replied, looking at him expectantly. "So what's on your mind, Luc?"

Satan scowled at her and growled, "Don't call me that."

"Isn't that your name?" Tori asked, innocently.

Satan stuck out his chin, defiantly and replied, "I have many names. I'm just not sure I like you using that one."

Tori looked at Satan, speculatively and replied, "Why? That's what Remy called you. Do you not like being called by your given name?"

Satan regarded her silently for a moment and then smiled, deviously. "I'll tell you what. I'll tell you what you want to know if you tell me what I want to know."

"What is it you want to know?" she asked, knowing where this conversation was leading.

"You didn't answer my question last time. We were talking about what it felt like when you were reliving the murder of that waitress in Chicago," he said, challengingly.

"She had a name, you know," Tori replied.

Satan rolled his eyes and sighed, dramatically. "Fine, Miss Ronin."

"That's better," Tori smiled, sweetly.

"Whatever. Why are you so afraid to tell me how you felt? Are you afraid you enjoyed it more than you should have?" he asked.

"Shouldn't there be a leather wingback chair and a couch for this kind of conversation?" Tori asked, sarcastically.

"If you feel that's necessary," he replied, calmly.

Suddenly, Tori found herself lying down on a dark brown leather couch, in a room that looked like an office, while Satan sat across from her, cross-legged, in a leather wing back chair, wearing a pair of wire-framed glasses, perched on the end of his nose. He had a notepad and a pen in his hands, poised in preparation for recording their conversation. "Now then, where were we?"

Tori sat up and scowled at him in frustration. "Nice magic trick. Is everything a joke to you? We're talking about someone's life here!"

"Why should I care about that?" he asked, glaring at her over the rims of his glasses. "She was just another face in a sea of millions."

Tori stared at Satan with her eyes widened in surprise. "Is that really all we are to you? Nameless faces, pawns for you to play with at your whim?"

"Pretty much," he quipped back. "The little flower boy is only one of many of those nameless faces I'm able to manipulate to act out my evil entertainment."

"That is the saddest thing I've ever heard anyone say," she replied.

"Stick around. I'm sure there are worse things you'll hear me say, eventually," he said.

Tori continued to stare at him, shaking her head slowly back and forth and said, "You're really serious, aren't you? You don't feel any guilt, remorse or responsibility for the people you hurt?"

"Nope, nope and nope!" he stated, emphatically.

"Then why do you do it? What do you get out of it?" she asked.

Satan smiled at Tori, placed the pen and notepad on the table beside him and sat back in the chair, comfortably. "Oh, where do I start? Is it the control and the power that drives me? Maybe it's the satisfaction that if I get to them before He does, that's one less victory for Him? Or perhaps it's the fear I see in their eyes when they realize who I am? Hmmm....I can't seem to decide which one I enjoy the most. I think I would have to say it's the fear."

"That's the most rewarding thing you get out of it, fear?" she asked.

"Of course!" he exclaimed. "It's the most powerful emotion there is."

Tori snorted a laugh and sat back on the couch, eyeing him distastefully.

"What?" he asked, confused by her expression.

"There's one emotion that's much more powerful than fear," she stated.

Satan rolled his eyes and groaned, "Oh here we go. This is where you give me the Bambi eyes and harp on how love is the most powerful emotion there is. Am I right?"

Tori raised her eyebrows, suggestively and shrugged her shoulders in acknowledgement.

"Blech," Satan spat, dismissing her. "Love is a wasted emotion by fools who believe in happiness and fulfillment in giving to others and blah, blah, blah..."

"Would you like to switch places?" she asked motioning to the couch where she sat.

"What so we can 'hug it out'?" he asked, using air quotes with his hands. "No thank you. I'll pass."

"Do you even know what a hug is?" Tori asked, sarcastically.

"Of course I know what a hug is," he replied. "I've seen people do it, although I have no idea why they seem to find it so comforting. It looks disgustingly uncomfortable and I imagine it would feel like a boa constrictor squeezing the life out of me."

"Seriously, we can switch places if you want to," Tori said starting to get up from the couch.

"Just sit down, that's not funny" Satan snarled.

"Fine, suit yourself," Tori shrugged. "Haven't you ever been hugged before?"

Satan stared at Tori with an astonished look on his face and answered, "Uh, hello? I'm Satan. Why would anyone ever have given me a hug before?"

"I don't know. Not even before you fell, when you were still an angel?" she asked, curiously.

Satan laughed and replied, "Regardless of what fairy tales you might have heard growing up, angels up in heaven do not float around on fluffy white clouds, playing harps and hugging one another."

"So what do angels up in heaven do?" she asked, innocently.

"I don't know! Why don't you go ask Remy? I'm sure he's thrilled to have someone to talk to now that you've officially met. Why don't you go hug him?" Satan exclaimed in frustration.

"I already did. It was nice," Tori replied.

Satan stared at Tori for a moment, surprised. "You hugged him? Why?"

Tori shrugged her shoulders and replied, "I don't know. The moment seemed appropriate so I just did it. It was nice."

"Blech," Satan spat again in disgust.

Tori looked at Satan thoughtfully and said, "I find it very interesting that you used the analogy of a snake to describe a hug considering the symbolism of you being named as the serpent in the book of Genesis. Don't you find that curious?"

Annoyed, Satan looked upon Tori's curious face, as the realization set in that she no longer feared him. *'If she no longer fears you, you no longer have control,'* he thought, angrily. *'And, she still hasn't answered your question!'* he thought more angrily to himself. "This conversation has begun to bore me," he said in a matter-of-fact tone. "We're done here. It's time for you to go."

Immediately, Tori felt herself wake as her eyes opened and she focused on the ceiling of her dorm room above her.

She turned her head to look over at Piper's side of the room and saw her roommate sitting in a reclined position, leaning back against the wall with her eyes closed. Not wanting to wake her, Tori quietly rolled over on her side facing the wall and went back to sleep.

As soon as she thought the coast was clear, Piper peeked over at Tori through her partially closed eyelids, and stealthily slid under her covers. Breathing a sigh of relief for not getting caught, she lay there quietly and smiled secretly, knowing that tonight, her friend's aura had not mixed with the darkness. *'She's beginning to figure it out,'* Piper thought, happily. *'She's learning how to face him without fear.'*

Taking one last look over at Tori, Piper snuggled down deeper under her covers, closed her eyes and quickly fell asleep.

Chapter 20

Early the next morning, Piper, Tori and Ben were heading North on the Blue Star Memorial highway towards Dover. Piper had offered to drive so the three companions sat crowded together along the bench seat of her vintage pickup truck.

While Piper sang along to 'Save a Horse Ride a Cowboy,' by Big & Rich, Tori searched the map view of Dr. Porter's neighborhood, to familiarize herself with the area.

Ben was sitting in far right passenger seat, eyeing the long, slender camouflaged case nestled in the gun rack behind their heads.

"Is there a rifle in that case?" he finally asked as casually as he could.

"Yep, that's my pride and joy," Piper replied, smiling. "It's a Remington 700 sniper rifle. My grandfather had it custom made for me. It was a gift for my twenty-first birthday."

Ben whistled lowly and replied, "Man, Logan would have a cow if he knew you had one of those. He's been talking about getting one since our first day of firearms training. What's the range?"

"About a thousand yards, give or take a few depending on the weather conditions," Piper replied.

"So how come you didn't join the sniper class?" he asked with a puzzled look.

Piper laughed and said, "Because I already know how to fire a rifle. It's my hand-gun experience that I need to work on."

"Bull, don't believe her," Tori interrupted looking at Ben with her eyebrows raised. "I've been standing next to her every day in class for weeks and she hasn't missed one target point yet. The girl doesn't need to work on anything that requires bullets."

"A girl has to be prepared for anything," Piper said, shrugging her shoulders.

"Is it legal to have that in plain sight?" Ben asked.

"I have a permit for it, don't worry," Piper advised. "Besides, I double-checked the state laws before we left this morning. Virginia is a shall-issue jurisdiction state, which means they shall issue a permit as long as certain criteria are met, which I have. Delaware is a may-issue jurisdiction state, which means they allow for a permit to carry a concealed weapon at the discretion of the local authorities."

"What does that mean?" Tori asked, curiously.

"That means if I ever decide to fire my rifle in the state of Delaware, I better be able to back up my reason with enough proof to prevent me from being arrested," Piper replied.

"There's your next exit up ahead," Tori interrupted. "Turn right onto Main and then about four miles down, you'll make a left on Halltown Road."

"Got it," Piper replied, checking her mirrors and signaling her move into the far right lane. She glanced over at Ben while she crossed over into the right lane and casually asked, "So, speaking of Logan. You guys have been hanging out a lot lately, haven't you?"

Ben nodded and replied, "Yeah, we have. He's a good guy."

"Is he seeing anyone?" Piper asked, looking straight ahead of her.

Ben looked over at Piper who kept her eyes fixed on the road. He then looked at Tori with a helpless expression.

Tori snorted a laugh and looked back down at her laptop, pretending not to be aware of the conversation. "Uh, not that I'm aware of," he replied, nervously.

"Oh my gosh! Relax, Ben. I'm not giving you the third degree about Logan's love life, I was just curious!" Piper laughed, watching Ben squirm.

Ben laughed uncomfortably and replied, "Okay good, because I really don't know anything about his personal life."

"Yeah, I know how you men generally communicate. No worries, it's no biggie. We're cool," Piper replied, wishing she hadn't said anything.

Wishing the same thing, Ben turned to look out the window as they entered the city limits. "Cool," he muttered.

~~~~~~~~~~

A half hour later, they were parked across the street from a row of brownstones, staring at one front door in particular.

"That's it right there," Tori replied pointing to the door flanked with large planters, overflowing with flowers.

"So what now, do we just walk up to the front door and ring the doorbell?" Piper asked, pulling out a pair of binoculars from a case under her seat.

"I guess," Tori replied, motioning to Ben to open the door.

"And say what, exactly?" Ben asked, turning to face Tori.

"If Agent Jayco really is missing, we don't know for sure that this Doctor Porter or his wife didn't have anything to do with it. Don't you think we should call Agent Hunter and ask him what he's found out before we go up there?"

Tori scrunched up her nose and turned back to the front door as she considered what Ben said. "I guess we don't want to tip them off to anything, if there's a chance they're involved."

"Well then, what do we do?" Piper asked again, focusing the binoculars in on the front door.

"I'm going to call Agent Hunter," Ben stated as he pulled his phone from his pocket, preparing to dial the number.

"Wait!" Tori exclaimed as the front door to the house opened. "Someone is leaving."

"That guy doesn't look old enough to be the good doctor," Piper advised. "Here, take a look," she added, handing the binoculars to Tori.

Tori took the binoculars from Piper and held them up to her eyes. As soon as she had the man in focus, she gasped in surprise. "Oh that can't be! That's him!"

"What?" Piper asked, doubtfully. "He's not old enough to be him."

Tori quickly lowered the binoculars and averted her gaze away from the building, "No, not Doctor Porter, it's him. The man from the visions! He's the man who murdered those women!"

"Are you sure, Tor?" Ben asked, trying to look at the man's face without being noticed.

"I'm positive!" Tori replied, confidently. "Look, he's getting into that van. What if he's the one who took Agent Jayco? We need to follow him!"

"If he is the killer, what if Agent Jayco's visit to the doctor and his wife yesterday tipped him off and we just saw him leaving another crime scene? What if he just killed them? Should we go check?" Piper asked, anxiously.

"We don't have time, what if we lose him?" Tori asked, watching the van begin to pull away.

"Okay, fine. I'm on it," Piper replied as she turned the key in the ignition while checking for oncoming traffic.

"Wait! We still don't even know Agent Jayco is missing, much less whether or not anything criminal has happened to the doctor or his wife!" Ben exclaimed, urgently.

"We don't have time to wait! Piper, go!" Tori demanded re-fastening her seatbelt.

"I'm going, I'm going," Piper muttered as she began weaving in and out of the lanes of cars, trying to keep the van in sight, yet not get close enough for him to see them. "Traffic is picking up ahead so you two keep your eyes on that van. If we get separated by a traffic light, we could lose him."

While Piper drove, Ben dialed Agent Hunter's cell phone which immediately went to voice-mail. "Hello, Agent Hunter, this is Ben Vincent. We're in Dover and we just saw the man Tori saw in the visions, leave Doctor Porter's house. We're following him now. Please call me back as soon as possible." He clicked off his phone and looked at Tori anxiously. "We're on our own for the time being."

Tori gave Ben a small smile and grabbed his hand reassuringly, "That's okay. We can do this, Ben."

He squeezed her hand back and smiled at her, "Okay," he replied. "I believe you."

"Shoot!" Piper exclaimed, hitting the steering wheel in frustration as she was forced to stop at a red light. "We got separated. Do you still see him?"

Tori nodded and replied, "Yep. I can still see him. You watch traffic. I'll let you know if I see him turn off anywhere."

"I see him too," Ben replied, keeping his eyes on the vehicle ahead of them.

Several street lights later, Piper pulled off the street into a parking lot. "We lost him," she complained, loudly.

Tori looked around them and noticed all the commercial buildings and warehouses up and down the street. "Well, why don't we drive around the block a few times and see if he parked anywhere? Look around us. Maybe he parked somewhere nearby and went into one of these buildings."

Piper looked around as Tori suggested and admitted, "I guess that's as good an idea as any." She re-engaged the truck into drive and pulled out of the parking lot, driving slowly as the three of them began looking down all the alleys and into any openings large enough for a van to fit.

Five blocks into their search, Tori spotted the van. "Look! There it is!" she shouted.

"Are you sure?" Piper asked, doubtfully.

"Positive! I memorized the license plate earlier, 45920. That's it! Pull over!" Tori demanded.

"Okay, okay. Hang on. Don't get your knickers in a twist," Piper scolded as she slowly pulled around the corner and parked her truck along the curb. "Now what?" she asked.

"Now we split up and start searching the buildings in this block to find out which one he went into," Tori advised.

"Uh, uh," Ben objected. "I'm not letting the two of you go off on your own."

"Seriously," Piper snarled. "You're going to play the macho card now?"

"Quiet! Both of you," Tori snapped. "We may not have much time so splitting up is the most logical thing to do."

She pulled her phone from her pocket and initiated a group chat message between the three of them. "Here, I've started a message window so we can keep each other updated as we search. When one of us finds him or Agent Jayco, text the building number but don't do anything until the rest of us get there. Agreed?"

"Agreed," Piper quickly replied.

Ben paused for a moment but realized Tori's plan was a good one, "Agreed," he relented.

"Good. Let's go!" Tori ordered as she removed her seatbelt and pushed Ben towards the door.

<center>~~~~~~~~~</center>

Agent Jayco turned her head towards the direction of the hallway as she heard the sound of footsteps approaching.

She shifted in her chair, and had to keep herself from crying out in pain as the muscles in her arms and shoulders objected to the unfamiliar position of being pulled back behind her back for such an extended period of time. She could feel the wet stickiness of blood on her wrists, now rubbed raw from her repeated attempts to free herself from the bindings holding her there.

"Well, good morning, Iris!" the man greeted her, mockingly. "Or do you prefer FBI Special Agent Jayco?" he added with a sneer as he walked up and tugged the gag out of her mouth.

Agent Jayco looked down and saw that he had her satchel and her badge in his hands. Saying nothing, she looked up and met his eyes, coldly.

"Still not talking, huh?" he asked, mirroring her expression. "That's fine, your choice."

He turned around and walked over to a desk in the corner of the room and calmly pulled the containers and related manila envelopes out of the bag. He laid them out one by one, in order by case number, and then turned to face her, calmly. "I have to admit," he said. "I was a bit surprised at what I found in your bag. The badge was a shocker as I'm sure you can imagine considering what I found in each of these envelopes afterwards."

Agent Jayco continued to stare at him, unmoving, trying to keep her breathing as calm as possible.

"Of course at first, I was furious. I couldn't possibly figure out how you could have such detailed information from each crime scene, down to the tiniest detail like whether or not I brought the flower with me, or had given it to one of the women beforehand. That's a very clever trick," he chuckled, picking up one of the containers and slipping the dried flower out into his hand.

He stared at the faded petals, trying to recapture the feeling he experienced with this particular stem, but the memory would not return to him. He sighed, regrettably and met her eyes once again.

Walking towards her slowly, he held the flower up for her to see and asked, "Do you really expect me to believe that this flower actually recorded the events of a murder? That this dried up, discarded, lifeless piece of compost can show you everything that happened?"

When once again, she refused to answer him, he angrily crushed the flower in his hand and threw it on the ground at her feet. "Answer me!" he shouted, furiously as he drew back his hand and hit her across the mouth.

Fighting back the stinging tears that sprang to her eyes from the pain, she continued to meet his deathly stare, feeling the slow trickle of blood begin to drip down her already swelling lip.

Debating whether he should just kill her now or continue to try and find out what else the FBI knew about him, he paused as he heard the creaking sound of a door opening from the other end of the building.

Unable to recall whether or not he locked the door behind him when he came in, he decided it was better to go check it out to make sure.

He roughly tugged the gag back up into Agent Jayco's mouth and threateningly whispered, "Not a sound out of you, do you hear me?"

When she still refused to acknowledge him, he snorted in disgust and quietly set off back down the hallway to investigate the source of the noise.

Chapter 21

Tori winced as the creak of the door echoed down the hallway in front of her. *'So much for the stealth approach,'* she thought to herself in irritation as she began to creep ahead slowly.

About halfway down the corridor, she heard a scraping sound ahead of her so she quickly darted into the doorway of a room off to her left.

She crouched down behind the door and waited there several minutes until she saw a shadow pass her in the hallway. A few seconds later, she heard the creaking again and the sound of someone turning the deadbolt. *'Great, now I'm locked in,'* she thought as she strained her ears, listening for the shadows owner to walk back past her door.

She waited until she thought the coast was clear and was about half-way out of her crouching position to peek around the edge of the door when suddenly it slammed into her forehead, knocking her down. As she hit the floor, she dropped her cell phone and watched as it slid underneath a rack against the wall.

"Hey!" she objected loudly, scrambling to get up off the floor.

As she stood, she felt the room sway beneath her feet and instantly felt the start of a headache beginning to form behind her eyes. As she tried to focus her eyes on the form standing over, she began to say, "What the heck..."

"What do you think you're doing? This is private property!" a male voice interrupted, angrily.

Tori looked up at the man standing over her and the first thing she saw was the dragon tattoo on the inside of his wrist. Continuing her gaze upwards to meet his eyes, the immediate recognition stopped her cold. *'Well this is great,'* she thought to herself. *'What are the odds that I picked the one building he was in? You better think quickly, Tor.'*

She rubbed her forehead a few times, stalling for time and replied, "There was this guy outside on the sidewalk following me. I got scared so I ducked into this building and was waiting for him to go away. The next thing I know, someone's slamming a door into my head. Why did you do that?"

The man sneered at her and replied, "Ever hear of being in the wrong place at the wrong time, sweetheart?"

Tori nodded her head and whispered, "Yes."

He grabbed her by the arm and began dragging her with him and replied, "Well today, isn't your lucky day. Come on, you're coming with me."

"Ouch, you're hurting me!" She objected loudly, trying to fight him.

Suddenly, as his hand made contact with her arm, visions began flooding into her mind, adding to the pounding headache she already had. She felt a wave of nausea wash over her, as images came to her of the man as a small boy alone and scared in an abandoned building. Then the memory of a man and a woman emerged, and Tori saw them bringing the boy into their home. There was love in that memory, Tori could feel it. It was a comforting feeling of love, safety and security.

Next, she saw the man showing a boy the process of splicing rose stems into cuttings in a greenhouse nursery. That too was a memory of love and nurturing.

Tori became so wrapped up in the visions and feelings of the man's memories that she didn't realize where he was taking her. Suddenly, the images stopped as he angrily pushed her into the doorway of a room and let go of her arm.

Immediately, her eyes were drawn to a woman tied to a chair in the center of the room. Tori tried not to let on that she recognized her and instead, she gasped and cried out, "What's going on? What have you done to that woman?"

Agent Jayco looked up, wearily and reacted in surprise as her eyes met Tori's. Tori minutely shook her head, 'no,' so Agent Jayco quickly averted her eyes to the man who was watching them both carefully.

He laughed, looking back and forth between the women and said, "Well neither one of you is going to get the best actress award this year. I hope you didn't have your hearts set on getting that."

He turned to Tori and glared at her angrily. "Now," he spat, bitterly. "Stop lying to me about some guy on the street and tell me the truth. What are you doing here?"

Tori looked at Agent Jayco apologetically and quietly replied, "I came here looking for her, Mattox."

Mattox's eyes narrowed angrily as he replied, "How do you know my name? Who are you? Are you another FBI agent?"

Tori shook her head and replied, "No, not exactly."

"What's that supposed to mean, not exactly?" he challenged.

"I'm uh...one of her students," Tori replied.

Mattox stared at her dumbfounded for a moment and then began laughing, hysterically. "Are you joking? Because that's the funniest thing I've heard all day!"

Tori shook her head again and shrugged her shoulders, "I'm not joking. Agent Jayco is one of my professors at the academy."

Mattox laughed again and said, "Oh, this is rich. You obviously should have paid more attention during your tactical defense training class because you just got an 'F' for a failed rescue attempt!"

He laughed again and turned back to Agent Jayco. He tugged the gag out of her mouth, ignoring her cries as the fabric pulled away the scab that was beginning to form on her lip, causing it to begin bleeding again. "Do you have any words of wisdom you wish to impart upon your prodigal student here, professor? I think now would be the perfect time for you to break your vow of silence, don't you?"

Agent Jayco licked her lip tenderly and glared at Mattox.

"Still not talking, huh?" he snapped. "Fine, you will eventually. One thing I've learned about women is once you get them talking, they never shut up."

Mattox spun around and strode off to the corner of the room and angrily grabbed the remaining chair by his desk. He brought the chair over to where Tori stood and demanded, "Sit!"

"Why? What are you going to do?" Tori asked, standing her ground, firmly.

"Oh don't get all high and mighty on me now, teacher's pet. Sit down or I'll sit you down myself," he spat, standing over her with his fists clenched.

Obediently, Tori sat in the chair and watched Mattox carefully as he pulled a length of twine from his pocket. He grabbed both of her hands, tugged them behind her back and began tying her up. As he did, Tori repositioned her hands so her thumbs and first knuckle were pressed up against one another and pressed her knuckles apart.

Oblivious to what she was doing, Mattox completed his knot and stepped around the chair, to stand in front of her.

"Comfy?" he asked, smiling sarcastically.

Tori gently relaxed her knuckles and felt the slack in the twine gently slip down her wrists. *'Didn't pay attention to tactical defense training, my butt,'* she thought. "It's perfect," she smiled back, sweetly.

Mattox stood there for a moment, uncertain as what he should do next. He looked at both women, thinking back to everything that had happened in the past several minutes and turned back to Tori. "So how do you know who I am? Where do you fit into this picture? I already know how she's involved," he asked.

Tori debated how much of her hand she should show and decided she might as well go all in. "I didn't know who you were until a few minutes ago, actually," she replied.

"What?" he asked, not following her.

"I didn't know until you grabbed my arm earlier. When you touched me, I saw things about you. Memories and feelings you felt as a young boy," Tori replied.

Agent Jayco looked at Tori curiously, wondering if Tori realized what she was saying.

Mattox scowled at Tori and said, "Bull. Try again."

"I'm serious," Tori exclaimed, "They were memories of you scared, hungry and alone in the apartment you shared with your mother. The apartment where one day she said she was going out for groceries and she never came back.

"The memories of the day you met Dr. Porter and his wife when they took you into their home. They showed you what it meant to feel loved and to feel safe and part of a family. What happened, Mattox? What changed that and turned you into this?"

Mattox stared at her in amazement and replied, "That's not possible. Someone doesn't just touch someone else and they see stuff like that. You're lying!"

"No, she's not," Agent Jayco whispered, hoarsely. "She's telling you the truth."

Both Mattox and Tori looked at Agent Jayco in surprise as she gently cleared her throat and found her voice.

"How is that possible?" Mattox asked, looking back at Tori, curiously.

Tori looked into Mattox's uncertain eyes and the realization came over her that this wasn't the man that she had seen in her visions. Not the complete man, anyway. For just a brief moment, she saw the boy again, scared and confused, not knowing what was going on around him. She wondered if there was any part of that boy left and whether or not he could be reached.

"Sometimes objects or people speak to me in ways that others cannot hear," she said, testing the waters.

"Speak to you, how?" he asked. "Objects like what?"

"Like flowers, for example," she replied, looking at the crushed stem on the floor by Agent Jayco's chair.

Mattox looked down at the flower too and then back up at Tori, "What are you talking about? How can flowers talk to someone?"

"I don't know how to explain it to you, Mattox. But those flowers that Agent Jayco brought with her, told me all about you and what you did to those women," Tori replied.

Mattox narrowed his eyes at her and said, "I don't believe you. You're trying to trick me."

"You read all those notes, didn't you, Mattox? The ones I had in my bag? The notes that clearly detailed who those women were, where you met them, what you did to them? How could anyone know all of that about you?" Agent Jayco quietly asked.

Mattox stared through her with unfocused eyes as he tried to reason in his head what he was hearing.

"Why did you start killing those women, Mattox?" Tori asked.

"I don't know," he whispered, quietly. "I was happy once, after Dr. Porter and Elaine took me in. I know they loved

267

me. They gave me anything I wanted. But no matter what I thought I wanted, it was never enough. There was this hole inside of me that I couldn't fill." Mattox stopped and became quiet as he stared back down at the crushed flower on the floor.

"What happened, Mattox?" Tori probed, gently.

"Everything was fine until one day, I saw her. We were walking in a crowd of people, laughing about something funny Dad said and then all of a sudden, there she was, like she didn't have a care in the world, laughing with some guy, walking down the street. We stopped at the same light, waiting for the cross walk to change and she looked right at me. She looked at me and didn't even recognize me," he replied, lost in the memory.

"How old were you, Mattox?" Tori asked.

"I was fifteen," he murmured.

"How old was the woman?" Tori asked.

Mattox looked at Tori in confusion and asked, "What?"

Trying again, Tori asked, "The woman on the street. The one you said was your mother. How old did she look?"

Mattox scowled at Tori, still confused and said, "I don't know, maybe early to mid-twenties. What does that matter? It was her!"

"No it wasn't," Tori replied, firmly. "Even if your mother had you when she was eighteen years old, if you were fifteen when you saw that women, your mother would have been in her early to mid-thirties."

"So!" he challenged.

"So how old are you now, Mattox?" Tori asked.

"Twenty-five," he said.

"Which means if your mother is still alive today, she would be about forty-five years old, right?" Tori asked.

"What are you saying?" he asked, uncertainly.

"I'm saying none of those women you killed were your mother, Mattox," advised Tori.

"Yes they were!" he argued. "They all were all her! Somehow, each time I kill her, she comes back!" Mattox began pacing the room, clenching and unclenching his fists as he walked. Tori could see beads of sweat forming on his forehead.

"Careful, Miss Cooper," Agent Jayco warned, quietly.

"I know what I'm doing," Tori whispered back.

Suddenly, Mattox stopped directly in front of Tori and shouted, "SHE LEFT ME! Why does she keep coming back? If she didn't want me, why didn't she just stay gone? WHAT DOES SHE WANT FROM ME?"

"I don't know, Mattox. I wish I did," Tori replied. She looked over Mattox's shoulder at the row of windows along the back wall, and noticed the frame of a large greenhouse directly behind the building.

"What about the flowers, Mattox? Is that where you grow them? Where did they come from?" she asked.

Mattox ran his hands through his hair, carelessly and replied, "Originally, I created them with my father. We worked on them together for years. They were going to be our mark on the world! Something we did together that no one else had seen before.

"Then one day, he found a flaw, something that no longer made them special to him. He couldn't have imperfection in his greenhouse so he threw them away! All that work, all those years caring for them, nurturing them, and he threw them away like they were garbage."

"Did you ask Dr. Porter why?" Tori asked.

"Of course I asked him," Mattox replied, angrily. "I told them we could still care for them create another type of flower and he said no, they had to be perfect. He didn't want anything that wasn't perfect. He couldn't understand what he had done wrong. He needed someone to blame. I could see it in his eyes. He blamed me!

"Then be began seeing me the same way, flawed and imperfect. He really didn't see me as his son. I was an experiment to him too, an experiment where something had gone wrong. Good thing I wasn't his real flesh and blood son, I was somebody else's garbage that they had thrown away. He became too busy for me after that. He

270

no longer confided in me and would disappear into his greenhouse for days, pretending that the rest of the world didn't exist."

"It was you, who took the flowers from the dumpster and re-engineered them. Wasn't it?" asked Agent Jayco.

"Yes," Mattox admitted. "I rescued them from the garbage. Then I brought them here. I fixed them! I took away their flaws and made them beautiful. I made them perfect."

"They are perfect, Mattox. I saw that with my own eyes. What you did was brilliant! Your father would be proud of you if you shared this with him," praised Agent Jayco.

"Shared this with him? Why should I be the one to share this with him?" Mattox replied angrily, his voice rising to a shout. "WHY SHOULD I SHARE ANYTHING WITH HIM? THIS WAS MY ACCOMMPLISHMENT! HE MADE IT PERFECTLY CLEAR THAT HE NO LONGER WANTED ANYTHING TO DO WITH ME! HE'S NO BETTER THAN HER! HE THREW ME AWAY LIKE I WAS GARBAGE, JUST LIKE SHE DID!"

"I know what your father is like, Mattox. I worked with him for several years. I know how important it is that things in his life are perfect and flawless. But you have to understand that he doesn't realize what he's doing," Agent Jayco reasoned.

"Don't apologize for him," Mattox, replied, glaring at her in warning. "He knew perfectly well what he was doing, and he did it anyway. I liked you better when you weren't talking. In fact, both of you shut up. I'm tired of talking."

Mattox began to turn away, but then paused as he heard a sound coming down the hallway. He listened for a moment longer and then turned back to Tori. "What is that sound?"

Recognizing the sound of the ringtone on her phone, Tori winced and replied, "That's my phone. I dropped it earlier when you hit me with the door."

"That's just great!" Mattox exclaimed, angrily. "Let me guess your phone has a chip that can track your location, right? So, what? Now I have to worry about the rest of your class showing up? I hope you backed up all your pictures and contacts, sweetheart, because your phone is history."

While Mattox angrily stomped off down the hallway to find Tori's phone, she raised her eyebrows at the ironic humor of the situation. Mattox was partially right about the locator chip, except that it was actually an implant in Tori's arm and not one located in her phone. *'That little college experiment sure has turned into a pretty valuable device. I hope the range clears these cement walls so Ben can find me,'* she thought to herself.

As soon as Tori felt Mattox was far enough away, she pulled her wrists free of the knot she had been working on while they were talking and rushed over to begin untying Agent Jayco from her chair.

"How did you get yourself untied so quickly? Ouch!"
Agent Jayco gasped as Tori began pulling at the twine
around her wrists.

"I'm so sorry," Tori whispered, shocked at the raw,
bloodied flesh that at one time was the porcelain delicate
skin of Agent Jayco's wrists. "I'll show you later. Right
now, I need something sharp to cut this twine."

She looked around the room, which was very sparsely
supplied and offered no viable option for her. She looked
at the door that led to the greenhouse and whispered,
"I'm going to go check the greenhouse. He has to have
something in there I can use."

"Be careful!" Agent Jayco whispered back. "He could
come back any minute."

"I will. I'll be right back," Tori replied, quietly.

She quickly ran over to the door and thankfully found it
opened easily and quietly. As she stepped into the
greenhouse, she stopped short, taken aback by the literal
sea of red around her.

Every direction she looked, she saw row upon row of rose
bushes, covered in deep, dark, velvety red flowers. It was
like looking into a glass of cabernet sauvignon, when held
up to the light.

Surprisingly, even thought the room was quite literally
filled with blooming flowers, the scent was deeply
aromatic, but not overpowering.

She spotted a small cutting table a few feet away and almost wept when she saw a pair of cutting shears.

"Thank you, God!" she murmured, quietly as she rushed over and grabbed them.

She quickly returned to Agent Jayco's side and had just cut the bindings on both her hands and her ankles when she heard Mattox's voice behind her.

"What do you think you're doing?" he exclaimed, holding the crushed remnants of Tori's phone. He threw the pieces down on the floor, strode over to the two women and grabbed Tori, angrily.

He noticed the shears in her hand and looked over to the open doorway of the greenhouse. Grabbing the shears from her, he shouted in her face, "HOW DARE YOU GO INTO MY GREENHOUSE! NOBODY BUT ME GOES IN THERE! DO YOU UNDERSTAND?"

Trembling, Tori replied in a quivering voice, "You have to stop, Mattox. I understand what you're feeling. I know you don't want to keep killing women. I know you're just trying to make your mother go away. Let me help you."

"DO I LOOK LIKE I NEED HELP? YOU HAVE NO IDEA WHAT I'M FEELING SO STOP TELLING ME THAT YOU DO!" he shouted.

"I do know how you feel. I can still feel it right now. I can feel how much you want it to stop," Tori replied.

Mattox quickly let go of Tori's arm and sneered at her. "The only thing I want to stop right now is to stop you from talking. And I can fix that pretty easily."

Forgetting that he still had the shears in his hand, Tori saw his arm begin to swing around toward her. For one brief moment, she saw the blow coming and raised her hands, defensively. As she did, she heard the guttural sound of Mattox grunting as he fell to his knees.

Tori looked up and saw Agent Jayco standing in front of her, holding her chair like a baseball bat. The moment of victory, however, was short-lived as Mattox quickly scrambled up off the floor and faced the two women.

"DID YOU REALLY THINK I WOULD GO DOWN THAT EASILY, PROFESSOR? DO EITHER OF YOU ACTUALLY BELIEVE YOU CAN STOP ME?" he shouted, furiously, holding the shears up like a sword.

"Maybe they can't. But I can," Piper announced from an opened hatch on the roof of the building above.

She quickly fired off a round from her rifle and immediately, Mattox fell to the floor, screaming in pain as a dark red stain began to form on the back of his left thigh.

Piper quickly tapped the earpiece she was wearing and said, "All clear, sir."

Tori looked up at the opening in the roof, her mouth gaping open in shock. Piper smiled down at her, waved and cheerfully exclaimed, "Hey, roomie!"

Tori waved back in a dazed manner and replied, "Hey, Piper."

Seconds later, a small explosion sounded down the hallway, followed by the sound of shouting voices and running footsteps coming towards them.

Agent Hunter was the first through the doorway using his gun as a pointer, followed by two uniformed officers. Once he saw Mattox's condition on the floor, he quickly shouted, "Clear."

Immediately, two teams of paramedics entered the room, each carrying a stretcher, follow by a very anxious looking Ben.

While one team rushed to Mattox's side to control the bleeding before taking him into custody, the other team began assisting Agent Jayco.

Ben pushed his way through to Tori and pulled her into his arms. "Are you okay?" he asked.

"I'm fine!" Tori exclaimed in relief, hugging him back.

Agent Hunter looked up at the open hatch and saw Piper sitting on the edge, smiling and swinging her feet. "Hello, sir," she called out cheerfully, waving to him.

Agent Hunter chuckled in relief, pleased that their plan had worked and waved back, "Nice job, Ms. Stirling!"

"Thank you, sir," she replied, enjoying the view below.

Tori turned to Agent Hunter and asked, "How did you find us?"

Agent Hunter smiled slyly, pointing to her arm. "That's the second time that chip in your arm has saved your life, Miss Cooper," he replied. "I'm beginning to think that little piece of technology is more useful than I originally thought. I might get one myself."

"I was worried that the close proximity of the buildings and the thick cement walls wouldn't be able to pin-point our exact location," Tori said.

"Well, you can thank Miss Stirling for that," Agent Hunter replied, looking up at Piper.

"It was the maniacal laughter coming out of this open hatch that did it. That and the shouting," Piper advised, casually. "That guy's got some serious anger issues. May I come down now?"

Agent Hunter nodded and replied, "Yes, you can come down now."

As Piper disappeared from view, Agent Hunter walked over to where the paramedics were treating Agent Jayco and gently asked, "Are you okay?"

Agent Jayco nodded her head and replied, "I'll be fine, Gabriel. Thank goodness Miss Cooper showed up when she did," she added, turning to smile at Tori, appreciatively. "She was brilliant. She has quite a gift for negotiating."

Agent Hunter raised his eyebrows in surprise and turned to Tori. "Is that so?" he asked.

"Speaking of gifts," Agent Jayco said, holding out her hand towards Tori. "Miss Cooper, would you mind trying what you did earlier with me?"

"What did she do earlier?" Agent Hunter asked, curiously.

"I would like her to show me," Agent Jayco replied as her eyes met Tori's.

Tori walked over to Agent Jayco and crouched down beside her. She gently took Agent Jayco's hand in hers, paused for a moment, looked into Agent Jayco's eyes and smiled. "I promise, I won't," she said, quietly.

"You won't, what?" Ben asked in confusion.

Tori smiled at Ben and replied, "I'll tell you later."

Agent Hunter looked back and forth between Tori and Agent Jayco and said, "What just happened? Did she read your mind?"

Agent Jayco shook her head and said, "No. She read my memories. I shared a memory with her and she saw it. Or perhaps felt it." Agent Jayco looked at Tori curiously, and asked, "Which one was it?"

Tori shrugged her shoulders and replied, "I'm not really sure. I think maybe a little of both?"

"Well, we can talk more about that later," advised Agent Hunter looking around the room. "We need to get Agent Jayco to the hospital."

"Wait! Before we go, may I please show Agent Jayco something first?" Tori asked, pleadingly, motioning to the greenhouse.

Agent Hunter looked at Agent Jayco and asked, "Are you up for it?"

Intrigued by what Tori wanted to show her, Agent Jayco nodded her head and replied, "Yes. I think I can."

Tori quickly came to Agent Jayco's side and while supporting her weight, she slowly guided her instructor to the greenhouse entrance. Opening the door carefully, Tori led Agent Jayco into the adjoining room. Agent Jayco stopped in mid-step as they cleared the frame and caught her breath.

She stood there for several seconds looking around her, shocked by what she saw. Tears began welling in her eyes as the realization of what she was seeing overpowered her. "This is the amazing," she whispered.

She looked at Tori and quietly said, "Poor, Andrew. This will crush him. When he realizes how close he was and that he gave up too soon, it will be the most painful thing he'll ever experience."

"I would hope there's one other painful experience, he regrets more," Tori replied, meeting her eyes, knowingly.

Agent Jayco looked around the room one more time and said, "Thank you for showing this to me, Miss Cooper."

"You're welcome," Tori replied, gently leading Agent Jayco back to the paramedics.

While Agent Hunter, Ben and Tori watched the paramedics lead Agent Jayco away, Piper joined them.

"Soooo..." she said casually with her hands in her pockets, rocking back and forth on her heels. "Are we done here? We totally skipped lunch and I'm starving. Can I talk anyone into bacon cheese burgers and fries?"

Ben's head whipped around in Piper's direction and he quickly replied, "Bacon? I could eat."

"Shocker," Tori and Agent Hunter replied in unison.

They both laughed at their joke, then Agent Hunter said, "I wish I could take you up on that offer, however I need to wrap up here and make sure arrangements for Mr. Porter are handled properly."

Turning back to Tori he added, "Miss Cooper, I trust the three of you can find your way back to campus without getting into any further trouble?"

Tori smiled, guiltily at Agent Hunter and replied, "We should be able to find our way back, sir."

"Good. I'll want to talk with each of you first thing tomorrow morning and go over every detail of what transpired here. This is the second time I've had to come to your rescue, Miss Cooper. Let's not make this a habit, shall we?" Agent Hunter requested.

Tori winced and with an apologetic look replied, "No, sir, let's not."

"All right then, I'll see you all in the morning," he said, quickly leaving the room.

Tori, Ben and Piper looked at each other and laughed nervously. They stood there silently staring at one another until Ben finally broke the silence and said, "So, food?"

"Yep," Piper quickly replied.

"Absolutely, let's go!" Tori agreed, leading the way.

Chapter 22

Tori stood in front of the mirror in her dorm room, scrutinizing her appearance, carefully. The dark navy suit and heels weren't something she was accustomed to wearing, although she had to admit, she liked the way it looked. She had debated what to do with her long auburn hair and in the end, decided to sweep it up into a braided bun.

As she began brushing a light coat of mascara on her lashes, Piper emerged from the bathroom, dressed almost identically to Tori, aside from her spiked, flame red hair, which she tamed a bit for the day.

"Well don't you look all suave and sophisticated," Tori teased, appraising her room-mate's appearance.

Piper smiled, gently tugged at the lapels of the jacket and replied, "I do look rather smashing, don't I?"

Tori laughed lightly and turned back to the mirror to finish applying her makeup.

"You look awesome! I love the braided bun. It's a nice touch," said Piper. "I wasn't sure what to do with mine. Is it still too much?"

Tori turned back to look at Piper and replied, "Thanks and no, it's perfect and totally you."

"Thanks," Piper beamed. She noticed Tori's hand was trembling slightly as she applied her lip gloss and asked, "So, on a scale of one to ten, how nervous are you?"

Tori chuckled and replied, "Oh, I would say about a fifteen!"

Piper laughed with Tori and said, "You're going to be awesome! Have I told you how proud I am that you were named class spokesperson? That is still so incredibly cool!"

"You've told me about a hundred times already, but thanks, Piper. I really do appreciate your support," Tori replied.

A soft knock on their door, interrupted their conversation as both women looked at one another, curiously.

"Were we expecting anyone?" Tori asked with raised eyebrows.

Piper shook her head, said, "Nope," walked over to the door and opened it a crack to see who it was. She laughed as she opened the door wider and said, "It looks like your welcome wagon! Look!"

Tori joined Piper at the door and was amazed by the number of people crowded in the hallway "Oh, my gosh! Hi guys!" she chucked.

"Surprise!" yelled Sarah, Aubrey, Ben, Meda, Karla, Tobias, Agent Nichols and Agent Jayco, in unison.

"Do you all want to come in? I'm not sure if all of you will fit, but you're welcome to join us," Tori replied, looking around the small space of her and Piper's room.

Sarah stepped forward and hugged Tori, fiercely. "I am so proud of you, honey!" She pulled back and looked at Tori's beaming face and added, "You look absolutely beautiful. I've never seen you so happy, sweetheart."

"Thanks, Mom" Tori replied, brushing a tear from her mother's cheek. "I'm just so happy. All the people I love most are right here to help celebrate today. Wait, where's Dad?"

"I'm right here, honey!" Tanner's voice called out from the back of the group. "Excuse me, please," he said, politely, as he slowly made his way forward and joined his daughter. "Congratulations, my beautiful girl. I am so very proud of you," he said, hugging Tori tightly.

"Oh, you made it! When did you arrive?" Tori asked, hugging him back.

"Just this morning," Tanner replied. "I had some last minute business to take care of before I could leave town."

"Well, I'm just glad you made it in time!" Tori said, happily looking at her parents.

"Speaking of time, Tor, it's time to get going," Ben interrupted pointing to the clock.

Tori looked over at her nightstand alarm clock and said, "Oh! I didn't realize it was already so close to Noon!"

"Told you she'd be late," Aubrey taunted from the hallway.

"I heard that, Bree," Tori commented back.

"I said it loud enough so you would," Aubrey teased in return.

"Girls, please. Not today," Sarah sighed, patiently.

Agent Jayco laughed, shaking her head in amazement and asked Ben, "Do you ever get used to that?"

"I haven't yet and I'm sure I never will," Ben laughed back with her.

"Okay, troops, head out!" Piper ordered, ushering Tori towards the door.

As Tori obeyed and began following everyone down the hallway, she asked, "How are we all getting there? Are we walking or driving?"

"It's such a pretty fall day, we decided we would walk," Sarah replied, taking Tanner's arm and walking beside him.

Tori looked over at Agent Jayco and asked, "How are you feeling? Are you sure the walk isn't too far?"

Agent Jayco smiled in reassurance, held up her bandaged wrists and replied, "I'm feeling almost back to normal. The doctor said I'm healing well and my bandages should be coming off in a few days. I think a nice walk, enjoying the beautiful fall color will be perfect."

"That's wonderful news, Agent Jayco. I really am glad you're feeling better," Tori replied, falling in step with her as they walked. "Have you talked to Dr. Porter?"

Agent Jayco sighed and replied, "Yes, actually I visited Andrew and his wife before I left town. I took them to the warehouse where Mattox was growing the roses."

"Oh," Tori breathed. "How did he take the news?"

"Pretty much as I expected," Agent Jayco admitted. "He and Elaine are devastated. The realization that their son was responsible for re-engineering the roses was bad enough. Then finding out that he murdered those women was such a shock to them both. It will take them a long time to recover."

"I am so sorry. That must have been so difficult telling him. What will happen to the re-engineered flowers? They're a successful new variety, right? Will Andrew get the credit or will it go to Mattox?" Tori asked.

"I've been asking myself that same question and I have no idea what will happen. Andrew has always been so driven by his work and being able to do something on his own.

It's beyond his capability to share recognition with someone else."

"I remember," Tori said, quietly, thinking back to the memory Agent Jayco shared with her. "He was your one great love, wasn't he? Is that why you never married?"

Agent Jayco gave Tori a sad smile and then looked up at the gold and crimson leaves overhead as they continued walking. She sighed deeply and looked at the group of people walking with them and replied, "He was, but we weren't meant to be. Just remember that as you and Mr. Vincent begin your lives together as agents. The job is very rewarding personally, but it can be very difficult on a relationship. There will be times when there are things you won't be able to share with one another. Not because you won't want to, but because you won't be able to."

Tori looked at Ben, who was having an animated conversation with her father, and smiled as they both laughed at a seemingly humorous comment her father said that she couldn't hear. "I'll try to remember that," she replied.

Agent Nichols fell back a few paces to join Tori and Agent Jayco and smiled at Tori, happily. "Hey! How are you doing? Are you ready for your big speech?"

Tori grimaced and replied, "Ugh, don't remind me. I'm trying to keep what little breakfast Piper forced me to eat in my stomach right now."

"Aw, you'll be fine. If there's one thing I've learned about you already, you're like a cat. You always land on your feet," replied Agent Nichols.

"Thanks. We'll see if you still think that after today. By the way, how did your trip to North Carolina go? Were Karla and Meda able to talk with Mrs. Foster's spirit?" Tori asked.

"Yes, although she really didn't give us more information than you were able to read from the flower," replied Agent Nichols. "And as we all suspected the amulet no longer works for Mrs. Neviah now that it has claimed you as its owner. At some point, you'll need to plan a trip out there to cross her over."

"Hmm, okay. I'll have to make that one of my first priorities after I join the team," Tori replied, mentally noting that in her 'to do' list.

"Speaking of joining the team, you are officially part of it now!" Agent Nichols beamed, proudly.

"That's right! I hadn't had time to think about that yet! I'm really looking forward to working with you again, officially!" Tori exclaimed.

"So am I," Agent Nichols agreed.

As the group approached the entrance to the auditorium, Tori saw Agent Hunter and Director Gibbs standing on the sidewalk, waiting for them. She smiled in greeting and said, "Good afternoon Agent Hunter, Director Gibbs. It's nice to see you again."

"Nice to see you as well, Miss Cooper. Congratulations on your achievements here at the academy. I think I can speak for both Gabriel and myself when I say that you have by far exceeded everyone's expectations," replied Director Gibbs while shaking Tori's hand.

"Thank you, sir," Tori replied, returning the handshake. "I remember what we talked about earlier this summer and I promise I didn't take what you said lightly."

"Apparently not," he chuckled.

Tori turned to Agent Hunter and met his praising smile. "Congratulations, Miss Cooper. I'm looking forward to having you on my team."

"It will be an honor for me as well, sir," she proudly replied.

"Well it's just about time to get started so everyone please go inside and have a seat. Miss Cooper, please join me on stage for the commencement ceremony," Director Gibbs instructed.

"Yes, sir," she replied, obediently following the director while she heard an assortment of 'good luck, Tori' comments trailing behind her.

Once inside the building, she followed him up a short flight of stairs to a stage where several of her instructors and other agents were already seated. Agent Hunter took one of the last two chairs and motioned for her to sit beside him as Director Gibbs approached the podium.

She sat down beside Agent Hunter and looked up at his face with eyes as big as saucers. Seeing how nervous she looked, he smiled down at her, patted her hand in reassurance and turned his attention to Director Gibbs.

"Good afternoon everyone," the director's voice boomed into the microphone. Within seconds, the room became completely silent. "I would like to thank everyone for coming today. It is an honor for me to be able to speak at today's graduation and join in the celebration of these fine men and women before me.

"The mission of the FBI is to protect and defend the United States against terrorist and foreign intelligence threats, to uphold and enforce the criminal laws of the United States, and to provide leadership and criminal justice services to federal, state, municipal, and international agencies.

"These are the core values of our profession. They are what make us a brotherhood and sisterhood capable of fighting crime and protecting freedom around the world.

"I want to congratulate each and every one of our cadets today, as they have worked hard, both inside and outside the classroom. They have excelled academically and they have learned new ideas and strategies that they can use as they begin their careers as agents.

"As you all know, each year, one cadet is chosen by his or her fellow classmates, one whom stands out from all the others as their spokesperson. One which they feel exemplifies notable qualities in humility; honesty; integrity and leadership.

"This year, not only has that student been deemed as class spokesperson, she has also been awarded the Director's Leadership Award. She is someone I have had the opportunity of getting to know the past several months, and agree that the award is well deserved.

"Ladies and gentlemen, it is with great pleasure that I introduce the class of 2013 academy spokesperson and Director's Leadership Award recipient, Miss Tori Cooper."

Chapter 23

While the room erupted with applause and shouts of celebration, Tori stared in shock at Director Gibbs as he applauded and smiled broadly at her. She turned to Agent Hunter and saw that he too was congratulating her.

"Go on," he urged, motioning her up to the podium.

With an unknown source of strength, she somehow rose from her chair and walked toward the podium where Director Gibbs was waiting for her. He handed her a plaque, shook her other hand and motioned for her to smile at the photographer beside them for a picture.

She smiled on command as the flash momentarily blinded her, and then returned her gaze back to Director Gibbs who seemed pleased that he had surprised her with the award.

He chuckled, patted her on the shoulder and said, "Congratulations, Miss Cooper." Motioning to the audience in front of her, he winked, mischievously and added, "They're all yours."

Tori paused long enough to read the inscription on the plaque and gently traced her name which had been elegantly inscribed into the metal surface.

She nervously looked around the sea of faces before her, scanning over them until her eyes met Bens. He smiled his crooked smile, winked at her, proudly and nodded at her in encouragement. "Go, Tori!" he called out which immediately made her laugh as he intended.

Taking a deep breath, she gently laid the plaque on top of the podium and placed her hands on either side of the base, in order to balance her weight. Thankful to be able to use the podium to shield her trembling knees, she said, "Good afternoon."

Clearing her throat gently and in a stronger voice she continued, "Thank you, Director Gibbs, and thank you fellow cadets, instructors, agents, family and friends. It is an honor for me to be able to speak at today's graduation as class spokesperson for the class of 2013, as well as being awarded the Director's Leadership Award. The honor of being able to address the class today was privilege enough on its own, without the added honor of being given such a prestigious award.

"As Director Gibbs said, the mission of the FBI is to protect and defend the United States against terrorist and foreign intelligence threats, to uphold and enforce the criminal laws of the United States, and to provide leadership and criminal justice services to federal, state, municipal, and international agencies.

"As students of the academy, we all came here with those same goals, to protect and defend our United States and to become leaders and to serve in our communities.

"Throughout the last twenty weeks, we continually faced challenges and in return, we were challenged as to whether we saw those challenges as stepping-stones or as obstacles.

"If we chose to see them as obstacles, then the challenges we faced were viewed as problems. Problems that needed to be overcome along with all the negative connotations associated with problems. A great deal of wasted energy can be spent focusing on a negative mindset like "I can't", "I don't want to" and "It's not my job".

"If however, we chose to see those challenges as stepping-stones, we saw them as opportunities that we encountered along the way for us to use, to "step on" in order to push ourselves beyond our comfort zones, discover new strengths and abilities we didn't know we had, and ultimately reach our goals of becoming FBI agents. A name that is synonymous with excellence, innovation, honor, integrity and outstanding service to our country.

"So, congratulations, my fellow academy-mates! Be proud of your accomplishments, but do it humbly and respectfully. Remember that enforcing the law will only be part of our job. The rest of the job will be being good family, friends, and neighbors in the communities which we will serve. Thank you."

The room erupted once again with a resounding round of applause and cheers as Tori and the Director of the Academy switched places at the podium.

"Congratulations again on your achievements, Miss Cooper. You have a great deal to be proud of," the director said, shaking her hand.

"Thank you, sir," Tori replied, returning his handshake.

She quickly retreated and returned to her chair beside Agent Hunter. Now thankfully out of the spotlight, she looked down at the plaque in her hands and once again read the inscription.

"That's quite an honor, there," Agent Hunter said in a low voice beside her.

Tori looked up to meet his eyes and solemnly replied, "Yes, it is, sir."

"Do you feel as if you deserve it?" he asked, curiously.

Tori thought for a moment and replied, "Not entirely, no, sir."

Pleased with her response, he smiled and replied, "Good, that's how you earned it, Miss Cooper. Never forget that."

Tori nodded in understanding and replied, "I won't, sir."

~~~~~~~~~~

After the graduation ceremony was over, the cadets and their families gathered on the lawn outside, showing off their badges and celebrating with one another.

Tori saw Ben and his parents standing with her parents, so she made her way over towards their direction.

On the way there, she saw Piper standing with two other women Tori assumed were Piper's mother and aunt.

"Hey, roomie!" Piper called out, motioning Tori to join them.

Tori smiled, walked up to the small group, flashed her new badge and replied, "That's Agent Roomie, to you."

Piper threw her arms around Tori enthusiastically and said, "I can't even begin to tell you how proud I am of you! First, class spokesperson, second, the recipient of the Director's Leadership Award, and then the top achiever in academics? My gosh, woman, is there nothing you can't do?"

Tori laughed with her friend, rocking back and forth in the hug and replied, "I can't see rainbows the way you can or fire a gun with my eyes closed. Or at least I should never, ever try that. Congratulations on getting top awards in firearms! I told you, you could beat those boys!"

"Thanks, Tor!" Piper replied, happily. Turning to face the two women, Piper excitedly said, "Mom, Sky, this is my roommate, Tori. Tori, this is my mom, Mallory, and my aunt Sky."

"It's so nice to finally meet you both," Tori greeted. "I've heard so many wonderful things about you. This girl is amazing!"

Piper's mother smiled and replied, "Yes she is. It's nice to meet you too, Tori. I'm sorry we got here so late. Someone wasn't paying attention to the gas gauge and we ran out of gas outside of town. Thank goodness that highway patrol officer came by and gave us a ride when we told him where we were going."

Sky rolled her eyes, dramatically and said, "We ended up with a police escort so what are you complaining about? Besides, he was cute. Did you happen to notice he wasn't wearing a ring? Anyway, it's very nice to meet you, Tori. It sounds like you and Piper being paired up the way you were was pure fate."

"I like to think of it as divine intervention," Piper teased, winking at Tori.

"Ha! Funny!" Tori laughed. "I'm going to go see my folks. Are you all going to be able to join us for dinner like we talked about earlier?"

"Yep, we'll see you there!" Piper replied.

"Great! We'll see you there. It was nice meeting you!" Tori said to Mallory and Sky.

"It was nice meeting you too, Tori," Mallory replied.

"Yes, you too!" replied Sky.

Catching Ben's eye as she approached their group, he quickly closed the gap between them and ran up to her, taking her in his arms and spinning her around in a circle.

"You are, by far, the most amazing woman I have ever met, Tori Cooper!" he exclaimed, laughing.

Laughing with him, Tori hung on to him tightly and said, "Thank you, Ben. Seriously you're making my dizzy doing that."

Ben swung her around one last time and planted her feet firmly in front of his. "Well," he said, "If you're already feeling light-headed, I might as well take advantage of the situation." He gently pulled her body up against his, dipped her body backwards and kissed her, passionately on the lips.

Caught off guard, yet not objecting, Tori sighed and responded as she felt Ben slowly trail one hand up the back of her neck, cradling her head in his hand.

"Get a room!" Logan jeered, slapping Ben on the back. "Are you two really that heavy into PDA? There's probably a support group for that."

Groaning his way out of the kiss, Ben straightened Tori back on her feet and turned to face his accuser. "Seriously, dude? Will you quit doing that?" he complained to his friend.

"Seriously, dude," Logan chuckled. "I mean look at you two. Your parents are standing right there!"

"You're just jealous. Everyone knows you have a thing for redheads," Ben teased, his eyes narrowed mischievously. "Well at least one redhead in particular," he added.

Logan's eyes widened in surprise as he whipped his head around to determine who was within earshot, "Come on, man!" he hissed. "You promised!"

"Hold on a second," Tori declared, eyeing Logan suspiciously. "Are you saying what I think your saying?"

"He hasn't said anything!" Logan quickly objected, punching Ben in the arm.

"Ouch! Hey, that is so not the way to make me stop talking," Ben laughed, enjoying the way his friend was squirming.

"Does that one redhead in particular know?" Tori demanded, poking her finger into Logan's chest as he stepped backwards in defense. "I know one redhead in particular who would want to know! So, tell me Logan, does she know?"

"Does who know what?" Piper asked as she approached. "What's going on and what did Logan do now?"

"Wait a second! Why do you automatically assume that I did something?" Logan whined in objection.

"Well, it is you and....yeah, that's pretty self-explanatory," Piper reasoned shrugging her shoulders.

"Ouch. That hurts me deeply, Piper," Logan said, dramatically.

"Somehow, I seriously doubt that," Piper replied. Turning to Tori she asked, "So, what's going on? Does who know what?"

Deciding to further punish Logan for interrupting her and Ben's kiss, Tori replied, "Oh, Logan has something he wants to talk to you about. So we'll leave you two to talk. See ya!"

While Tori and Ben quickly walked away laughing, Piper turned to Logan with a puzzled expression and asked, "What just happened? What's she talking about?"

~~~~~~~~~~

Later that evening, after dinner with their families, Tori and Piper returned to their dorm room which was now randomly stacked with boxes and suitcases containing their belongings.

Pausing only long enough to kick off her shoes and place her plaque and badge on her nightstand, Tori plopped face down onto her bed and groaned, wearily. "Oh, I'm so tired right now. I don't even want to take the time to change out of my suit. And I ate too much! Why did I let you talk me into that piece of chocolate cake?"

Kicking off her shoes and lying down on her bed, Piper laughed and replied, "Hey, no one twisted your arm forcing you to eat it."

"Well it just looked so good, staring at me like that. I couldn't let it go to waste," Tori complained.

Both women lay quietly for a few minutes, each thinking back on the events of the day until Piper's giggle broke the silence.

"What's so funny?" Tori asked, peering at Piper with one eye.

"We're FBI agents, Tor," Piper giggled again. "This is our last night as dorm-mates. Tomorrow, when we leave here, we'll be leaving as FBI agents!"

"I know, Piper," Tori murmured.

"And we've both been assigned to Agent Hunter's team," Piper marveled. "How on earth did that happen?"

Tori rolled over onto her side and smiled at Piper, happily. "Well, Ben and I already knew we would be assigned to his team. Obviously you've impressed him with your aura readings and your shooting abilities. Plus he's really big on team chemistry so he already knows we all work well together. It just makes sense that you joined the team too!"

Piper smiled, dreamily and replied, "This is going to be awesome! Dinner with everyone tonight was fun."

"Yeah, it was," Tori replied.

The room was quite again for a few minutes until a moment suddenly came back to Piper. She rolled onto her

301

side, facing Tori and asked, "So what's with the creepy staring thing that Agent Hughes does. Is that normal? I caught him staring at me a couple of times during dinner."

Tori laughed out loud and replied, "Yeah, unfortunately for him it is normal and it does creep everyone out at first. I seriously don't think he's aware that he's doing it. Once you get to know him, he's really a nice guy."

"So what's his story?" Piper asked. "He has a strong orange aura, which is good because it indicates someone who is courageous and powerful, but there's also a rim of deep blue around him which tells me he's struggling with sadness within him that he hasn't yet resolved. Do you know what it is?"

Tori frowned and rolled onto her back, looking up at the ceiling above her. "Yes, I know what it is. He and Agent Neviah were in a relationship together before she died. They were in love with one another. I guess in a way, they still are."

"Oh," Piper breathed. "That explains why he was with Mrs. Neviah so much today. He must still talk to Agent Neviah, huh? That makes me sad. I can't even imagine how horrible that is for both of them!"

"Yeah, it is," Tori agreed having seen the way Karla still looked at Agent Hughes.

Finding one last burst of energy for the day, Tori pushed herself up onto her feet and said, "Okay enough of that. It's time for me to change out of this suit and get ready for bed."

"Okay," Piper yawned. "Go ahead. I'll just lie here until you're done. Then I'll get ready too."

When Tori emerged from the bathroom a few minutes later, her face and teeth freshly cleaned, she looked over and saw Piper sound asleep on her bed, still wearing her suit.

Seeing the peaceful expression on her friends face, she decided not to wake her. Tori quietly hung her suit in her closet then settled in her bed.

Stifling a yawn, she turned off the light, snuggled under her covers and drifted off to sleep.

Chapter 24

Tori smiled and opened her eyes as she felt the gentle mountain breeze blow her hair away from her face. The warmth from the setting sun still had enough reach to keep the chill out of the air a few minutes longer, as it descended towards the familiar mountain peaks.

She breathed in deeply, savoring the clean scents of pine and wild sage and leaned back against her boulder, enjoying the grainy texture of the rock beneath her hands.

As she sat there quietly, enjoying the sounds of the earth preparing itself for transformation from daylight to night, she felt a new sensation around her as she realized she was no longer alone.

She smiled, gently and said, "Hello, Remy."

"Hello, Tori," he laughed quietly in response behind her. "How did you know I was here?"

She turned to face him and replied, "I could feel your presence. The air changes when you're near me."

"Ah," Remy nodded as he looked over at the mountains where the sun was now hovering. "Looks like He painted you a pretty sky tonight."

Tori looked back at the sunset and smiled again as the colors further deepened into shades of plum and apricot.

"I've always said that God has the most magnificent pallet," Tori breathed, marveling at the colors. "No artist could ever come close to the purity of color that He creates."

"Amen, to that," Remy drawled as he sat down on the boulder beside her.

They sat a few minutes longer watching the sun disappear, when Tori asked, "So?"

"So, what?" he replied, innocently.

"So, why did you bring me here?" she asked, curiously.

Remy reacted in mild surprise and replied, "I didn't bring you here, Tori. You did!"

"I did?" she asked. "Huh!"

"So what's on your mind?" he asked, patiently.

Tori exhaled a deep sigh and replied, "What isn't? I feel like I have the weight of the world on my shoulders and I don't have anyone who could even begin to understand to talk to!"

Remy scowled at Tori and exclaimed, "Well what am I – chopped liver? You sure know how to hurt a man's ego!"

Tori groaned in frustration and bumped against Remy's shoulder, teasingly. "You know what I meant," she laughed.

"Yeah, I know. I'm just giving you a hard time," he teased back.

Tori shivered slightly as the chill in the air claimed victory now that the sun moved on to the horizon on the other side of the earth.

Seeing her shiver, Remy gently placed his arm around her shoulder and encircled her with his wings to keep the air from reaching her.

She leaned against him, rested her head on his shoulder and looked up to watch the stars begin to blink on like tiny flashlights in the sky.

"Is it true, Remy? Am I the prophecy?" she asked, quietly.

"Yes," he replied.

"So now that the statue and the amulet have ended their silence, does that mean the time of the enlightenment has begun?" she asked.

"Yes," he replied.

Tori drew in a sharp breath as the reality of his simple admissions began to fill her with apprehension.

"What do I do?" she whispered.

"I don't know," Remy replied. "But I promise, whatever happens, I will never leave you."

"What if I'm not strong enough?" she worried.

"Not strong enough? Have you not been paying attention? I've watched you go up against two serial killers head-on, and you defeated them both!" Remy exclaimed.

"Well, there is that," Tori joked.

"And even more importantly, you've managed to confuse the one being on this earth who has always believed that he's the scariest monster of them all," Remy noted.

"Confuse? What do you mean?" Tori asked as she shivered again.

Remy chuckled, pulled her closer against him and said, "I know Luc better than he realizes, and I've seen the way he acts around you. Don't get me wrong. The first encounter the two of you had, he definitely got what he wanted. He scared the ba-geezers out of you."

"The night I first felt the feathers," Tori reminisced, gently running her hand along his wing.

"Then the next time the two of you were together, you were still scared, but you got angry too. That anger made you brave and you stood up to him. He didn't like that," Remy advised.

"The time you first brought me here," Tori recalled.

"Yes," Remy replied.

"Huh, that's interesting. So have none of your previous descendants ever stood up to him?" Tori asked, curiously.

Remy shook his head and replied, "Not the way you have, nope."

"So then the last time he and I were together..." Tori began when Remy interrupted her.

"Hang on a minute, there was another time you were with him?" he asked, pulling away from her to look at her face.

Not understanding the concern on his face, Tori replied, "Yes! It was shortly after you brought me here. He and I talked again, but that time I think I annoyed him more than anything. He didn't like it when I mentioned that I hugged you."

Remy's eyebrows shot up in surprise and he asked, "You told him about that? And he got annoyed? Oh, that's actually kind of funny. Hang on. Where exactly did the two of you meet? I've been watching the garden for you and I don't remember seeing you."

"Well, we started off in the garden, but then I might have provoked him into recreating a psychologists' office so he took me somewhere else," Tori replied.

"Huh." Remy grunted, looking back up at the stars. "Well I guess that's only fair considering I bring you here. Well at least I used to bring you here, this time you brought me here. How did you do that, by the way?"

Tori shrugged her shoulders and replied, "I have no idea, honest."

"Well, you'll probably want to figure that out. It obviously could work out to your advantage since it doesn't seem like we need the garden anymore," Remy said.

"Speaking of which, what is the significance of the garden anyway?" asked Tori.

"It's the beginning of the end of mankind. The origin of sin and where man first died," Remy noted, solemnly.

"Agent Sullivan was right!" Tori marveled. "What about the woman? The one I saw you and Satan arguing over?"

"Elsbet," Remy said quietly.

"That's her name, Elsbet? What about her? Is her spirit still on the earth?" Tori asked in earnest.

"Her punishment was to walk the earth until judgment day," Remy confirmed.

"Where is she? Do you still talk to her?" Tori asked.

"I don't know. Once her spirit left her, I could no longer see or hear her," Remy replied, sadly.

"Maybe I can find her!" Tori exclaimed, excitedly. "Maybe there still a chance for her redemption!"

"And that's important to you? That someone you haven't even met has that chance?" Remy asked, smiling, proudly at her.

Tori smiled back at him as her mind went to work and she replied, "She's your daughter and my sister, Remy. And even if she wasn't, everyone deserves a second chance."

Seeing the look of determination on her face, Remy's eyes narrowed suspiciously and he asked, "Everyone?"

Smiling slyly back at him, Tori replied, "Everyone!"

"So you think you're ready?" he asked.

"Better now than never," she replied.

A short distance away, Satan stood in the shadows of the trees, rubbing his hands together, grinning, wickedly.

"Very well, dearest, Tori," he crooned, "Let the games begin!"

Note from the author

Here we are, at the end of the story. Or are we?

In all seriousness, I really do hope you are enjoying being a part of Tori and Ben's lives as much as I am.

Each day that goes by, I discover something new about my characters that I can't wait to share with you! So, please be patient as the continuation of their story unfolds in book three.

Also, many of my fellow readers/foodies have commented about the frequent food references I write about and asked me for the recipes.

I thought that was a great idea, so I've posted the recipes from 'First Sight,' book one in 'The Tori Cooper Novels,' on my website; readvickistewart.com.

The recipes from book two have been included on the following pages, and will also be made available on my site.

Bon Appétit!

Recipes from 'The Enlightenment'

Meda's Caramelized Onion, Mushrooms and Gruyere Quiche:

Ingredients:

       1 medium onion, sliced into half-moons
       1 pound sliced Cremini, Shitake and Portobello
           mushrooms
       4 tablespoon olive oil
       1 tablespoon chopped fresh thyme
       ¼ teaspoon dry mustard
       3 large eggs, yolk and whites separated
       1 cup milk
       1 cup grated Gruyère cheese
       Kosher salt
       Fresh ground pepper

Directions:

1)   Preheat the oven to 350 degrees.

2) Heat two tablespoons of olive oil in a large nonstick pan over a medium heat. Add the onion and cook, stirring occasionally, until golden brown and caramelized, about eight to ten minutes. Transfer the onions to a bowl.

3)   Add the remaining two tablespoons of oil to the pan and heat over a medium heat. Add the mushrooms and cook, stirring occasionally, until they have released their water and begin to brown, about six to eight minutes. Add the onions back to the pan, stir in the salt, pepper, mustard and thyme.

4) Whisk together the eggs, egg whites and milk in a small bowl.

5) Spray a nine-inch pie dish with cooking spray and spread the mushroom-onion mixture into an even layer. Pour the egg mixture on top and then sprinkle the Gruyere cheese on top.

6) Place the dish in the oven and bake it for thirty-five minutes or until knife inserted in the middle comes out clean.

7) Remove the pan from the oven and let it rest for five minutes before cutting.

Tori's Cooking Therapy Night:

Bacon-Wrapped Cherry Pepper Poppers

Ingredients:
- 1 jar hot cherry peppers
- ½ cup cream cheese, softened
- 1 jalapeño pepper, diced, and seeded
- 12 slices thin bacon, cut into thirds
- Toothpicks

Directions:

1) With a sharp knife, gently slice into one side of each pepper and scoop out the seeds and membrane.

2) Mix the diced jalapeño into the softened cheese and fill each pepper with the cheese mixture.

3) Wrap the filled peppers with a piece of the bacon until just the ends overlap and secure it with a toothpick.

4) Arrange the stuffed peppers on a baking sheet and place in a 350 degree oven for twelve to fifteen minutes or until bacon is crisp. Remove from oven and serve the peppers warm.

Gruyère Cheese Gougères

Ingredients:
>   1 ½ cups of water
>   1 stick of unsalted butter, cut into cubes
>   1 teaspoon sugar
>   ½ teaspoon salt
>   1 ½ cups of flour
>   8 large eggs, beaten
>   1 cup shredded Gruyère cheese

Directions:

1) Preheat oven to 400 degrees and line two baking sheets with parchment paper.

2) In a large saucepan, combine the water, butter, sugar and salt, bringing it to a boil

3) Reduce heat to medium and add the flour all at once, stirring vigorously with a wooden spoon until the dough pulls away from the sides of the pan. Remove pan from heat.

4) Add the beaten eggs to the dough in small batches, stirring thoroughly in between each addition, until eggs are incorporated and a thick, glossy pastry dough remains.

5) Transfer the dough to a piping bag fitted with a ½ inch tip and pipe 1 ½ inch mounds of the dough onto the parchment paper, one inch apart.

6) Sprinkle each mound of dough with the shredded Gruyère cheese.

7) Bake the Gougères in the oven for thirty minutes, until browned and puffed.

Sweet Chipotle Dressing

Ingredients:
> 2 cloves garlic, diced
> 1 Roma tomato, diced and seeded
> 1 small onion, diced
> 2/3 cup rice wine vinegar
> ½ cup olive oil
> 2 tablespoons Liquid Smoke, Mesquite flavor
> 2 tablespoons chipotle puree'
> 2 tablespoons Dijon mustard
> 2 tablespoons cilantro, chopped
> 2 tablespoons honey
> 1 teaspoon salt
> ½ teaspoon cumin
> ¼ teaspoon black pepper

1) Place all ingredients except for the olive oil in a blender and blend until smooth.

2) With the blender on, slowly add the oil in a thin stream until the mixture is fully emulsified. Keep chilled until ready to serve.

Pan-Roasted BB&J Mussels (Bacon, Bourbon and Jalapeños)

Ingredients:

    4 dozen mussels
    2 jalapeños, seeded and chopped
    2 cloves garlic, chopped
    ½ cup shallots, finely diced
    ½ cup bacon, diced
    ¼ cup bourbon
    ¼ cup clam juice
    ¼ cup half and half
    2 tablespoons unsalted butter
    2 tablespoons parsley, chopped

Directions:

1) Scrub and de-beard mussels and then place them in cold water for at least 15 minutes.

2) In a large, deep pan, cook the bacon over moderate heat until the bacon is crisp, about ten to twelve minutes. Remove bacon from pan with slotted spoon and transfer into a bowl.

3) Add the shallots and garlic to the pan and cook until they are softened and the garlic is just beginning to look 'toasted.'

4) Add the mussels and bourbon to the pan, and simmer until the bourbon is almost evaporated.

5) Add the clam juice and cover the pan, cooking the mussels until they open, about five to eight minutes.

6) Transfer the mussels to a serving bowl, discarding any that have not opened.

7) Add the half and half, jalapeños, parsley and bacon to the pan and simmer until the sauce has slightly thickened, about two minutes. Add the butter, stirring the sauce until it is incorporated and then pour the sauce over the mussels.

Serve the dish warm with crusty bread to soak up the broth.

www.ingramcontent.com/pod-product-compliance
Lightning Source LLC
Chambersburg PA
CBHW071105250626
47159CB00002B/609